To Keith Skipper,

In memory [...]
over Radio Norfolk on 19 July 1994

Fred Gee..

THE ROAD TO RUIN

The Road to Ruin

F.C. Gee

The Book Guild Ltd.
Sussex, England

The Book Guild Ltd.
25 High Street,
Lewes, Sussex

First published 1993
© F.C. Gee 1993
Set in Baskerville
Typesetting by Ashford Setting and Design Services
Ashford, Middlesex
Printed in Great Britain by
Antony Rowe Ltd.
Chippenham, Wiltshire.

A catalogue record for this book is available
from the British Library

ISBN 0 86332 845 8

1

You would need to be a geriatric, like me, to remember what life was like in this country before the advent of television.

The story I am about to tell began in those far-off days at the end of our Second Great War, in a remote East Anglian village several miles from the sea, on a quiet stretch of river, with a population of a mere hundred or so warm-hearted but cautiously insular country folk, whose tuneful undulating dialect was in bright contrast to the flat, featureless landscape which surrounded them.

Some say that Norfolk and Suffolk are an acquired taste, but there is no taste at all in a Norfolk dumpling until it is placed in a stew. For those who know the counties, there is a feast to be enjoyed in the good nature of a people who have learned to live by their wits, and to treat all strangers as suspect until they have proved otherwise.

The residents of Little Missington had plenty to be miserable about had they been so inclined, but happily only a handful of them were of that disposition. Six years of war had left them a little weary and no better off for their victory. The general appearance of the village scarcely differed from the days of the First Great War. Nothing of note had been added to the scenery within living memory and little had been taken from it. Cornfields had undergone an annual change of crop and the hedgerows had thickened here and there, but the physical likeness of fathers and sons, and mothers and daughters, maintained a familiarity about the place that gave the illusion of timelessness.

Charming as that may seem to us now, looking back from an age where change is forever happening, it had, as W.S. Gilbert once remarked, its inconvenient side. The road, for instance, from Myrtlesham to Puddlethorpe was fit for neither beast to pound nor fowl to cross. Since the loss of its toll-gate, and keeper, in the Great Flood of 1906, nothing had been done to repair the road surface, nor to prepare it for the growing weight of vehicles that was to pass along it with the coming of the motor car. Repeated complaints and demands for action had been lodged by the residents of neighbouring towns, motoring organizations, and the Ramblers Association, but parishioners of Little Missington were unmoved by such representations. If the Lord had meant there to be motor cars in their part of the world, He would surely have built their encampment on rock instead of mud!

The day came, however, when an election of county councillors brought a new party to power and introduced a change of Chairman to the Highways Committee. Then, as the new broom swept along the various highways that came within his jurisdiction, it came to rest, as did most of the vehicles that went that way, upon the thoroughfare at Little Missington. The sequel was a letter that featured on the agenda of a meeting of the Parish Council one night in the spring of 1946.

Chairman of the Parish Council was Cyrus Galleon, a farmer whose dairy herds and cornfields kept many parishioners in work, if not in luxury. Mortimer Lockett, the Treasurer, was a watchmaker and jeweller by trade, accustomed to dealing in small denominations. Clerk to the Council was Syd Stubbles, the village barber, well-placed to report and record the local gossip.

6

Between them these three gentlemen and seven ordinary members managed the affairs of the parish to the satisfaction of those who elected them. The remainder of the electorate were apathetic and had offered no opposition at the hustings. Active among the ordinary members, but careful not to hold office lest it should prejudice his trade as a builder and part-time undertaker, was Benjamin Digby, a man of enterprise and imagination.

* * *

There was a breath of thunder in the air as Digby dashed through the front gate of his rose-lined cottage overlooking the river, to the opposite end of the village where a dilapidated church hall served as home to the Parish Council. Hanging over the building, as he approached, was a huge cauliflower cloud which experience had taught him would bring thunder to the village if it came their way. Having read the agenda, he fancied that a storm was about to break inside the hall whatever happened to the cloud above. Not only was Little Missington being called on to modernize its road for the passage of traffic it did not particularly want, but it was being asked to pay for it as well.

A flash of lightning split the air as Digby thrashed at the thought of such an imposition. Drenched with vows of indignation he strode into the hall impatient to precipitate his views upon his fellow councillors ... only to find he was the first to arrive.

It offended Digby's sense of economy when people were late for meetings and he sat in the gloomy cheerless hall which he had played no part in constructing, and calculated the cost per minute of their collective lateness. It would have bought him, he reasoned, a month's supply of tobacco for his pipe or the Chairman a week's ration of hay for

7

his horses.

Next to arrive was Patrick O'Hachetty. He had inherited a butcher's business from his father, an émigré from Ireland, now resting with his soul at the bottom of the churchyard. Pat O'Hachetty, senior, had taught his son to avenge the wrath of Cromwell with every swing of his chopper. His eyes brightened when he saw Digby and he grabbed him by the elbow.

'Did yer read this?' he cried, waving a copy of the letter from the County Council. 'I vote we bury the postman and deny we ever received it!' Digby, the undertaker, liked the idea but hoped he wasn't serious.

Before the butcher could embellish his theme, George Whackett the schoolmaster appeared.

'Reckon you wouldn't give many marks for whoever wrote that letter, George,' said Digby anxious to divert the conversation.

'I'd give him six-of-the-best!' said Patrick resuming his belligerence.

'I noticed he couldn't spell *thoroughfare*,' said George, 'for I don't suppose he meant *throughfare*: nothin' ever gets through!'

'Hope you weren't talking about me, George,' said Frank Morse, laughing as he entered, for Frank ran the General Stores and Post Office where he was responsible for telephones and telegrams.

The level of chatter increased as they vied with each other to denounce the proposition they had come to debate. By the time Ted Brewer joined the gathering, it was reminiscent of the public bar, behind which he normally resided at the Coach and Horses.

The two remaining ordinary members of the Council did not leave the Coach and Horses until the publican was already in his seat alongside the schoolmaster. Sam Waterman and Harry Carter were among Ted's regular

8

customers and as a result they not infrequently missed the Parish Council meeting, but this meeting was one they were determined not to miss. Sam had been a boat builder in his younger days and now maintained his interest in the water by operating a strange-looking craft called a weedcutter which he steered up and down the river to keep it navigable by boats and swans. Harry, on the other hand, was a landsman whose life had been devoted to horse-drawn transport. What they now shared in common, apart from patronage of the Coach and Horses, was time on their hands in retirement.

When Cyrus arrived he was flushed and out of breath, as much from hurrying and a last minute tot of toddy as from indignation, and he took a moment or two to compose himself before he opened the meeting.

'Have we a quorum?' he asked at length.

'We've a full house!' cried Patrick.

'Well, then,' he began, 'I'm sure we've all read the letter so let's get that out of the way first. Would anybody like to suggest a reply?'

Mr O'Hachetty made a sign like he was raising a chopper.

'We can't afford it,' said the Treasurer, not waiting for an estimate.

'We don't need it,' said Syd, hoping that would settle the matter.

'I don't see why we should pay for someth'n' we don't need,' echoed the publican, oblivious to the effect his remark might have upon the brewing industry were it to be quoted out of context.

'I aren't agoin' to pay any more on th' rates,' said Sam. 'If they gets any higher we'll need a horoscope to see 'em!'

'You mean a telescope, don't you, Sam?'

'Do I boy? I'd have thought "horror" were the right word!'

9

Cyrus reminded them that the letter had said the County Council would withdraw their authority for maintaining the road if they failed to look after it properly and repairs would then be carried out by the Highways Committee at Little Missington's expense.

'From what I can see,' said Digby, 'there's no way out of it but we've got to do something about the blasted road.'

'Ahem! said the Clerk, not used to such language in the church hall.

'He means like the blasted oak, I expect Mr Stubbles,' said the Chairman.

'I mean the blasted road!' repeated Digby, unrepentant. 'If we don't do something about it soon we might as well pack up our belongings and move in to another parish. We certainly couldn't afford the rates once that new Highways Committee got its hands on our road. It's so long since it had anything done to it it'd cost a fortune to put right the way they would tackle it... I vote we do it ourselves.'

There was an uneasy silence for a few moments and then the Clerk looked up from his table. 'Are you agoin' to lend us your cement-mixer, Ben?' he asked. 'I can let yer have a bucket an' spade if that'll help!'

'I've got some plasticine,' cracked another wit, but the Chairman could see from the look on Digby's face that he was serious.

They spent the next twenty minutes listening to Digby telling them how to repair a road. The Clerk winced every time he came to terms like 'blinding' and 'bottoming', but it took a craftsman to recognize a craftsman and he soon realized that Digby knew what he was talking about. 'Bottoming', said Digby, would be necessary to prevent the road being squeezed by downward pressures into the ditches on either side, a phenomenon unlikely to have occurred with the present road where the ditches ran across as well as along the highway. He explained how 'pitching stones' would need to be placed by hand and the gaps between filled in with broken rubble to bind the stones together. 'Blinding', he said, was the term used by the trade to describe this part of the operation.

'That's all very interesting, Mr Digby,' said Cyrus, anxious to re-assert his role as the Chairman, 'but who can we get to do it?'

'My idea,' said Digby, 'was that we should do it ourselves.'

'Well, you're a builder, I see that, so I suppose it wouldn't be improper for us to commission you to do it for us. But have you got enough men for the job?'

'No,' said Digby, 'and you couldn't afford them if I had. The point about my suggestion, Chairman, is that we should literally do it ourselves: each one of us give a hand, and all of us round up some volunteers ... and equipment.'

They began to see what he meant.

The vicar, they said, had a roller. According to the less devout he used it to flatten his figure more than the vicarage lawn. But they were sure they could borrow it.

Sam Waterman had plenty of tar, though he needed it, he said, for 'bottoming' his boats rather than the road. However, he thought he could spare a pot or two.

Digby said he would supply the earthenware pipes needed to drain water that would collect when it rained and Ted Brewer said he had an old pump he would lend them to get rid of the water that was already there.

Harry offered his cart to carry the stones and rubble that Digby had been talking about and George Whackett said there was an old wheelbarrow on the school playing-field which they could use.

Cyrus saw the opportunity to turn the idea to his own advantage. There was an ugly hollow in one of his fields from which building stone had once been extracted when

11

they were erecting a local malthouse. He saw the prospect of restoring to pasture a part of his land which had lain fallow for many a year and offered the remainder of its contents to the enterprise

A vote of thanks was passed to record his generosity.

By the time the meeting closed euphoria had set in and they all went home assured that the job was as good as done. The clouds had dispersed and only the distant roll of thunder, punctuating shallow flashes of far-off lightning, reminded them of the storm that had earlier threatened their proceedings. One would have thought they had voted themselves into a fortune instead of such a rash commitment.

2

Mrs Veronica Digby was not at all convinced that her husband had spent the entire evening at the church hall. There was something particularly unusual about his attitude that she could not associate with his return from a Council Meeting. He was talkative and excited and full of remarks about a new crusade.

Had he got back at nine o'clock, say, instead of half-past ten, or left the particulars of his scheme until the morning she might have believed him, but coming back at this significant hour and carrying on the way he did she was sure he had been to the Coach and Horses and not at all inclined to humour him.

Such, however, was Digby's overwhelming satisfaction at the way he had steered the meeting out of their predicament that he hardly noticed his wife's reaction. Pacing the living room from end to end, he terrified the tabby cat which leapt from chair to chair as he passed, and not even the appearance of his daughter in her latest fashion pyjamas could release him from his vision.

Sally went back to her room without the customary token of affection from her father and Mrs Digby returned to face him with a cup of strong black coffee.

'You've forgotten the milk, dear.'

'No, Benjamin, I have not!'

'Oh, my! I must be getting tired. I thought it looked

13

blacker than usual.'

Prepared to ignore the coffee altogether for a minute, he placed the cup on the table and took his wife by the arm. Leading her to the fireplace he pointed to an old print they had on the wall above. It showed a group of Ancient Britons, headed by Boadicea with trident raised, chasing the backs of a line of chariots, charging the slopes of a gleaming valley, and trampling the dust of their native land. It was not clear whether the action represented the victorious rout of an invisible foe, or the headlong retreat from invading hordes, but the spectacle of England's ancient warriors defending their country in time of war was one that inspired Benjamin to great heights of pride and oratory.

'Look at that, my dear. That's what we need now. A new spirit of adventure, drawn straight from the blood of our ancestors. I'm going to see that every lad in our village knows the peril of the present situation. I shall rely on them to form a band of men that will stand strong and defiant on the boundaries of our land and face the challenge of the day triumphant.'

What Boadicea had done against the Romans, they would do against the County Council. And what the Romans had done to build roads across the lands of England they would do again, in Little Missington, themselves!

'Drink your coffee, Benjamin, and we'll go to bed.'

'Coffee? Bed? How can you stand there and talk about such things when there's work to be done, thought to be given to the tasks ahead, inspiration needed for the rallying of our forces.... Mrs Digby, this is the crucial hour of our lives, the testing point of our solidarity! If we fail it could mean the collapse of a community that has remained inherited and compact for countless generations....'

'Well, I'm going to bed, anyway. You can follow up later

14

when you're sober!'

The impact of her remark did not register. Benjamin looked after her as she slammed the door as though she were part of the invisible army that was left out of the picture over the mantlepiece. His trend of rhetoric broken, and without an audience, he remembered the cup of coffee and refreshed himself with several sips before the flavour reached his senses.

'But it *is* black, I tell you, Vera,' he spluttered. 'You *have* forgotten the milk.' Rushing to the pantry he remedied the omission from an earthenware pot that stood on the brick-lined floor.

* * *

Benjamin slept very badly that night. The visions of crusading choir boys shovelling the rubble from a country road and converting it into a modern concrete highway faded as the light of dawn brought the first doubts to his mind, and the twittering chorus of the birds which normally delighted him came now as dripping water on his tortured brow. The full scale of his awful commitment was slowly breaking on his consciousness and reddening his countenance as the cold light of understanding caught up on the clouds of imagination which had been floating higher and higher through the night. The glow which confronted him warmed only to embarrassment, and then like the sharp snap which follows the sunrise, a chill breeze gripped his thoughts in icy horror.

Where on earth was he going to get the men to do the work he'd promised?

All the enthusiasm and elation of the night before had disappeared by breakfast time and Mrs Digby was even more convinced of her diagnosis than ever. Benjamin was as quiet and morose behind his boiled egg and piece of toast

15

as he had been flamboyant and boastful of his intentions when she went to bed.

'I'd better fetch the doctor to your dad,' she remarked to Sally as they watched him dipping the marmalade spoon into his cup of tea.

'Oh dear, I've sugared it already!' He half-smiled at them and added apologetically, 'I'm getting absent-minded in my old age.'

'You're not old yet, so don't try hiding behind that one, Benjamin Digby, or I'll remind you how old I am by forgetting to cook your dinner!'

'Your mother will have her little joke, won't she?' He looked up from the table as he said this and turned to Sally for support. Seeing them both staring at him intently he began to fidget a little, for fear they were hostile about something.

'She doesn't look any older than the day I married her.'

Strange how a remark which in certain circumstances can warm a woman's heart rouses her in others to anger!

'There now! That's a proper insult that is! If I looked like this the day I married you, you must have been dafter than I thought you were!'

'Not a bit of it,' said Digby, struggling, and again looking towards his daughter for support. 'You didn't look much older than young Sally here — and see how lovely she is!'

'There's no need to bring her into it either. If you go putting ideas into her head about wedding days and things like that she'll be going off and marrying the first young handsome who comes along. It'll be soon enough before she goes as it is.'

'Oh Mum. How can you say that?'

'She's pulling your leg, girl. Don't take any notice of her. You're far too young to think about things like that.'

'She's eighteen! At her age I'd had two proposals of

16

marriage and refused both of them.'

'Oh, Mum, you shouldn't say that.'

'Why not? It's the truth. Your father wasn't the only beau I had, by a long chalk.'

'You were the only girl I had.'

'I never knew anyone lie like your father. Have some more toast.'

'No thank you.'

'How many times have *you* been proposed to?'

Benjamin's question did not take Sally by surprise. 'So many I've lost count. They ask you the first time they meet you these days. I bet they didn't do that when you were a girl, Mum.'

'Your father did.'

'Which goes to show what a quick judge I was of character. And any fellow who sees our Sally's likely to do the same. She's the prettiest girl in the village; it's little wonder they fall for her. Who's the latest, Sal?'

'Leave the girl alone, Ben. She doesn't have to tell us who she's going out with.'

Benjamin, who had succeded in diverting the conversation, looked slyly at his wife and then winked at Sally. 'She gets right upset though if you don't tell her.'

'Ben!'

'Yes dear? Well, who is it, Sal? Who's the lucky feller this week?'

'Dad! I do *not* have a different ''feller'', as you call him, every week. I only change friends if I feel different about them.'

'Or find someone you like better?'

'That's not fair, Dad, and you know it.'

'Well what happened to that Bertie you used to see a lot of?'

Sally turned her head coquettishly towards the corner of the ceiling. 'I still see him.'

'Oh. So it's still on, then?'

'I said, I still see him.'

'I see. So it isn't anyone else this time: it's just that you feel different about him, like?'

'Ben, leave the girl alone. You shouldn't torment her.'

'Well, you started it.'

And so Digby escaped his threatened visit from the doctor. But all that day he worried about the plans he'd made for re-surfacing the road, and in particular about how he was to get the volunteers he needed for a labour force. Prospects of persuading the young men of the village to rally to his call did not appear half so promising when he came to consider them individually as they had done the night before when he saw them only in fantasy. Those who had recently returned to civilian life from the armed services were unlikely, he thought, to regard a spell of manual labour as a fair reward for winning the war. Conversely, he doubted whether those who were still too young to have served their country would consider a course of stone-laying as a useful qualification for their future. That left one or two who had been spared the experience of military service by a measure of physical disability and Digby failed to see how they could be expected to overcome their handicaps in time to be much help.

* * *

In the Coach and Horses that evening Digby was greeted by a group of villagers who were keen to learn at first-hand what had really been decided at the Council Meeting on the previous night. Rumours of a mammoth project had been circulating since the early morning and there were some among them who had been shrewd enough to wonder who was going to pay for it all. In a village the size of Little Missington it does not take long for gossip to travel and, although there was no local newspaper to announce it, the whole village had been aware of Digby's proposition before the breakfast things were off the table.

Of course, such means of distributing news are prone to inaccuracy. Even a modern national newspaper is more reliable than the pre-Lutheran methods of conveying information.

Some of the messengers at Little Missington had become so extravagant in their exaggeration of Digby's plan as to include a bridge and tunnel in their account of it, and no-one had really appreciated that it was to be a 'do-it-yourself' affair at the absolutely minimum cost. Digby's first task, therefore, was to put the record right on what it was he actually intended to do.

As he came to discuss the mechanics of how the job was to be done he mentioned the need for volunteers and explained that upwards of fifty pairs of hands would be needed if they were to make any headway at all. In the hope that it might induce some of his contemporaries to set an example, he explained his fear that they would not get a very enthusiastic response from the younger generation, and this started a series of recollections to illustrate how attitudes had changed since they were boys.

One memory led to another to show that in their day they did all the right things, like raising their hats to ladies in the street and going to church on Sundays, whereas today they saw none of these courtesies practised.

To have pointed out that few of the present generation wore hats at all and that half their elders had stopped going to church once they got to the 'age of discretion' would have no effect upon their convictions. The youth of today was irresponsible and unchivalrous, superficial and untidy and, one would have imagined, unguided by inheritance, for it was all the things their fathers were not, and none of those they were.

Yet the most significant change of all in youthful habit over the past half-century seemed to have passed unnoticed: there was not a single one of them in the Coach and Horses that evening to defend himself. It said much for the resourcefulness of youth that this was so, for there were very few other places in the village where they could meet and pass their hours of leisure. Dances were held in the church hall on Fridays and Saturdays, and there was a film show there on Wednesdays. A youth club with table tennis facilities functioned at the vicarage most nights of the week (except Sundays) and there were occasional whist drives and socials at the school house, but other than these there were no organised or regular gatherings in the village to which youth might be attracted and no single place of entertainment, built as such, where they could go. Some who were shy, or averse to dancing, went fishing on the river and others who had no aptitude for games laid snares across the fields and woodlands.

The problem which faced the population of Little Missington in respect of its application to leisure was the same as that which faced countless millions still in the so-called backward areas of the world, where modern civilizing methods of mechanical recreation had yet to do their playing for them. Wherever the hour of rising was very early, and the working day vigorous and hard, the inclination to active pastime in the evenings was very small. It is a sobering thought, therefore, that whereas in the village of Miang Mai in Central Thailand, or Wong Ho Chin in the heart of China, the human birth-rate was increasing yearly out of all regard for decency, the influence of western civilization and puritanical thought had maintained the population of Little Missington at a pretty constant level for the past couple of hundred years.

The thoughts of those in the Coach and Horses were neither puritanical nor particularly civilized that evening for they were becoming increasingly vindictive towards youth. If it did not occur to them that they were being unjust in accusing their young men of worthlessness, it mattered even less that they were the fathers who had reared such children. As if they were haranguing Solomon for the sins of his wives, the elder statesmen of the village kept up their vitriol in defence of bygone days, forgetting that when *they* were young there was a generation before them to make the same charges on their account.

The bar was in danger of overflowing with its melancholy when an old man got up and made a remark which was to cut the atmosphere clear of its smoke and misery, and leave a mark upon the village history as surely as the architects who built the church — or Cromwell who defaced it.

Bob Blackett thumped the table with his glass. 'If them young 'uns ain't game enough to swing a shovel for the sake o' this parish I reckon we old 'uns ought to show 'em how to do it! If we can't persuade 'em, shame 'em, that's what I say!'

Digby was thunderstruck. Bob Blackett was a pensioner who hadn't done a day's work for years and this was the first time he had been free of gout to make an animated contribution to the conversion for just as long. Bob's normal place was in the corner farthest from the bar, where he could sit propped against a stick and wait for the beer to be brought to him when anyone called a round. When his turn came to pay he usually staggered forward and fell just short of the bar until somebody took pity on him and sent him back to his corner.

Tonight, in the excitement of what he had to say, nobody noticed it had been his turn when he got up to speak and he found himself suddenly surrounded with brim-full tankards in a splash of celebration.

Digby's project was well and truly launched. In the

heat of emotions which had built up during the evening every man-jack among them volunteered to lend a hand. It was a foregone conclusion that the rest of the village would follow, for it would have been too much for their curiosity not to have and too bad for their pride to be left out.

3

Sally, who had earned her keep since leaving school by helping her mother about the home and her father in the office, had not exactly told the truth when she insinuated she was tired of Bertie Woodfellow. What had really happened was that her pride had got the better of certain other emotions because Bertie had forgotten her birthday. Instead of being flattered by his remark that he never wanted to think of her being a day older than when he first saw her, she was indignant that he had not remembered the date. After all, she had mentioned it often enough as the day approached.

The immediate post-anniversary period was marked by a long spell of self-imposed quarantine during which time Sally's fever grew steadily worse. As invariably happens in such cases, it was Bertie who gave in first. The night after Bob Blackett had thrown down his challenge in the Coach and Horses, Bertie appeared at the Digby's cottage with a bunch of roses and forget-me-nots. These he thought were the appropriate flowers for the occasion. He asked shyly for Mr Digby when the door opened.

'Why, come in, Bertie,' said Mrs Digby, 'he's upstairs changing his collar just now but he'll be down in a minute.'

Sally, who had seen him coming, slipped quickly upstairs to her father and startled the life out of him by appearing at his bedroom door while he was changing from one pair of trousers to another.

'Daddy, come quickly,' she said, not noticing his embarrassment, 'there's somebody down stairs to see you — with a bunch of flowers.'

'Who the devil has died, then? We haven't booked a funeral for tomorrow, have we? Who is it, Sally? And why didn't you knock before you came in?'

'I couldn't. The door was open.'

'Well, you should have called out or something...'

'Ssh! I didn't want to be heard. Tell him I'm out, or I've gone to bed, or whatever you like, but I don't want to see him.'

Just then her mother opened the door which led on to the staircase from the living-room. 'Sally dear, do come down. There's a friend of yours waiting to see your father.'

Sally's expression was an exact replica of her father's on many an occasion when her mother had said something he did not want to hear. She went slowly and sulkily downstairs.

'Hallo, Sally. I didn't think you'd be at home. I... I've come to see your father about some business...'

'Oh, then I won't disturb you. I'll go back to my sewing.'

'No, please don't... I mean, won't you wait till your father comes. ...I've brought these for you, as a matter of fact. They're sort of a ... late birthday present, if you see what I mean!'

'Oh, isn't that sweet of Bertie?' said Mrs Digby, putting her foot in it a second time. Sally was not yet ready for the reconciliation.

'Thank you,' she answered coldly, 'they'll go very nicely with the ones I had last Saturday.'

Before he could retrieve the situation, Bertie was face to face with Mr Digby and a hurried awkward explanation followed of why he had come to see him.

'I thought you'd come to see young Sal, here, not me,'

24

said Digby rather unhelpfully. 'A few minutes later and you'd have missed us, you know. We were just going out, Mrs Digby and me, weren't we, Vera?'

'Oh, I'm sorry, Mr Digby. I didn't mean to keep you. I can call back some other time.'

'My dear feller, not a bit of it! You're here now, you can stay now. We're not in that much of a hurry. It's just that I thought . . . ,' and a sly look at his daughter made him choose his words carefully, '. . . we ought to tell you so you wouldn't be offended if we went out and left you in a minute or two, like.'

The door to the staircase closed rather sharply and Sally disappeared upstairs with her roses and forget-me-nots.

'What is it you wanted to see me about? Has it got anything to do with Sally?'

'On no, Mr Digby, it's nothing like that.'

Mrs Digby's heart turned over. Benjamin relaxed.

'Well then, is there something I can do for you?'

'No sir, it's rather the other way: you see, I thought perhaps there was something I could do for you, like. I believe you were looking for someone to help build a road?'

Poor Digby! He was flabbergasted. Then suddenly the wickedest of thoughts occurred to him. If only his daughter were a little more promiscuous he might have all the labour he was looking for!

'Looking for someone, did you say? I've been looking for lots of someones. I need a whole brigade of someones. Do you know what we mean to do?'

'Yes, I've heard about your plan, sir. It's a very good idea.'

'Of course it's a good idea! It'll save us money. It'll keep the rates down, and keep those ruddy county councillors off our doorstep. It's not just a necessity, it's a matter of life and death for Little Missington.'

'Can I join in then? You've still got room for some

more helpers?'

Digby's eyes filled with tears. 'My dear feller! What a good feller you are! More room did you say? I certainly have got more room. We'll need every able-bodied man in the village if we're to do the job properly. There's a lot to be done, you know. It's not like putting down a path to a farmhand's cottage. I've had plenty of volunteers, mind you. Don't think that I've not had offers. Only one or two, to tell you the truth, are a little bit past it now and I'll have to put them on the lighter jobs. But that's just between you and me! What I need are more chaps like yourself who can stand up to a bit of heavy work without complaining or sloping off when I'm not looking.' Digby uttered this without the slightest trace of cynicism. He was obviously carried away by Bertie's gesture and off-loading some of the thoughts which had been troubling him as he had turned over the problem in his mind during the past few hours. 'Are there any more of your pals, do you think, who might be wanting to volunteer if they knew there were still vacancies?'

By the time Sally emerged from her bedroom Benjamin and Bertie were in animated accord about recruiting arrangements and her father was busy explaining the difference between constructing a road on the Telford and Macadam systems. To demonstrate what he was saying Benjamin had brought in a window box from outside and placed it on the table in the centre of the room. Sally looked aghast at the little pile of pebbles on the green baize table cloth.

'Daddy! What *are* you doing?'

Digby looked equally surprised at his daughter's tone of approbation. 'I am showing Bertie how to make a new road.'

'Well, I hope you know how to make a new tablecloth. Mother will be livid if she sees that!'

26

Fortunately Mrs Digby was cheerfully pottering about in the kitchen, under the impression that she was being tactful in leaving the two men to discuss their business matters alone.

Sally started to remove the models from the table and Bertie helped, albeit uncomfortably, by pushing a handful of rubble into his jacket pockets. Mrs Digby returned to find Sally's bottom protruding through the open window and Benjamin and Bertie at opposite ends of the fireplace, suspiciously poking the fire.

Before she had time to discover what was going on, Digby had taken his wife affectionately by the arm, winked misleadingly and said, 'We'll be off now, Vera, and leave these two young ones to sort out their own affairs.'

Sally looked round angrily to stem her father's meddling, but only succeeded in banging her head on the base of the window frame.

'It might as well have been there as on the wall!' she muttered, sitting down with a bump.

Bertie looked anxiously at the door. Seeing that her father and mother had gone, he rushed over to find if Sally had hurt herself.

'No, I'm all right. Thank you. A few knocks on the head won't hurt me.'

Bertie sensed there was an edge to that remark and dodged it.

'I hope you liked the flowers...'

'The roses were lovely.'

'I plucked the forget-me-nots myself.'

'Did you? I had forgotten about them.'

Sally hated being thrust into a situation like this. She had been left alone with Bertie unexpectedly and was not prepared for the encounter. If she had known that her mother and father were going out, and had asked Bertie to call in their absence, it would have been different. But

27

now she felt her parents had conspired against her and she was tactically at a disadvantage. In consequence, her defences took much longer to break down than would otherwise have been the case.

'Sally... I'm sorry about last Saturday. I didn't mean to forget, you know. I was only joking when I said...'

'Oh, that's not important! I'll have plenty of birthdays. Besides, why should I care if you remembered it or not? It was *my* birthday, wasn't it? I don't expect people who are not in the family to remember my birthday — I'm not a child any more. I don't have cakes with candles on. It's all over now and past, so don't say another word about it.'

If Bertie had not been so busy wondering what to say next he would have seen a vision of Mrs Digby before him at that moment, but he ignored the spectre of years to come and plunged his arms impulsively round Sally's shoulders. On such occasions as this actions are so much more acceptable than words.

'Will you come with me to the dance next Saturday?'

'I might ...'

Bertie saw the first glimpse of relenting in her eyes and drew her closer.

'You will come, won't you Sally? I've been so lost without you all this week — I couldn't bear to go another week like that.'

Their eyes met now for the first time and warm tears welled up to melt the ice that had come between them. Sally waited to be kissed.

* * *

In the Coach and Horses Digby was buying a drink for his wife and listening to the latest gossip-of-the day from Mrs Brewer.

'They say old Bob's been acting queer-like all day. He's

even been down to the forge without his stick, and that's something he hasn't done for twenty years — as long as I've known him!'

'Go on, Daisy, you old fibber! You know darn well you can remember further back than that!'

Benjamin hesitated a moment between the tantalizing expression of his old sweetheart behind the bar and the instinctive awareness that his wife was in the room behind him. It was not that any animosity existed between the two women, for they had both been sweethearts to too many of the same men in the village who were still alive to tell the tale, but Digby felt a twinge of conscience every time he flirted in the presence of his wife. Perhaps it wasn't conscience but self-consciousness, though whatever it was he felt uncomfortable, and there was no fun at his age in encouraging discomfort.

All the same, old Daisy was a good sort, he thought, and Daisy felt the same about him.

'How'd you like to put the clock back twenty years?' she asked him. 'Bet you and the missus wouldn't be in here havin' a half-pint together, eh? Just about the time you were countin' on young Sally, wasn't it?'

Mention of 'young Sally' caused Digby to confide in Mrs Brewer that he had left his daughter at home with 'the Woodfellow feller.' 'They get on well together, you know, if they're left alone. Make a nice pair, they do. Not that I'm interfering, mind, but encouragement goes a long way, I always say.'

Daisy Brewer was horrified. 'Young Timber and your Sal, eh? Left them alone, did you say? Blessed if I'd leave a daughter alone with a fellow of his age. Times aren't like what they used to be. Kids of today know more at five than we did at fifteen!'

'Exactly, Daisy — that's exactly what I reckon. If we'd been left alone at their age we'd have had plenty to find out about. But they know it all already, so there's no curiosity. Besides, young Sal's no fool. She won't stand any nonsense. And, anyway, the boy's not like Old Timber, his father, was: he's a perfect gentleman... He brought her flowers!'

'Good God, man; he can't have been up to any good!'

Digby grinned. He read Daisy's thoughts by the look she gave him.

'What was it I used to bring you? Buttercups?'

'And daisies!'

'Good Heavens!' Tossing his head and roaring with laughter, Digby gathered his glasses and turned to look for his wife. Instead he came face to face with Cyrus and Gladys Galleon. 'Well, if it isn't the chairman. What will you have?'

Daisy dispensed the order while Digby excitedly told him how Bertie had promised to round up some volunteers. 'Young Woodfellow is setting a fine example. He'll rally them all, I promise you, before the week's out. There won't be one of them blacklegging, I bet you. That lad's got spirit...'

'That daughter of yours must have something too, eh, Digby?' Cyrus paused for a moment to let the remark take effect. 'She must be worth her weight in gold when it comes to diggin',' he added artfully. He was a devil for a joke like that!

Mrs Galleon, meanwhile, had slipped away to Mrs Digby who had taken up quarters in the corner furthest from the bar. 'You poor thing! I bet you've been here for hours? I can tell you have by the rain on your coat; it stopped raining ages ago.'

'I get used to it. He must have his little nonsense with Daisy. Then he gets conscience-stricken, and I get a double gin and orange. It's been that way for years. He's harmless!'

30

Gladys encouraged her to continue. 'I don't know how you manage to look so young, Vera. With those husbands of ours I wonder we don't both look like corpses. Cyrus is talking now about taking exercises in manual labour. Have you ever heard of anything so ridiculous!'

'That's nothing! Benjamin wants to play at Roman soldiers. He led off at me last night and said I was Boadicea or something. Frightened the life out of me, he did. I knew he'd been drinking, mind, but it worries you just the same. You never know when their mind's going to turn and stay like it. Still I suppose he's had a lot on his mind since the County started interfering with their parish affairs. Ben says there'll be a revolution soon.'

'A revolution?'

'Yes, that's what Ben says. There'll be a revolution, he says: those councillors at County Hall on one side and him and your husband on the other. While we've got the initiative, he says, it's all right, but if we ever lose it, it'll be a massacre.'

The two men returned, perplexed at overhearing the last part of the conversation without knowing to what it referred.

Digby gave his wife her double gin and orange and looked the other way. Cyrus stared sheepishly at Gladys and offered her a double creme de menthe. The women exchanged glances but wisely held their tongues.

After the crispness of the atmosphere had worn down to the level of matrimonial pleasantries, Benjamin and Cyrus broke away again, though only conversationally this time. While their wives sped through the repertoire of local gossip their attentions turned to matters of municipal importance.

City executives, if they so desire, can conduct their business over luxuriant luncheon tables, but Little Missington had no place where a man could pay to rest his elbows on a table-cloth; the saloon bar of the Coach and Horses was the nearest one could get to a public meeting place suitable for mixing work with pleasure.

Cyrus and Benjamin met there once a week for just that purpose.

Digby was confident now that he would have sufficient labour to start work in a few days. In fact, if the offers he expected were forthcoming it was imperative he should have a plan worked out so that everyone could be allotted tasks immediately. He knew enough about human nature to realize that enthusiasms do not mature on keeping.

Cyrus rather fancied himself as a strategist and began to see the opportunities open to him. 'Line them all up in the Church Hall on Wednesday evening, Digby, and we'll sort them out into shapes and sizes. Tall ones for the picks and shovels, sieves for the short ones...

Benjamin had been an N.C.O. in the First World War and too often at the receiving end of a strategist's whim to take kindly to ideas like this. 'They won't stand for regimentation, Cyrus. You can't expect it. They're civilian volunteers, remember — unpaid! We'll have to get our discipline another way.'

'Be kind to 'em, eh? Say "please" to everything and raise your hat before you ask? What do you want, Digby, a crowd of chorus girls?'

'I want a labour force that'll stay to the finish. Cyrus, we'll have to be subtle about it. You'll see what I mean in a minute. What would you say was the greatest spur to industry? What is it you're always talking about at election time? Free enterprise, isn't that it, and competition? That's it, isn't it — that's what you believe in? Well, that's what we'll use to do the trick on this job. The first thing we've got to do is clear the road and dig up the surface. How it's done I don't mind so long as we get it cleared quickly and ready for rebuilding. I reckon we should put half the force at one end of the village and the other half at the other end and tell them to race each other to the middle. 'That's what I mean by competition.'

It was no manner of speaking that the Coach and Horses stood at the centre of the village. Digby knew his local geography.

Cyrus thought for a few moments and pulled harder at his pipe. He liked the idea, especially the bit about free enterprise, but he wasn't too sure about the outcome of the competition.

'Were you thinking of a prize for the first team home?'

'Well, I daresay we could persuade old Ted to open up a special firkin'. There was a twinkle in Benjamin's eye as he saw the remark register.

'I don't think the vicar would like that much. . . a new road built on the foundation of beer and bribery!'

Cyrus chewed his words and chuckled as he relished the thought, then knocked back his drink with a flourish that startled the ladies.

Digby had triumphed again.

* * *

Next morning the offers came tumbling in. Bertie, who had recently been demobilized after four years of somewhat frustrating ground duties in the Royal Air Force, had embarked on his new-found crusade with enthusiasm and cunning. After first meeting the kind of reaction that Digby had imagined, he found ways of overcoming resistance which, if Digby had applied them, might have been counter-productive.

A rosy-cheeked youth in the church choir objected on the grounds that strenuous exercise in the open-air would affect his vocal chords, to which Bertie retorted 'Not half as much as my knee would in the right place!'

33

Billy Fowler was fond of football and argued that digging would damage his feet. Bertie demonstrated how it had not affected his feet in that way by placing one of them swiftly in the seat of Billy's pants.

Jimmy Brewer rather fancied himself as a 'ladies man' and complained with a grin that getting his hands scratched and dirty would affect his philandering. Bertie convinced him that a reputation for over-cleanliness could be construed as under-manliness, and Jimmy relented. Thus, by similar tactics, were the youth of Little Missington recruited.

Benjamin was soon bubbling with excitement. Only a short time ago he had been in danger of having insufficient labour with which to put his plan into operation; then it had looked as though all his volunteers would be old age pensioners. Now it seemed that youth would outnumber the elders after all, but news of the free beer spread quickly and soon a balance of power was restored.

Balance was indeed a function of power and not of number, for there were more men in the village over middle-age, than there were below it. Permitting a liberal interpretation of 'youth', Digby announced that the competition would be a straight race between the young men who would start at one end of the village and their elders who would dig up from the other.

The boys were not afraid of being outnumbered for they were confident of their strength to win. Moreover, they were less concerned with the barrel of beer than with the kudos they expected to earn from their feminine admirers.

All over the village a catch-phrase began to appear, on brick walls and fences, tree trunks and cowsheds, pungent and mysterious. Everyone was talking about it, most of all the ladies. Whetted with wonder were their appetites at what might be in store, and hungry indeed were they all to see the outcome of so great a promise.

'The Road to Love...' wrote Bertie, and they all repeated it with varying degrees of uncertainty as to its meaning,... "THE ROAD TO LOVE ... IS AN OPEN ROAD ... SO DIG IT!"

It is interesting to speculate if this was, perhaps, the origin of an expression that gained currency in later years, far, far beyond the walls of Little Missington. But only those who understand the ways of youth will 'dig it'.

4

The Big Race, as it soon came to be known in the village, was due to start at two o'clock on Saturday. Bertie, having lost the toss at the call-over on Wednesday, was made to work his team from the bottom of the hill so that they would have the slope against them.

Digby agreed to captain the team of elders, although it was understood that he would be taking charge of the whole lot of them the moment they embarked on stage two of the proceedings, which was to build up a new surface. That was scheduled to start on the following weekend.

Instructions to both teams were very simple. They were to dig to a depth of two feet from the existing surface and sieve from the rubble all stones over an inch and a half in diameter. The stones thus salvaged were to be piled along one side of the thoroughfare and the residual rubble along the other. These would be needed for stage two.

Late on Friday night a small contingent went out with hurricane lamps and placed diversion notices at appropriate junctions round the village, ready to come into use the following day. Not a great deal of thought was given to the alternative routes selected, for those responsible for placing the notices were confirmed pedestrians and entirely unaccustomed to the peculiar needs of the motorist.

A cold air of hushed expectancy hung over the street as dawn broke on the Saturday morning. It was as if the surface knew that its hour of doom had come, and like the prisoner on his last march to the scaffold, it was reflecting back to the air the cold fear that it had struck into so many hearts when they came upon it in its trail of terror.

Throughout the morning flags appeared at windows on the route of action, and one or two old ladies placed sixpences for luck along the mud-baked road-way, as they did in Christmas puddings, for the benefit of those who could find them. People were walking about the street with a carefulness and reverence as though they were trampling through a churchyard, and when one man spat upon the gutter, as he'd done for years without a protest, he was set upon and made to feel ashamed.

From all outward appearances, work in the fields and barns went on as usual, but inwardly there was not a man or youth in the village who had his mind on anything except the road.

Even the women were sensing the occasion. There had been an extra bite in the goodbye kiss for many of them that morning and they knew that much was at stake besides the barrel of beer. Stoves were throbbing with the boiling stewpots and ovens roared around the roasts and pies. Dainty puddings followed fancy pastries to the pantry shelves and dusty bottles from the darkened cupboards came up with their contents of exciting brews.

Despite all the tenderness of preparation there was many a meal devoured in haste with never a heed for later comfort.

No local football derby, nor the annual cricket match, could have aroused such a common interest or invoked such a clash of favourites. Where mother had husband and son competing in the race, and sisters had brothers in opposing camps, there was bound to be divided loyalty and only the fine spirit of common purpose for which the whole race was designed kept the families from falling out.

37

Not many husbands helped with the washing-up in Little Missington even on a normal Saturday, but on this remarkable day not many housewives bothered either. Dishes were stacked to one corner and pots left on the hob to soak. Dogs went without their dinners and chickens sat on their eggs for want of fetching.

The big hand of the church clock dropped from a quarter to half past one, and everything in the village was dropping with it. While the hand climbed back up the other side of the face to a quarter to two a procession was slowly making its way to the starting lines.

It was a fine clear day, late in the month of May, and a full six hours of sunlight lay ahead to shine upon twelve hundred yards of highway that was soon to be disinterred.

The teams formed up at their respective ends and all was set for the start of a road race that had no parallel in the history of modern sport.

There was not a vehicle in sight.

The festive spirit which had been evident among villagers since early morning had infected the teams as well and many contestants of all ages had turned out with coloured garlands and gay rosettes, to say nothing of fancy socks and patches on their trousers. Along the footpaths spectators stood with flags and rattles and showed their favours according to which end of the village they selected.

Bertie's Boys were there so early, and got so excited at the sight of their sweethearts and particular fancies, that they formed themselves into a long chain and marched up and down the roadway on their half of the track for fifteen minutes while the men at the other end were limbering up and disentangling themselves from their wives.

A strange array of digging instruments was piling up by the boundary markers which had been carefully identified from an Ordnance Survey map provided by George Whackett, the school master, in conjunction with

38

an old print which hung on the wall in the Coach and Horses. Spades, forks, picks and shovels; trowels, rakes, hoes and scrapers... the only thing which seemed to be missing was a pneumatic drill, and this would hardly have been an asset for the road was far too brittle to break up from that form of attack.

As the cheers of the onlookers mingled with the chimes of two o'clock Cyrus Galleon emerged from the bar of the Coach and Horses. Engaged as umpire and official starter of the undertaking, he was allowed no personal participation in the enterprise, which suited Digby just as much as it did Cyrus himself. The disadvantage of losing a labourer in this manner was outweighed in Digby's reckoning by the half-dozen it might have taken to repair the damage he was likely to do by interfering.

Swinging a shotgun from his shoulder and a pint of beer from his elbow, Cyrus stumbled on to the rostrum which had been specially built for the occasion and from which he was ultimately to toast the winners. 'May the best team win!' he shouted, far out of earshot of any it concerned, but readily applauded by the group of small boys and wizened old ladies who stood right in front of him. Raising his tankard he drank to the sentiment, then, remembering his need to be strictly impartial, raised it again with the opposite elbow. '... And never forgetting', he bellowed, 'a health to the losers!'

Smacking his lips, he looked wickedly down to the bottom of the hill, but what he saw did not encourage him to rest his eyes for long.

Bent forward behind a strip of white tape borrowed from some sweetheart's pigtail, a row of half-naked bodies crouched as if ready for a sprint. At the other end, though Cyrus could not see them because of a bend in the road in that direction, a silent group of sweating 'old 'uns', stood puffing like a herd of cattle just released from an overcrowded truck.

Taking up the shotgun Cyrus loaded it with a live round, 'for luck', as he told the children. Possessed of the wildest impulse he aimed at a rook on the topmost branch of the oak tree opposite. Round him the crowd began to sway like wheat in a whirlwind, and overhead the rook sat harmlessly watching.

Suddenly he pulled the trigger and a song-thrush sitting in the bushes underneath the oak tree died an operatic death.

Bertie and Benjamin plunged their picks to the ground and the old road from Myrtlesham to Puddlethorpe was on its way up.

5

The only bus that came to Little Missington was an 11b and that did not run on Sundays. Saturday, on the other hand, was usually a busy day and the little single decker Leyland that plied to and fro between the neighbouring towns reckoned to pass through Little Missington once every three or four hours. It was about as often as the driver's nerves could stand.

It was not unusual to find the road obstructed by uprooted trees or straying cowherds, sometimes even a shallow flood to ford, but the sight of a diversion notice was something new to the driver's experience. Rounding sharply where the arrow indicated he went straight through a five-barred gate held open by a pitch fork and signposted to Puddlethorpe. His wheels locked neatly in the furrows of a fast growing cornfield and came to rest about twenty yards from a hayrick.

Passengers from the bus mingled with spectators on the upper part of the course and tried to borrow spades to dig out the bus, but every attempt to get hold of an implement was greeted as a deliberate act of hostility by the locals. Eventually they gave up and set out to walk.

An hour and a half later the companion bus from Puddlethorpe was met at the other end of the village by a footsore and leg-scratched group of passengers who had stumbled through back lanes and brambles, over Little

Missington's lovely countryside, following the diversion notices put out the previous evening. Not one of them would have guessed that these signs had been erected in all sincerity to aid the driver of their vehicle.

Fortunately, most officials of the Corporation Transport Department were away at weekends, availing themselves of a privilege to travel free, though it was unlikely any ever used the facility to visit Little Missington. Complaints, therefore, had there been any, would have been more than usually useless. In fact, by the time passengers from the stranded bus had reached their destinations they were either too exhausted to lodge a protest or too bewildered to explain what had happened. One or two thought later of writing to the local newspaper commending the walk through the village in preference to the bumpy ride which they usually endured and for which they were charged a fare.

So, apart from an empty bus in the corner of a cornfield, and a good deal of harmless gossiping in the neighbouring townships, there was nothing to draw attention to the damage being done to one of England's ancient highways.

At about half-past four the womenfolk came forward with hot mugs of tea, dispensing them with cakes and muffins. One young lady at the lower end slipped on to the track with a flask of brandy, an act which could have had serious repercussions had it been seen at the upper end of the course.

The appearance of the road by this time was superficially little different from what it had always been, except that it was now two feet deeper in places. Periodically Cyrus marched up and down between the parties imparting words of encouragement at one end and impatient platitudes at the other. Then one of Bertie's team, swinging a mighty pick-axe, sent him headlong into the nearest ditch. After this escape he reduced his stint to the 600 yards between start and finish at the up-village end. The Coach and

Horses opened at 5.30 and he wanted to be on hand to send back any defaulters.

By the first sign of sundown youth was getting a little impatient. Progress had been slower than expected and they were painfully aware of how few stones had been salvaged from their rubble.

A scout was despatched to report on the size of their opponents' tally.

Mistaking his motive for a quick call on the publican, Cyrus seized the lad and offered to release him only on condition he 'paired' with one of the other party. Knowing nothing of parliamentary procedure, the lad thought he meant something quite different and ran all the way back to his comrades without the intelligence he had been sent to collect.

Actually the upper end of the road was disintegrating faster than lower down for, helped by the force of gravity, it had responded well to Digby's hazardous and haphazard attack. Not all his team faced the same way and picks were swinging as indiscriminately as pendulums in a pawnbroker's shop. They needed more than the earth's magnetism to set them in the same direction, but nobody came to grief from decapitation and only the arthritic suffered.

One effect of this random onslaught was to isolate a number of humps and hollows, giving the floor of the road an artistic quality that modern sculptors would have envied. To the onlookers it was curious how, when the short men stood on the humps and scooped in the hollows and the tall ones trod in the ditches and hacked at the escarpments, they all looked the same height.

Bertie, on the other hand, had organized his team with commendable foresight and they were moving forward in echelon determined by the toughness of the ground. Those in the front ranks were swinging with pickaxes, followed by 'scoopers' with shovels and spades, who passed the loads back to 'buckets and wheelbarrows', which were fed in continuous chains to the road side where 'sievers' were busy with separations. It was a breathless undertaking. Every half hour the ranks moved round so that no one got an unfair share of the duties.

Digby's trouble was getting some of his team to move at all but he had more bodies to make up for the dead-weights and over all his output was greater. Cyrus measured the distance they had covered so far or, rather, uncovered, and assured them that the barrel was as good as theirs. He prophesied that by sundown on Sunday the two ends would be together and a great celebration in progress at the Coach and Horses. How long it would then take to put a surface back again so as to make the highway passable did not concern him.

As dusk began to fall it was the cue for Cyrus to reappear on the rostrum and at eight o'clock he took an even wilder aim with his shotgun to announce the end of the day's proceedings.

Those accustomed to the drone of rooks and pigeons in the evening twilight and the frightened flutter of feathers when a shot is fired felt there was something odd about the silence which settled on the scene when Cyrus put his gun away. Perhaps there had been so many worms unearthed along the track that afternoon that the birds were overfed, but it seemed more likely they had taken stock of the situation at two o'clock when the first volley had been fired and migrated. Only the cries of weary workmen panting towards the Coach and Horses were heard to break the spell of rural silence.

Bertie had other ideas for his followers and they were scattering in all directions. At first sight this looked like a sign of weakness and disunity, but in fact appearances are often faulty guides to truthfulness, and the real reason for their hastiness was a desire to get home and change for

44

the village dance that evening in the church hall. It said much for their stamina that they could think of standing on their feet again all evening after so strenuous a day on the road.

The organizer of the Saturday dances was a Mr Christopher Hopper, owner of the malthouse, which accounted for them being known as the 'Weekly Hops'. He had anticipated a poor attendance that Saturday due to prior claims to everybody's energy, and he had cut down on all supplies as a prudent economy. He used the end of an old roll of tickets for admissions; there were fewer sandwiches and cakes and bottles of pop for the interval; and there were not so many chairs for sitting out, so that nothing could be done to curb his excitement when he saw the number of young people converging on the premises. Rushing about from end to end of the building, waving instructions to everyone in sight, he lived up to his name and looked more like a lonely dancer abandoned by his partner than a master of ceremonies in command of the situation. The poor man's agitation was no less for the fact that a few minutes earlier he had been alarmed at the almost total array of unescorted females in the hall and had been on the verge of phoning the nearest Air Force establishment and the County Barracks for reinforcements to redress the balance.

It was not as if the 'hop' had always been a sell-out. Many were there that night who had never danced in their life before and it was no secret that they had come to acquaint themselves with the ladies rather than learn the steps of the waltz. The word had got around and young ladies of the village were there in force. Some of the lads brought their usual partners, but they did not all survive the competition and it is sad to reflect that one or two of the more attractive young ladies proved unfaithful under the pressure of demand.

Bertie, as one might expect, was busy making up to Sally

and, to her credit, she stood by him throughout. This was no sentimental legacy from their bygone glories, for she had watched him with growing admiration all afternoon and was astonished at his power of leadership. No girl can resist the limelight and when there is a handsome-looking fellow she knows in the middle of it she has to be there too. Bertie was undoubtedly the hero of the day's proceedings, so far as everyone at the dance was concerned, and Sally revelled in the glare of envy which came from all the other girls as they danced together. Bertie, for his part, was delighted to have Sally back for she was, he believed, the prettiest girl there. It has to be said, however, that his preoccupation with the following day's problems may also have had something to do with his lack of attention to the host of other admirers.

Before the evening was too far under way and the pairings too far removed from the dance floor, Bertie passed the word round to his supporters that he wanted to see them outside for a few minutes during the interval.

* * *

Meanwhile at the Coach and Horses, Digby was facing a troublesome argument from the surviving members of his team. That is, from those who were not stricken with lumbago and groaning in bed. (Cyrus was too far gone with exhilaration from his arduous and important duties on the touchline to contribute anything useful at this stage, except an occasional pound note to keep the liquor flowing.)

There was general dissatisfaction at the way things had been going, both from the point of view of strategy and the progress they had made. Chief dissenter from their method of attack was Pat O'Hachetty. With his animated Irish prosecution he flayed the opinion of Digby and others that it was better they all did of their best and dug for dear life than that someone should regiment them the way it had been reported the lads were doing.

'You can dig like the Devil and never reach Him if you don't co-ordinate! We might as well be diggin' sand-pies at the seaside as go on the way we're doing. Why don't we form up into squads like the lads have done?'

'What — and strip to the waist?' asked someone.

'Strippin' ain't proper,' Syd protested. 'Suppose one o' their braces giv's out in front of all them women?'

'They weren't wearing braces,' Cyrus told him, perhaps a little spitefully.

'Then it's disgustin'. What do they keep 'em up with?'

'Will power,' said one. 'A deep breath', said another. 'A hip bone', said someone else, and that was enough to set Syd Stubble off all night.

'Nothin' but trouble ever came from a hip bone,' he grumbled and the response he got was more sympathetic than he expected. 'There's a proper lack of "properiety" these days,' he went on. 'No modesty like there was in my day.'

'You took your hat off to a lady, didn't you, Syd?'

Someone else in the audience was being unkind now. 'Well, they've progressed a bit since your day. They take their . . . shirts and vests off now!'

There was a great roar of laughter from those who had thought he was going to say something else, and Syd was submerged in a buzz of ribaldry that he tried not to understand.

They had got some way from Digby's project and the atmosphere looked a little brighter, but the Irishman was determined to bring them back to the earth they'd been working on.

'It's not will-power we need, nor manpower neither. It's horse-power we want! We're not building the pyramids! We should have a plough and a horse to pull it, or we'll be a month o' Sundays. What are we doing now? Just scratching the surface, when we ought to be getting our teeth into the job.'

Patrick's typical muddle of metaphors alarmed the sexton so much that his top plate nearly fell on the table. The thought of being expected to get his teeth into those rocks quite unnerved him, but it was the 'month-of Sundays' remark which troubled him more.

'It's bad enough that you should be thinking o' working tomorrow,' he muttered, and it was clear to Digby that at least one able-bodied absentee might be expected from their ranks the next day.

* * *

Buns and coffee in the church hall had to wait while Bertie briefed his followers, and the poor organizer, who had somehow managed to get more sandwiches cut and a fresh supply of cups and saucers introduced, trembled when he saw the young folk queuing up for passes-out.

When they were all assembled in the field outside Bertie asked if the ladies would leave them and it was extraordinary how well they responded. It was not until they were back inside the hall that some of the girls thought it curious why Bertie should have needed to call them all together to perform a function they were perfectly capable of handling alone. This was carrying regimentation too far and they felt rather indignant about it, but much too well-mannered to say so. Some of the lads were deceived as well, of course, and by sheer force of habit made the most of their opportunity, but Bertie soon had them buttoned up and attentive to his message. Things had gone too slowly, he said, and if the rate of progress was not speeded up it would be Christmas before they reached the Coach and Horses.

48

What had chiefly kept them back they agreed had been the miserable pace of sieving and they offered all sorts of ideas for increasing the output, from trebling the number of sieves to stretching a length of wire-netting across the road. Then someone had an inspiration. 'What are we wasting our time for, saving stones from the rubble, when there's plenty of all sizes on Shingleton Beach?'

The weather that weekend was gloriously fine and warm and there was no lack of volunteers to go down to the beach at midnight, but the problem was how to get there and back with the load they wanted. For reasons which have already been made clear, there were not many vehicles of modern vintage in the village and a relay of wheelbarrows over fifteen miles to the coast was thought to be excessive even to these enthusiastic youngsters. Then Bertie remembered. There was Mr Digby's hearse. The big question was how could they borrow it without him knowing? A twinkle in Bertie's eye suggested he knew the answer. All that remained was to win her over.

* * *

It was after midnight when the procession set out for Shingleton and half an hour before they reached the beach. Sally had borrowed from her father's trousers the keys to both his vehicles: the lorry he used for building and the hearse for burying. She was thus able to report that he was fast asleep and, so long as they wheeled the vehicles out of earshot of the cottage, would get away unspotted. Bertie took charge of the 'Black Chariot' and Sally drove the 'Covered Wagon'.

Sieves, shovels, buckets and spades were loaded on to the lorry together with sacks, barrels and empty water butts, and around this collection of implements sat Ernie Miller, Bernie Coman, Allan Hopper, Betty Mason, Jill Fowler and Lilian Byfield.

Bunched up inside the hearse, reluctant companions to a coffin, and substitutes for wreaths and bouquets, rode Kathy Whackett, Mollie Coman, Mary Tyler, Jimmy Brewer and Jeremy Archer. Having no partner, Sammy Carter sat in front with the driver and a wicker basket full of food to fry and sticks to burn.

On arrival at the beach the first task of the girls was to build a barbecue while the boys piled pebbles in their casks and formed a chain to carry them shorewards to the road. Bertie stayed down on the beach supervising the sifting of shingle from sand and Jeremy Archer controlled the loading of it onto the lorry. Jimmy Brewer slipped away with Kathy Whackett but was later found behind a breakwater when little Sammy went there to break wind.

Meanwhile a fire had been lit within a wall of stones set neatly in the sands and the smell of sausages and spam and eggs soon spurred on the workers till their truck was full. Then, in the cool night air, with the sea lapping rhythmically behind them, they relaxed and ate a welcome meal. Even to the girls, whose physical efforts had been less strenuous, it tasted good and the sight of so many bare chests shining in the moonlight, either from sweat or sea spray, made them aware of a greater appetite.

Sally gazed at Bertie's strong arms and broad square shoulders and felt a great urge to attach herself to them, as molluscs do to the hulls of ships.

'All right, then, let's be having you! Last one aboard's the loser!' It was a boisterous call from a voice that could be so romantic.

The first glow of dawn was lighting the eastern sky as they re-entered the village and, despite their growing fatigue, they set about the task of depositing their load with both speed and system. Leaving the hearse in a narrow lane not far from Digby's cottage, they removed the coffin, and Bertie, Jimmy, Jeremy, and Sammy carried it to the part of the road they were excavating. Here they tipped its contents of pebbles into discreet piles by the roadside and then took the now empty coffin across to the lorry where they held it under the tailboard while those on the lorry shovelled in the load which they had brought back from the beach. The 'pall-bearers' then deposited their second load of pebbles by the roadside and returned the coffin to the hearse.

In a gesture of mock solemnity they all stood still, silently surveying the scene. They were surprised to see what little there was to show for their efforts once the load had been scattered, but they knew that each pile so placed would relieve them of the need to sift their rubble when the race resumed and they could simply toss it to one side and make faster for the finish. Nothing in the rules said where the stones were to come from, only that they should be collected.

All that remained now was to push the two vehicles into their garage, exchange pleasantries with each other, and retire to bed before their parents discovered they had been out all night. Bertie gave Sally a goodnight kiss when the others had gone and thanked her for being a brick. Jimmy, on the other hand, had just dropped one, on his way home with Kathy, and was receiving a smart slap in the face.

A bleary-eyed Sally at breakfast confessed to being late to bed on account of attending a beachside barbecue with Bertie and a crowd of others on their way back from the dance. Not being quite sure what a barbecue was, and associating it in her mind with the word 'barbaric', Vera Digby was very frightened and asked Benjamin if Sally ought to see the doctor.

Benjamin was more concerned with how they got there.

'I did come to ask your permission first', said Sally, skating away from where the ice was thin, 'but you were asleep.'

'How do you know I was asleep?'

'Because I opened your door...,' Sally could see the crack before she got there and waited for the splash.

'Not the sort of thing you usually do when you don't want me to say "no".... Why were there tyre marks in the yard this morning? I don't remember using the truck yesterday.'

And so it came out. Or, at least, that much of it which concerned the part Digby had unwittingly played in transporting his rivals to the beach at Shingleton. He was still a long way from suspecting the real purpose of their journey, however, and although he intended to punish his daughter for betraying his trust and invading his pocket, he secretly believed the adventure would give immeasurable advantage to his team by tiring out the participants and was not as severe with Sally as he might have been.

* * *

It was Cyrus who first stumbled on the truth. He fell headlong over a pile of sea-smoothed pebbles on his way to the firing point, pulled the trigger involuntarily, and started the second day of the race five minutes ahead of schedule.

At the top of the village a fierce argument was in progress about whether they should be using horsepower or manual labour and it was as well for the finer feelings of the Sexton that he was not there to hear them. Digby, however, was cheering them up by telling them the dance had been such a success the previous night that most of the youngsters would be unfit this morning and give little opposition.

The news which Cyrus brought was, therefore, shattering. All the work stopped and there was much 'blastphemy'!

52

What the boys had done amounted to a breach of the rules, not because of the way they had cheated to avoid the sifting, but because they had worked after close of-play. This was enough to disqualify them, and a strong case was made for calling off the race immediately and claiming the barrel of beer. Digby's reminder that the object of the exercise was to clear the road and not the barrel did not go down very well and it took him a long time to persuade them to continue.

O'Hachetty wanted to form a union and put this sort of thing on a proper basis once and for all, but Cyrus had a better idea. He felt that the boys had cheated themselves into a false position. They had abrogated their right to fair play and he was no longer constrained to regard himself as impartial. He would throw in his lot with the elders.

This was the moment Digby had dreaded. Before anything further could be said, however, Cyrus disappeared. Twenty minutes later he returned on the back of a horse. Behind him trailed a plough. 'Stand back, gentlemen,' he cried, and steering the animal into the gulley created by their erstwhile efforts, shouted for someone to grab the handle.

Robin Thatcher was a farm hand, and he jumped at his master's call, but he had never ploughed a road before and he underestimated the condition of the surface. The great wrought-iron teeth bit into the mud and rubble and the poor horse gave a grunt and a snort which almost shook Cyrus from the saddle. 'Come on there, Daisie,' he roared and tugged harder at the reins. Daisie plunged into a pot-hole in front of her and, sweating with fear, reared up and raced off at a gallop, the plough still harnessed to her. Robin remained with them, dragging on the handle so that the teeth of the plough dug deeper into the road. Suddenly there was a spurt and a gush and a splash and a shout, and water squirted everywhere, drenching them all.

Digby grabbed for the harness and cut it adrift but he could not stop Cyrus and the horse, who beat it together towards the far end of the course where Bertie's team assumed they were being charged in anger.

'Down everybody, get down!' but it was too late; they had most of them gone already.

'Come back, come back,' cried Bertie when he saw who was on the horse, 'it's only the umpire,' . . . but as the beast got nearer he, too, flung himself into the nearest ditch and shuddered as the hoofs went by above his head.

Meanwhile Digby's team was struggling with a water main that had been uprooted and no amount of plugging with the materials they had to hand would stop it gushing. Then Digby noticed huge bubbles rising through the water which had now flooded the road as deeply as they had dug it. Thinking at first it might be somebody drowning, Digby dived into the mud head-first and emerged a moment later very frightened.

'Stand back,' he cried, 'it's the gas main gone as well.'

Nobody really stopped to think if a match would ignite it in the flood but every smoker stubbed at his lighted end, whether or not it had been extinguished a moment earlier in the douche.

* * *

Back in the cottages, chaos was hitting the kitchens. Ovens were being prepared for the Sunday joint and sinks (where they had any) were full of vegetables for scraping. Suddenly the supplies of gas and water ceased.

'I always said the pump was more reliable,' Mrs Miller moaned as she unscrewed the tap off its moorings.

There was no lunch for anyone in Little Missington who relied upon the modern gas stove. Only the kitchen range and oil-stove owners carried on. The others waited.

Ted Brewer was first to the rescue on the stopcocks. He had them all off and under control while the others were struggling in the water looking for punctures.

Sam Waterman went for his boat, for the road was now like a river and the lads at the lower end saw the flood as a further act of retribution, like the charge of the horseman a few minutes earlier.

Bertie went off to complain and when he failed to return the others followed him.

It was a hectic morning ahead for all of them. Half the village was down in the trenches looking for broken pipes and half on the top looking for tools with which to repair them. Spare pipes were fetched from odd corners and a mixed team of young and old grappled wildly in the mud for the damaged sections which had to be replaced. Nobody was quite sure what they were doing but Digby and the publican were giving orders and others were fixing and fussing about.

Cyrus had not returned, so he could not add to the turmoil, but in view of the manner of his departure it could be assumed that wherever he was he would be making as big a commotion as anyone there on the roadway.

Back in the kitchens a little later something stranger than ever began to happen. From somewhere in Mrs Carter's parlour a weird hissing noise was coming, and when she struck a match to see if the gas had come back to her cooker a long sheet of flame shot out from the taps in the sink, and not only the hot one either!

Mrs Whackett was putting her meat in the oven. She had not noticed that there had been a stoppage and when she opened the tap and bent down to ignite the gas a spray of cold water struck her between the eyes. The jets from her burners gushed with mud and when she tried the taps on the top of the stove they produced a spectacular fountain.

Out on the road to Puddlethorpe a huge explosion shook

55

the neighbourhood and a new hole in the highway appeared. Somewhere else, in the direction of Myrtlesham, a chasm opened where the pipes lay buried and down at the sub-station, further on towards the gasworks, dials and counters were swinging about like watch-springs.

If only they had thought of it before! This was surely the perfect way of breaking up a road.

6

Although it was the Tuesday after Whitsun, there was a Monday morning feeling among the employees of the County Council, and it was not until coffee had been round that news of the Little Missington disaster reached the Highways Department.

They were busy preparing for a meeting of the Committee that afternoon and an item was promptly added to the agenda:

'Report on breakdown in communications at Little Missington.'

Rescue squads from the Gas and Water Boards had been out all night and their reports were awaiting the departmental heads when they arrived. Like health officials acting in the emergency of an epidemic their first instinctive orders were to sever all connections with the danger area and Little Missington went back to its pump-and-primus existence.

Digby had a depressing day and most of his loyal supporters were hard put to it to defend him against the sneaking feeling, gaining ground wherever they went, that 'Benjamin had put his foot in it!' That this was an oversimplification of what had actually happened did not occur to them, but Digby sensed the air of censure which hung over him and took to the fields, where he fell in behind the hoe with Cyrus Galleon and contemplated the prospect of higher taxes.

An emergency meeting of the Parish Council was due at half-past seven and it was difficult to know what to suggest now to prevent the intervention of the county authorities. They were back to where they started several weeks ago, except that now there was not only a road to repair but gas and water mains as well.

'We must resign,' said Digby, lifting his feet heavily out of the furrows.

Cyrus ploughed on solemnly, unusually silent, except for occasional 'Woas' that were probably more an expression of his feelings than instructions to the horse.

Digby deduced that Cyrus did not want to resign. 'Well, if *you* won't I will,' he added, slipping to the other side of the farmer.

'Woa there!' roared Cyrus, heaving on the reins, obviously this time meaning the horse to stop. 'Woa!' He looked at the backside of the animal for some moments and watched it flicking flies from its flesh with the scraggiest of tails.

'Do you see that?' he asked Digby at length.

'What?' said Digby.

'The way those brutes get tormented. If they'd only learn to keep their tail between their legs the flies couldn't get in and bite them!'

'I don't see what that's got to do with our problem.'

'It has, you know. We must keep the authorities out. When they came at us the first time we panicked and flicked our tails. Now look what has happened. We've got sores all over our backsides! What we ought to do is stick fast and keep our tail between our legs. Don't let 'em in!'

'Even a horse has to lift its tail sometimes,' Digby argued. 'We'll never keep them out altogether.'

'How big are those holes at each end of the village?' asked Cyrus, ignoring the builder's protest.

'The one you dug is bigger than the other one,' said Digby sourly.

'Then we'll make the other one deeper,' said Cyrus. 'I mean to keep them out like our ancestors did round their castles — with a moat.'

Digby stumbled, but recovered quickly. 'We can't cut ourselves off completely from the world outside or we'll starve to death for want of supplies.'

'But we can stop them coming in to repair the road,' said Cyrus.

'What about the gas and water?'

'We didn't have either when I was a kid. We could do without them now.'

'It would give us more time to put things right ourselves,' Digby agreed.

'Well, that's settled. I'll just finish the field, then we'll take the mare down and plough up the end of the road I missed!'

* * *

There was no controversy on the Council that night for by then the job had been done and Cyrus was able to report that everything was under control. 'All we have to do now is keep going,' he told them, 'until the new road is finished. Then we'll re-open the two ends and let the traffic flow again.'

Bertie was meawhile struggling with his team of volunteers. They had suffered that evening from menial duties, like carrying water from wells and preparing the paraffin lamps, which had long since passed from their experience except in rare moments of emergency. The prospect was not encouraging.

'Why don't we pack up and leave the place to rot?' asked Gordon Tyler.

'Let them as messed things up put 'em right again!' cried Allan Hopper.

'Let's get on with it and stop grumbling,' said Bertie. 'The sooner mended the sooner we can live in comfort again.'

'What do you mean "again"?'

'What comfort will there be with buses and lorries and fast cars going through all the time?'

It was surprising how reactionary some of the young folk of the village were, or what innocent mimics of their elders.

'Do you want things to stay as they were all the time?' asked Bertie. 'There's such a thing as progress, you know, and we can't live in the past for ever.'

'Why not?' said someone . . . and that set Bertie thinking.

* * *

The Digby's were not expecting company that evening and Sally had washed her hair. Her mother was ironing. Neither had taken the slightest notice of warnings to conserve water and Mrs Digby's wash that day had been bigger than usual on account of Benjamin's activities the day before.

Sally answered a knock at the door and let out a cry of horror when she saw Bertie standing there. 'B..but I thought you were busy tonight,' she stuttered.

'I have been,' said Bertie. 'That's why I've come to see your father.'

'He's not back yet,' Sally told him hastily. She sounded unaffectionate.

'I'm sorry if it's inconvenient,' said Bertie. He was embarrassed but not daunted. 'It's important, so I'd better wait.'

Sally twisted a towel round her head and showed him in. 'I didn't mean you to see me like this,' she protested as they went into the living room.

At that moment Mrs Digby held up a pair of Sally's panties from the ironing-board and Bertie probably mistook what Sally had meant.

Benjamin returned from his meeting a little earlier than he had done the last time the Council met. Bertie was glad to see him back.

'What's this? Doing your penance for driving my chariot?' Bertie took refuge behind the pail of water he was carrying.

'Just filling up the bath to keep you going tomorrow,' he puffed. 'The ladies said they'd used all that you put in this morning.'

'Not surprised,' said Digby, looking at his daughter curled up before the fire like a Persian cat, her hair splayed out to dry.

'Daddy, Bertie's got a wonderful idea,' she purred. 'Tell him, darling.'

'Well, it's very simple, really. You see, I've been thinking perhaps we've been going about things the wrong way round ...'

Digby frowned and began to wonder whether he'd make such a welcome son-in-law after all.

'If we make a new road and let traffic pass through the village they'll go on to Myrtlesham or Puddlethorpe and I don't suppose many will want to stop here. Now that's bad for trade. What we want is to encourage people to come to Little Missington, then they'd spend their money in *our* shops and buy *our* property and we'd all be better off.'

'I see,' said Digby, warming to him again. 'What you mean is we ought to block up one end of the road only.' Digby had his mind on Cyrus's solution which had just been endorsed by the Parish Council.

'No, I don't,' said Bertie, surprised at the suggestion. 'We want them to come from all directions, from far and

61

near. So we've got to give them something to come for. What we need is a monument or something — something old and quaint that people would come for miles to see, out of curiosity. Tourists, sightseers, holidaymakers. . . '

'But what would they come to see,' asked Sally, not having thought of this the first time he told her.

'Bob Blackett?' Digby grinned facetiously, but he began to fathom the young man's thinking.

'Suppose we haven't got any monuments, or relics worth coming to, we ought to be able to make some, oughtn't we?'

'That's just what I was coming to,' said Bertie, pleased now at his encouragement. 'You being a builder and me a carpenter, we ought to be able to construct something somewhere that would look like, say, a ruin.'

Sally looked up to see which way her father would take the remark then laughed when she saw him beaming.

'My word, lad, you're a bright feller! We could do with you on the Council. I don't know, though, maybe you're better off off it. You'd be suffocated by that devil O'Hachetty or persecuted by Stubbles or just sat on by the Chairman! We can do better together, lad, from this side of the chamber.'

'The only thing about the idea,' said Bertie, trying to ignore the praises, 'is that it calls for secrecy.'

'Ah, yes,' said Digby, looking quickly to see if his wife was still in the room. Sally rolled over on her tummy and pretended she had not been listening.

'If the word gets out that we're faking our history we'll never draw a soul,' Bertie added. 'That's why, if you agree, I think we should keep the plan entirely between these four walls.'

They each glanced round, as if to check Bertie's calculation that the room had four walls, and saw Mrs Digby entering the room with a trayload of coffees.

'Mum's the word!' said Sally, forgetting her previous

subterfuge.

'How long have you been out there, Vera?' asked Digby.

'I've been as quick as I could,' she replied, handing her husband the only black one she had made, 'and we'll have none of your sergeant-major stuff this evening. You just get on with this and be thankful you didn't have to make it yourself.'

Digby winked at young Bertie and they knew it had been all right.

It was rather a shock to Sally and her mother to hear Benjamin offering to walk home with Bertie.

'I could do with a bit of fresh air,' he said, unconvincingly. 'Can't take the dog for a walk as we haven't got one so I'll come with you instead.'

'Thanks!' said Sally, in proxy for her friend.

This manoeuvre robbed her of the goodnight kiss she had expected but Bertie blew her one as he went out. Digby took him firmly by the arm as they stepped into the yard.

'Come with me, my lad, we've got a call to make before you go home.'

* * *

Cyrus was decanting his 'bedtime tonic' when they reached The Willows. This was the farmhouse most people in the village said was haunted, but no one had ever seen the ghost and Cyrus, who had lived there all his life, kept the superstition alive as a kind of extra insurance against unwelcome visitors. Gladys had already gone to her room and was fidgeting with the curtains when they rang the bell.

'Good gracious, Digby, what's the fellow done?' cried Cyrus seeing him standing on the doorstep with Bertie on his arm.

'He's done a great deal,' said Digby mysteriously, 'and if you're not too sleepy to listen you'd better hear what he's got to say'.

Curiosity was a failing with Cyrus as it is with most people and he hurried them into the study, eager to learn what it was that brought them there at such a time of night.

'Are we alone?' asked Digby, a little unnecessarily for he had seen Mrs Galleon at the window, but he wanted to heighten the drama.

'Go on, man, of course we're alone!'

'Shut the door, then, Cyrus. It's important that no one should hear us. Can you keep a secret?'

Digby would never have taken the risk had he not needed the farmer's help, but being landowner of more than half of Little Missington it seemed essential at this stage to bring him into the picture and enlist his support.

If they were to build their ruins it was necessary to find ground to build them on, and Digby had already thought of a field by the river where Cyrus had an old cowshed that was falling to pieces for want of repair.

'Let me convert it, Cyrus, into something historic. It won't take long and it couldn't inconvenience the cows more than they've suffered already.'

'I don't like it.' Cyrus grumbled and it looked as though their plan had been wrecked. 'History and ancestry and all that kind of thing ought to be sacred. It's not like converting a house or a farmyard into something more modern and useful. What you're suggesting is . . . well, it's like putting the clock back.'

Cyrus thought for a minute. 'Of course, if you were just restoring a ruin, so to speak, by putting one back where it used to be . . .

Digby recognised the mischief in his voice and knew that all would now be well.

7

The Highways Department of the County Council had to deal with the situation now that no traffic could pass from Puddlethorpe to Myrtlesham.

They began by organizing diversions over more navigable routes than the local inhabitants had arranged, but such was the nature of the minor roads in that part of the country that they ran out of diversion notices in the Highways Office before all the turnings could be marked. The result was that motorists got lost much sooner than they would otherwise have done, but they did so with official 'direction' from the County, as distinct from the incompetence of a mere parish council.

Gangs of workmen were sent to the village to repair 'essential services' but found themselves more often repairing their vehicles. The reception they got from the villagers was not at all what they had been led to expect. Women fed them all day with pies and cups of tea, children asked them interminable questions, and the amount of work they accomplished was extremely small. The more astute among them got the impression the village was not in a hurry to restore its communications with the outside world.

No one from the Council attempted to resurface the road. Two young men from the Surveyor's Department came with theodolites and set about measuring the levels. Their results were so unconvincing and incompatible they decided there was something wrong with their instruments and went back to the office to recalibrate them.

The do-it-yourself enthusiasts also had lost their enthusiasm, and their leaders, Benjamin and Bertie, were busy in other directions; in particular to the south-westward on a meadow which Cyrus had made over to them for the perpetration of their plot.

Known in the village as Galleon's Meadow, it stretched from a thick plantation of pine trees at one end to the river at the other and was approached on one side through a five-barred gate and on the other over a stile. A narrow footpath ran alongside the hedgerow of hawthorn and brambles, separating it from the plantation, but few people ever passed that way because it was eerie and unsettling, especially at night. The trees made it gloomy and around nightfall, when the mist moved up from the river, it had a reputation for being haunted. Occasionally some intrepid lovers would walk that way but more often than not they stopped at the stile and departed as dusk descended. A derelict cowshed stood in the middle of the field where Cyrus allowed his cows to graze but it gave little shelter and was seldom used.

The river bank at the edge of the meadow rose about a foot and a half from the water and was slowly being eroded for want of protection. Fishermen had staked their boats to it to stop them drifting with the current and water rats had burrowed into it to build their living quarters. On the opposite bank there was an open field of barren marshland over which cattle never roamed and only birds, butterflies and wildflowers flourished. It was therefore a stretch of the river which offered little attraction to the local inhabitants but an ideal location for Digby. Being adjacent to his meadow, it was known as Galleon's Reach.

Lest anyone should stray that way while they were working on it, Digby and his accomplice decided to seal off the approaches, both to the Reach along the river and to the meadow along the footpath. It was also essential to their plan that neither of them should be seen in the vicinity. Whereas in digging up the road they had encouraged everyone in the village to participate they were now engaged in resurrecting an ancient ruin and the illusion they wanted to create required the black cloak of a magician to conceal its preparation.

Diversion of motor traffic is easily achieved by putting up a notice, which drivers will accept philosophically, but for a pedestrian to be persuaded to take an alternative route requires something better than the written word nailed to a tree trunk or propped up in the middle of the road. In certain circumstances a stretch of barbed wire might have achieved their objective but not without rousing unwanted curiosity and the risk that some intrepid traveller might see it as a challenge to be overcome.

Digby decided, therefore, to re-route a footpath which went through the meadow so as to take a traveller round the meadow instead. It was fortunate that Cyrus owned the adjacent fields for it enabled him to shift the familiar five-barred gate on one perimeter of the Meadow and the stile on the other to the fields alongside, making the approaches look familiar one field sooner from each direction.

To add credence to the deception, Digby moved the dead trunk of a tree which had fallen near the entrance to the Meadow, on the village side, and arranged for some cows to be grazed in the neighbouring field.

Hedges around the meadow itself had to be filled in so that no one would be able to see through them. Some gaps were plugged with branches and foliage stripped from nearby thickets, but others were more obstinate in their transparency. Attempts to transplant whole hedges were not successful and some sections had to be filled with cultivated varieties of bush and creeper. To give extra cover from the side nearer the village they spread fertilizer among the weeds and put birdseed in the branches to encourage the birds to build nests.

In their efforts to keep prying eyes out, they almost committed the folly of boxing themselves in. Moreover, they forgot for a time the fact that they would need to get in and out of the meadow themselves with supplies of materials for their work of reconstruction. To achieve this they made a large 'gate' out of twigs and twine which could be lifted in and out of position, and camouflaged it totally with freshly gathered foliage.

While Benjamin was concentrating on closing the meadow, helped from time to time by Bertie, Bertie was busy behaving like a beaver trying to dam the river so that the meadow could not be approached from that side.

One of the oddest sights on the water had for many years been a craft with a broad beam, a flat bottom and a protruding stern, known as a 'weed-cutter'. It was owned by the River Board and designed to keep down the growth of weeds on the river bed.

The man whose job it was to ply this vessel up and down the river, to sharpen its blades whenever necessary and see that a navigable channel was kept open for public users of the waterway, was Sam Waterman, a retired boat-builder and now a member of the local Parish Council. For the same reason that bus drivers are supposed not to take their holidays on board a bus, Sam did not often go fishing, but when he did it *had* to be in a boat. Not the weed-cutter, which had an outboard motor, but a simple oars-and-rowlocks rowing boat. 'It's no good sittin' on the river bank waitin' for 'em to come to yer — yer has to get out arter 'em,' he said, and the sight of him setting out for his quarry was enough to frighten not only the fish below but every fellow fisherman within striking distance of his tackle. His cast was a spectacle much talked of in

68

the angling community. It started with a slow sighing noise as he drew a deep breath and pulled out the slack on his line. Then came the brisk ripple of waters as he stood up in the boat, followed by a shrill swish as he flourished the cane above his head. Then a long whine while the line ran out with the float and sinkers chasing the bait to the end of their tether. Finally, a dull plop as the lead-weights of the sinkers fell savagely to the bottom of the river.

The miracle was that any fish remained to be hooked in the face of so many warnings. Some said he hooked more above water than below it, but Old Sam certainly knew how and when to fish.

It was a cunning ruse to dodge the chore of carting cans of water about the cottage that took him to his fishing tackle one evening shortly after Whitsun. While husbands and sons elsewhere were helping their womenfolk overcome the failure of the pipes, Sam set out in his little tub of a rowing boat to where a large pike had been reported earlier that day. Meditating about the size of the fish he was approaching and the domestic drudgeries from which he had escaped, Sam rowed vigorously on, oblivious to all else. He knew that part of the water so well that he did not bother to turn his head as he took the bends of the river in his stride. A harder pull on one oar than the other and the boat would swing gently round, keeping along the centre of the stream as if an unseen rail were guiding it.

But it was an unseen tree that sank it.

Lying across the river from the bank at the beginning of Galleon's Reach, a large oak had dipped its trunk, like a huge flagstaff at the salute, damming the water and trapping everything that floated on its way downstream. Sam's boat hit it with a violent thud and, like an iceberg in the ocean, the submerged tree tore holes in the sides and bottom of his craft.

'Beavers, I'd say it was,' declared O'Hachetty when

Harry Carter told him the story.

'Sam reckons the place were haunted,' Harry added, and said, 'when he got up on the bank them cows was capering about the field like demons demented.'

'Good job old Syd weren't there, then,' laughed Ted who had been listening from behind the bar.

When Digby heard the story he was delighted. It proved to him that one of their defences was effective and it revived the old superstition that there were supernatural goings-on in the vicinity of Galleon's Meadow.

He was now ready to start moving materials on to the site.

* * *

The first load of sand and cement to go up to the meadow was more exciting to Bertie than his trip to the beach at Shingleton. On that occasion he had shared his danger with sixteen others and only Sally's parents had to be avoided. Now it was he and Digby against the entire population of Little Missington and the penalty for being seen was the ruination of all their plans for. . .the creation of a ruin.

Benjamin had been in favour of carrying the sand and cement up in bags but Bertie remembered how many separate journeys there were in a lorry-load of pebbles and persuaded him to take one big risk rather than several hundred little ones.

Bertie's experience with the lorry also reminded him not to leave tell-tale tyre tracks on the approaches to the meadow. To avoid this meant driving across the field on duckboards. Starting with two boards ahead of each of four wheels, the back set had to be taken to the front each time the lorry moved forward the distance of one duckboard. By the time they had dropped the invisible gate into position from inside Galleon's Meadow, they were as near to exhaustion as if they had adopted Benjamin's original idea and carried the bags by hand.

Even then their troubles were not over because the same procedure had to be adopted on the return journey after the lorry had been emptied. However, by then, with the target reached and the load ejected, they returned to the village in better spirits than when they left it.

Thinking things over that night, in the fertile few minutes before falling asleep, Benjamin realized how vulnerable they would be if anyone approached the meadow while they were taking their lorry across the neighbouring field. He resolved there and then to play up the power of the supernatural and provide so many examples, like that to which Old Sam would bear witness, that people would not dare to go within a mile of the haunted meadow.

* * *

It is one of the sad facts of life that the innocent individual often suffers at the hands of the public-spirited.

Young David Coman was the third of Fred Coman's sons and the black sheep of the family inasmuch as he wanted nothing to do with cows. He was a shy and sensitive lad who liked collecting things, but the things he looked for were not those usually sought by collectors. Whereas most people want different specimens of whatever they collect, David looked for similarities of a kind: stones of identical shape and size, twigs of the same order of branching; leaves of precisely repeated structure and so on. It was as if he were bent on destroying the sanctity of the individual and had been overinfluenced by his childhood games of 'Snap'.

Too young yet to earn his keep, he managed to save money to buy books and support his collections by delivering the morning papers for Syd Stubbles. With so many members of his family rising early to attend their animals, he had no difficulty in getting up in the morning and he liked to be out on his own.

Once a week he had to forego the freedom of leaving the farm for a few hours because Sydney insisted he should have one day off. To compensate for this he usually sat up late the night before so that he would have an excuse for not getting up to breakfast the following morning.

It was just David's bad luck that he should have chosen one of these nights on which to stray into the neighbourhood of Galleon's Meadow. He knew from previous visits that this was a place where he could be sure of solitude, and he went there in search of a replica of the five-lobed foxglove leaf which he had found in the meadow a year ago. Being so independent, he had not got to hear of the strange goings-on in that vicinity.

The fact that he was actually searching in the wrong field probably made little difference to his chances of finding what he wanted, but the sun had gone below the skyline before he was prepared to give up and go home. Then, just as he admitted to himself that there was insufficient light to see, he heard a noise like the flapping of wings coming from the next field. Thinking it might be a flight of geese, or swans, he walked over to the hedge, pulled back some foliage and peered inside.

What he saw, or rather what he thought he saw, was not at all what he had expected.

Unlike his brothers, he had learned his nursery rhymes by heart, but it was a long time since he had believed in them. Now he could see one being enacted before his eyes.

'Hey diddle diddle, the cat and the fiddle;
The cow jumped over the moon.'

There, on the other side of the hedge, a cow was gliding

72

up towards the moon which was just beginning to light up that part of the evening sky. He did not wait to look for a little dog laughing, and was too dazed to think of a fiddle: he just ran for all he was worth and went straight to bed when he got home. For the whole of the following day he stayed in bed in a state of considerable shock.

Two victims were now in bed as a result of their being near the meadow and word soon got about the village that something ought to be done to protect the women and children.

It was disputed whether the vicar or an officer-of-the-law would be more likely to secure their safety and, of the two, Digby would have preferred the latter. Oswald Lawless was a good policeman but he was not noted for his personal bravery and Digby had less to fear from his interference than from Norman Harper, the vicar, who was quite likely to take his responsibilities very seriously and set about eradicating such manifestations of the Devil, as he had been heard to call them.

When consulted, Digby had a better idea to offer. 'The man to see, surely, is the man who owns the land and, after all, he's your Parish Chairman. Why don't we ask him to do something about it? He's got dogs and guns and . . . well, we all know how well he fought in the last war.'

So it was decided to ask Cyrus to mount a guard on his meadow and see to it that no more of the villagers came to harm.

When Digby put it to him, and explained how vital it was to prevent any nosey-parkers getting a preview of their work, Cyrus remarked that he was not yet convinced about the ethics of the plan and did not want to be party to a fraud. Since Benjamin and Bertie had first spoken to him on the subject he had spent hours looking through the local literature, both in his own and in the County Library, but so far he said he had failed to find any historical support for the idea. There was no evidence that Little Missington ever had an edifice worthy of reconstruction, even as a ruin and, unless they could prove that inadequate records had been kept of the district to account for this, he would have no alternative but to insist upon the restitution of his cowshed.

Digby went back to his cottage very disturbed. He, too, had spent hours searching for clues that would lead to at least a suspicion of something they could salvage from the past. He had studied the map on the wall in the Coach and Horses, from which George Whackett had traced the boundaries of the village for the Big Race, but it yielded nothing except the conclusion that his own ancestors had not been long in the building trade, for there were few signs of habitation and only such symbols as stood for a ford, a footway, a horse trough and a village pump.

Sensing that her husband was not in the best of humour as he walked in, Mrs Digby called out to Sally to clear away her pins and needles so that her father could sit down.

Benjamin was used to finding his daughter surrounded by patterns and pleats but this time it was parchment and pliers and pieces of wire.

'Look,' she said, holding up a half-finished lampshade against the naked light bulb. 'It's the latest thing-to-do. I read about it in a magazine.'

Digby could hardly believe his eyes. It was like a magic lantern show — with the accent on the magic. Instead of the usual flower or peacock design, there was the outline of a map, ornately bordered and obviously very old. Before Sally could stop him he had stripped the parchment off the frame and stretched it across the floor.

Vera returned to find her daughter in tears and her husband on all fours, scrambling around like a dog with a bone and slipper.

'What on earth are you doing, Ben?' she asked.

'Helping Sal...' he began vacantly.

'Then why is she crying?'

Digby hadn't noticed.

'I thought he would like it.' Sally whimpered.

'I do — of course, I do. I like it very much. Can you see a castle on it, or a cathedral, or a monastery, or a battlefield ... you know, something historic?'

Sally exchanged glances with her mother and they fancied they were in for another difficult evening.

When Digby discovered that Sally had bought the parchment from a shop in the market-place at Myrtlesham he insisted on her going back the following day to see if she could buy some more, but she was empty-handed when he met her on return at the bus stop.

'I asked him where he got the one I bought yesterday,' she said, 'hoping that would help, but he couldn't remember. He said people were always coming in with rubbish like that after they had cleared out their attics and emptied old cupboards.'

Digby was thoughtful for the rest of the way home.

* * *

Vera did not take kindly to her husband engaging in the rag and bone trade! She was not a snob, she assured herself, but Benjamin could do better than that.

'My dear, you don't understand; there's money in this business today.' he assured her. 'People don't always know the value of what they throw out.'

'Then you're cheating the poor,' she said, 'and deceiving them. If you know what somebody's throwing out is valuable you should tell them.'

This reminded Benjamin why he did not usually discuss his business affairs with his wife.

Notwithstanding the strictures of a scandalized spouse,

Digby continued to make calls around the village, offering money for rags and bones, and praying that out of some vase or casket there would fall a parchment map of Little Missington with a castle on it.

Meanwhile Cyrus was scouring his loft and cellars on a similar quest, without knowing of Benjamin's latest commercial venture. More concerned with finding a literary reference to the local past than a graphical one, he had taken a second look at the County Library and was all set for the British Museum when Digby arrived at the front door with his little cart and an enormous handbell.

'Any old bones?'

'My God, man, has it come to this?'

8

With the boss away all day, swinging a bell and pushing a handcart, miles from the site on which they had started work, most employees would have swung the lead and pushed off home. But not Bertie. While Digby was calling at remote cottages, gathering in the bric-à-brac from every corner of the village, Bertie was labouring alone, carrying bricks and flint stones up to the meadow on his back.

Alone, that is, until one day a head appeared through a hole in the hedge as he was about to stack his sack at the end of another journey. A voice called '*Drop that*' and, to the surprise of the caller, he did: and disappeared.

Bertie who had watched how the skylark eludes its pursuers, dropped to the ground immediately he was disturbed.

For a moment Sally might have believed the tales they were telling in the village for, having followed him up to the meadow from her father's yard, she knew it was Bertie she had shouted to and yet suddenly he was nowhere to be seen. Undaunted by the evidence of sorcery and magic, she wriggled the rest of her body through the hedge and rushed forward to where he had stood when she called to him.

Still chasing the vision which had gone from view, she scoured the horizon and stumbled, sprawling over a sack of stones on to the prone body of a man. It was not the first time she had fallen for Bertie, but she vowed it would be the last if she ever came upon him in that manner again.

There were heated exchanges while they challenged each other to explain what they were doing there, but after a truce had been declared Bertie decided to knock off for an hour or two and they spent the rest of the day together in what was by now the most secluded spot in Little Missington.

* * *

Benjamin was too preoccupied with his rag and bone trade to pay much attention to anything else and spent most of his spare time in the back shed putting away the junk he had collected, searching every article as if it were prehistoric. Sometimes he would go over the items he had put away the night before just to make sure he hadn't missed some recess or other where a parchment might have lodged. The shelves of his shed began to sag with the weight of ornaments and the walls became draped with old clothes whose linings had been ripped. With the musty smell of accumulated rubbish the atmosphere in the place reminded one of a museum and if Digby had only thought to charge people to come and walk round he might have spared himself the trouble of inventing an ancient monument.

One evening after he had returned with a particularly useless load of local junk he found Sally sitting in the twilight by the fire stroking the cat. It was an unusual occurrence.

Benjamin switched on the light. 'Why are you sitting there in the dark? Somebody might have fallen over you.'

Sally said nothing.

There was something equally unusual about the room, and Benjamin sensed it. 'What have you been doing to the lights?'

Illumination no longer came from the centre of the room but from a standard lamp in the corner between the fireplace and the window. Sally's features stood out sharply against it and Benjamin noticed the look of expectancy upon her face.

'You've been up to something, young lady, haven't you? Re-made the lampshade, I see. Looks very nice.'

'Aren't you going to have a closer look at it?'

'I've seen it before, haven't I? Isn't it the one I pulled to pieces? I can tell it is from here by the parchment and that old lettering. Glad I didn't spoil it. It makes a nice decoration. Now can we have the proper light on, it's gloomy without. You save that for when young Bertie comes.'

Sally was delighted with her father's response. 'I think Bertie might have been more observant than you were.'

Benjamin looked to see if she was wearing a new dress or had another hairstyle, but he didn't notice anything different about her, except that at this time of day she was usually helping her mother in the kitchen. Then he saw that she was fingering the lampshade.

'It isn't the same one, you know,' she told him. 'The parchment got torn so I had to find another piece.'

Digby rushed over to the fireplace and grabbed at the standard, holding it up in front of him as if he were bearing the Olympic torch. Mrs Digby walked in with a tray of cutlery ready to lay the table. Sally jumped up to help her and the cat, who had premonitions there was going to be trouble, made a quick exit through the open doorway.

Vera was just about to ask her husband what he thought he was doing when he gave a shriek and hoisted the lamp into the air again.

'Whoopee!' he cried and spun himself round on one leg, pulling the flex out of the socket and plunging them all into darkness.

'That's got Little Missington and Great Missington and Missington St George and goodness knows how many other Missingtons... It's a treasure! It's what I've been searching the village for. Sally, wherever did you find it?'

Mrs Digby reappeared with a candle, two aspirins and a bottle of Alka Seltzers. Benjamin took no notice of her.

'Where did you find it, Sally?'

'I picked it up among some of the rubbish you brought home one evening. Guess you must have missed it!' There was a musical ring about the intonation with which she expressed herself.

Digby sat heavily in the chair and couldn't believe it.

'When? Where? Which night? What rubbish? Whose rubbish was it?'

'Hey, steady on,' Sally chuckled, 'I don't remember all that, any more than that dealer remembered where he got the other one. I just went into the shed one evening to see if you were home yet and a moment later there it was lying on the floor in front of me.'

'No! I don't believe it!'

'Well, you don't think I made it up, do you?'

Digby looked hard at his daughter. Her eyes were clear and sparkling and her cheeks flushed with pride and happiness. He had never seen her look so lovely... or innocent... or grown-up. It was difficult to detect who was being the more naive: Sally with her simple faith in the story she had just told, or her father for believing her.

The fact was that Sally *had* picked the parchment off the floor of the shed, for she had put it there herself, only momentarily, but enough to establish the truth of her story. Without realizing it she was beginning to learn the truth of truth itself, that black and white have many shades and words can carry undertones not always recognized by the listener.

Benjamin had been deceived, but not unworthily. Sally

had worked hard to copy the style of the map she had come by accidentally and it had taken her another trip to Myrtlesham to find the parchment which was to make her efforts look authentic. Much imagination had gone into the drawing and the result was no mere replica of the original with names transposed or roads re-routed; this was a fine work of art, based on the latest map of the village and reconstructed with suitable omissions, embellished with coats-of-arms, and surrounded by fancy borders. On the site of the present church there was a spire with a cross, and on the village green a maypole. Over Mr Galleon's land where his house, The Willows, now stood, there appeared the symbol of a gallows, giving credence to the rumour of its being haunted, and to Benjamin's immense delight, by that stretch of the river, not far from the gallows: a garrison shown by crossed swords and the outline of a castle.'

Digby appeared at The Willows that evening almost beside himself with joy. Cyrus accepted the evidence without the remotest show of surprise but with the most enormous pride. He said he knew it was only a matter of time before the full heritage which his ancestors had left him would come to light and he poured Benjamin a large glass of port from his oldest decanter.

They studied the map excitedly round a mahogany table overlooked by a portrait of Cyrus's grandfather, and the old gentleman's expression was such that had he been called upon to verify the accuracy of this assumption he would not have needed to change it one twist.

Neither Cyrus nor Benjamin had any thought of disputing the authenticity of the map and nothing could detract from their pleasure at feeling historical support for their enterprise had been established.

Satisfied in their minds that a castle had once existed in the neighbourhood, and overjoyed that it should have been somewhere near the spot where they were planning to resurrect it, their curiosity now turned to what it had looked like. In this respect Sally's map was unhelpful for her representation of it had been by means of a symbol only.

The two men spent some time debating to which period of English history the castle might have belonged and each one aired the fullest extent of his knowledge on the subject of fortress architecture. Then Digby realized that since it was only a ruin of the place they were going to reconstruct it did not really matter what it had originally looked like, so long as the public would recognise the 'remains' as those of a castle. Cyrus was grateful to his friend for pointing this out and recharged their glasses with his vintage port.

'You're right, my friend, of course, but they must recognize it as a genuine ruin.'

'Surely you're not suggesting we should rebuild the whole castle and knock it down again? That would be asking too much!'

'It might be necessary. Certainly it would be more honest. But let's try it out first on a model.'

Cyrus led his perplexed companion, now scowling more fiercely than the portrait, up four flights of stairs to the attic. Here Digby's anxieties were swiftly overtaken by fascination for what he saw. Laid out over the floor in front of him was a complete track of miniature railway with stations, bridges, signal boxes, level crossings, tunnels, locomotives and every variety of rolling stock. Beyond this, against the wall farthest from the door, a display bench of model ships and aeroplanes, and nearest the window, beneath the sloping roof, a baize-top table covered with toy soldiers in battle array attacking the four walls of a castle.

All this presented an insight into Cyrus Galleon's character which Digby had never suspected and it stirred him very much to think that the man he had known only as a farmer and Chairman of the Parish Council, with deep prejudices and a strong tendency towards pomposity, should after all possess a softer underbelly of a sentimental nature.

Anxious not to offend his host by betraying these thoughts, Digby bent down to touch one of the miniature locomotives. Cyrus did not notice him but was gazing vacantly about the room.

'I've kept all these toys ever since I was a kid in the hope that one day I'd have a son and heir to pass them on to. But we never did.'

Benjamin looked up at him with a warm glow of fatherly understanding. 'I've kept some of mine, too. But they weren't much good for a daughter.'

'Some of these I inherited from my father,' Cyrus went on, picking up a fine model of an old windjammer. 'Its sails are a bit torn but it's still in good condition. We used to call it the family heirloom: Galleon's galleon! My ancestors were seamen, of course.'

Next he pointed to the table of toy soldiers. Some were mounted, some marching, some crouching with guns raised, some shooting from the shoulder. 'Those were all mine. Every bit of pocket money I ever had, I should think, was invested in lead.'

Digby followed his attention to the table and in particular to the solid model of a castle that was its centre-piece. Cyrus took it in both hands and lifted it off the table. 'This is our model, my friend. I built every bit of it myself with a carpenter's outfit and a book of instructions. Now we can take it to pieces and see what a real ruin ought to look like.'

If Cyrus was the architect of the 'ancient monument' about to appear in one of his meadows, Benjamin and Bertie were its builders. They set to work with renewed enthusiasm once they had some plans to work to and Cyrus had carefully scaled up the effect produced by his crumbled model so that they would know exactly where to place each fallen stone and what to omit as buried rubble.

Yet it was not as simple a task as they had first imagined for the problem of building backwards was that one had to leave structures unsupported and to finish off with all the appearance of decay and erosion.

It came hard to a man who had always taken pride in what he did to deface his work deliberately but Digby found pleasure in trimming the edges of his walls to give them the semblance of age, and delight in little touches like planting moss between the stones and painting slime on those nearest the ground to indicate damp.

Bertie was amazed at his elder's diligence and learned much from his attention to detail. It might not have pleased Digby, however, to know that his teaching was being applied to a closer study of his daughter. His observational faculties sharpened by Digby's example, Bertie was paying more attention to those intimate curves and prominences on Sally's body which he had either never noticed before or which had perhaps not previously been so well-developed. Sally was aware of the attention she was getting and not at all embarrassed as she would have been had the straying eyes which surveyed her belonged to any other man. Now that she had discovered the whereabouts of their lair she made the pilgrimage to the meadow every morning around half-past eleven to take Bertie and her father their lunch, and frequently stayed on through the afternoon to give them a hand with their manual tasks.

Bertie watched her with a mixture of admiration and wonder, for he was too shy and inexperienced to be guilty of lust and Sally, conscious of the effect she was creating, gave grace and beauty to every movement. Encouraged by her father as well as Bertie, she became adept at laying stones. Digby thought of letting her do this because he believed the unskilled hand of a woman might produce an effect similar to the ravages of time, but he was wrong. She soon became so good at it that he realized he could give her a job in the family business and not be ashamed of her.

Bertie, however, was beginning to have other ideas about her future. He even went so far as to consider completing and furnishing the castle so that he and Sally could live in it, but doubted if it would be finished before they reached their middle-age.

His thoughts, however, were in advance of his actions for he had not yet broached the subject of marriage with either Sally or her father. Perhaps he had just reached that stage in life when marriage was a matter to be considered without reference to any particular partner, but whenever he stood before Sally with her hair rippling in the wind or her cheeks flushed with exertion, he knew that he had found the person with whom he would be happy to spend the rest of his life. One day, he reminded himself, he would have to ask her to marry him.

The opportunity nearly came one day when they were digging a large pit, euphemistically described by Digby as 'excavating the dungeon'. Sally and he were deep below the surface filling buckets with earth, while Digby was struggling at the end of a block and tackle hauling them up and emptying them. By filling three or four buckets in quick succession they were able to snatch a rest while Digby pulled the buckets one at a time to the top. Exhausted with these sudden bursts of energy, Sally slumped into Bertie's arms and wrapped herself around his trembling body. It was about as much as the lad could stand. He kissed her fervently and felt the limp fingers of her hands stroking the back of his neck.

'Would you like to live in a place like this?' he whispered.

'No I wouldn't!' she answered hotly, thinking of the

damp dark dungeon they were in and not the image that was in Bertie's mind.

Bertie, whose thoughts had returned to the splendour of a full-sized castle, felt the drawbridge slam in front of him and pursued the quest no further. They returned to the next bucket-load without Sally ever knowing how close she had come to her first proposal.

The dungeon dug, and fragments of the fortress in position around it, they now faced their hardest task — the moat. Cyrus insisted on a moat. No one would believe there had been a castle, he protested, unless there were a moat. Moats had become his fixation.

Digby, however, had dug enough. He was prepared to go on placing stones and pillars in perpetuity but he wanted no more trenching. Trenches were in Cyrus Galleon's line with all his war experience. Henceforth, only work above the ground was Digby's responsibility; below ground was not. Even undertakers were not expected to dig graves! Bertie and Sally, who had enjoyed some of their subterranean moments, neverthless paid in labour for their pleasure and were ready for a change of habitat. Digging was downright hard work and that kind of spadework — unromantic.

Ignoring their objections, Cyrus determined to have a moat. If he had to recruit every mole in the district he was going to have a moat. Digby could throw in his hand if he wanted but he, Cyrus, was going to see the job done properly. If he could cut a gash in the road with a frightened horse and a twisted plough, how much easier he reckoned it would be to draw a furrow through his own field with the proper implements. Benjamin left him to it, except to exercise a stricter guard on field security for fear the whole village would move in like birds behind the ploughman if he began to carry out his threat.

But Digby underestimated his Chairman's resolve. For

the next two weeks Cyrus worked unceasingly, changing his horses every day. First with the plough, then with the rake; after that with scoops and hoe; he dented the perimeter of the ground until the semblance of a moat appeared. It was not a very deep moat and no one would have had much difficulty in crossing it today, but as Cyrus pointed out, there had been plenty of time for it to have filled up with debris of collapsed walls from the castle and sediment from the surrounding countryside.

So Cyrus achieved his aim. Galleon's girdle had been drawn around the castle ruins and the moat of Little Missington was there for all to see. Cyrus, Digby and Bertie stood back to admire their work and congratulate each other on what they surveyed. On one side of the moat there were ragged sections of a stone wall rising two or three feet above the ground, forming almost a semi-circle in which there were signs of what might have been the base of a watch tower or outer gateway. It was here that one could see a length of broken chain and a long bar of rusty iron, just visible in the mud, suggesting the site of a drawbridge. Scattered about the stumps of flinted stone were blocks of brick and mortar, shaped like a square-based 'U' which appeared to have fallen from turrets off the battlements.

On the other side of the moat were the remains of an inner wall of smaller radius in which had been another gateway leading to the castle itself. Here there were steps which led downwards to a dungeon on one side of which the word 'HELP' had been scratched in the stonework. Above ground, more steps led to a rectangular section of wall, about five feet high, which appeared to be the bottom of the keep. On this, Bertie had mischievously placed a Union Jack.

Digby said the scene reminded him of a well-made sandcastle just after the tide had come in. Cyrus said it needed another six months to 'set' properly and Bertie said that made him think of a jelly mould. They were clearly in high spirits and delighted with their enterprise.

There now remained the question of how to unveil the masterpiece.

* * *

October had been a fine month, with mostly clear skies and warm air, which had made life in the 'Haunted Meadow' very pleasant. The evenings had grown progressively shorter and the mornings gradually colder but the absence of rain and strong winds had given Digby and his team an uninterrupted run of working days 'in the field'.

While Cyrus and his horses had been dragging their machinery round the field and Digby had been putting finishing touches to the superstructure, they were thinking about the kind of ceremony they ought to have to introduce their handiwork to the public. It had to be suitably spectacular, yet the revelation ought to be plausible enough for people to believe in it. Having been frightened away from the area once, the village folk had now to be induced back again and provided with a story which they could pass on with sufficient conviction to bring others from far afield to see for themselves.

It was some time before the inspiration came.

During all these days while they were busy in the meadow, neither Benjamin nor Bertie had been seen in the village until after nightfall. Once or twice each week Benjamin had managed to get to the Coach and Horses before closing time and by suitably phrased remarks established the alibi that he and Bertie were busy on a far away project which would keep them out of circulation for some time. It was not unusual in the summer months for Digby to be away from sunrise to sunset, nor did it surprise anyone that he should be working outside the neighbourhood. Few people in the village could afford a builder to do more than repair a broken drainpipe or leaking roof, so most of Digby's income, from this side of his business, came from the wealthier inhabitants of surrounding areas.

Although it did not arouse suspicion, Digby's absence from the village put him out of touch with the local gossip and he had to rely heavily on his daughter for news of what was being said about the meadow. Whenever it seemed that interest was flagging he had to inject a new stimulant in the form of a fresh scare or rumour, at the same time keeping up the pretence that Cyrus had the area under patrol, and that no harm would come to those who kept away.

One day Sally arrived on the site with news that the boys in the village were gathering wood for a bonfire on Guy Fawkes Night. They were pitching their sticks on the Common.

'There's to be dancing and fireworks and a barbecue afterwards,' she added, glancing at Bertie to see if he remembered their last such adventure together.

Digby seized upon the news with great excitement. 'That's just exactly what we want,' he chuckled. 'A diversion!'

Bertie's memory switched to the chaos of their previous diversion exercise and he looked from one to the other with much misgiving. Digby drew them closer and explained what he had in mind.

Cyrus arrived at the meadow on the fourth of November, not with any machinery for gouging the earth, but with a cart load of fireworks.

Digby, who had been dumping wood there vigorously for several days, matching stick for stick the combined efforts of the lads of the village, added the last supporting struts to his beacon and carefully placed a petrol can at the base. Into the neck of the can he plugged a fuse and backing away towards the hedge with the line between his fingers, his eyes twinkling like a schoolboy's, he bumped into Bertie.

'What's that?'

'Sh! You'll see tomorrow.'

'Looks like you mean to be blasting something.'

'Now, lad, thou'd better not let th' Sexton hear thee!'

* * *

On the Common next evening Syd Stubble was having a hell of a time! Not that he would have described it that way but, translated, that is what it meant. All around him was hell fire: burning, glowing, sparking, fizzing, popping, banging. Little boys whom he had turned out of his shop because they were too young to be sold fireworks chased him with Roman Candles they had bought elsewhere. Older fellows whom he had once dressed as choirboys now whistled at him as Tuppeny Thunders exploded at his feet. The youth of the village had gone berserk and were revelling in the orgy of noise and incandescence.

Only a few of Syd's contempories were out on the Common and they laughed at his antics thinking he was enjoying himself with the children. Most of his age group were fortifying themselves against the hazards of the occasion round the bar in the Coach and Horses.

Syd, however, had a mission. He had heard there was a move afoot among certain high-spirited young gentlemen thereabouts to lead a procession of torch bearers to the Haunted Meadow in an attempt to exorcise the ghost. Taking the line that it was pagan to patronize the Devil he sought out the ringleaders and urged them not to proceed.

'No good can come of it,' he told them, 'for those who

deal with damnation shall themselves be damned. You'll need more than a torch to burn the tail off Beelzebub,' he added, hysterically, 'and if *he* catches *you* it'll be purge-atory!'

Catherine wheels, Jack-in-the-Boxes, squibs, Thunder Flashes, rockets continued to go off all around him and Syd burned himself out before the display was over.

The big attraction was, as always, the bonfire and that was to be saved until the last so as to show the fireworks to their best effect against the darkness. The suspense of waiting, however, was too much for one small boy who aimed his rocket out of a lemonade bottle horizontally at the pile of sticks and set them alight prematurely. Soon the whole sky was aglow with soaring flames and the heat and crackle of burning twigs sent everyone a long way back for safety.

* * *

Up in the meadow four figures were lurking about in the undergrowth. Each had had great difficulty in getting there unseen for the frequent cascades of bursting rockets had lit up the skyline like flares on a battlefield. Cyrus had arrived suffering from simulated shell-shock and recovered only after taking several swigs of brandy from a hip flask. Bertie had enjoyed the fun of flinging himself to the ground with Sally every few yards but both were exhausted and bruised by the time they reached the ruin.

Digby alone had completed the journey unscathed. He had camouflaged himself from head to foot with branches, and stood still in his tracks every time the sky brightened.

Now they lay huddled together around a hole in the hedge watching the periodic bursts of light from the direction of the Common. When these changed to a steady glow it became evident that the bonfire had been lit and their cue for action had arrived.

Digby lit the fuse to his petrol can. Cyrus turned the handle of a perforated contraption he called The Banshee, which was nailed to a tree trunk. Bertie and Sally ignited the blue paper and withdrew rapidly from the tails of two rockets aimed to go up above the ruins.

For a moment all eyes were on the rockets for they were to herald a series of dramatic illuminations designed to attract attention and give the impression that something like a volcano was erupting.

There was a fizz and a swish and up they went. A couple of dull 'pops' were heard but nothing was seen of the falling stars and streaks of glory which had been promised. Cyrus muttered ruefully about their cost and the twisting fraudulence of the man who had sold them to him.

Bertie and Sally rushed to ignite the second batch. A pause, and the same thing happened.

'They're duds!' cried Digby. 'Don't bother about the others. Get moving with the flares. The "bomb" will go off in a minute: the fuse only takes five minutes.'

This was the first they knew about a 'bomb', but Bertie remembered the petrol can and hurried towards the moat. Every few yards along the curve of Cyrus's excavation they had placed a large triangular firework described as Aurora Borealis. This, it said on the label, would glow several colours in succession and end with a loud puff. Customers were warned to stand well back and not to hold in the hand.

Bertie, Sally and Benjamin each took a segment of the circle and ran with their tapers, touching off the perilous pyramids, while Cyrus went on turning the handle of his Banshee. Bright peaks of flame followed the runners until the ring was completed and a dark outline of the ruins could be seen in the centre.

Benjamin gasped and stood admiringly waiting for the colours to change. Suddenly he remembered the 'bomb'.

'*Watch out!* he called. '*Keep away from the bonfire.*'

Cyrus looked up and noticed it was not yet alight. Before he could comment to this effect there was a brilliant flash from the bottom of the pile and a long jet of flame snaked towards him.

Dropping the handle of the Banshee he raced to the cover of his moat and let out a wail which took over from the descending tones of the siren.

Instead of bursting with a bang and setting the bonfire ablaze, as Digby had expected, the petrol can inflated like a balloon and became airborne. Packed with a length of inflammable celluloid, scavenged from the last film show in the village hall, it emitted a fierce flame from the open neck and was jet-propelled.

Missing the tree where Cyrus had stood, it rose into the air and passed out of the field towards the river. As it went, trailing fire like a comet, the whole sky was lit by a vivid flash of lightning and a tremendous crash of thunder shook the air. Cold gusts of wind swept over the meadow and within a minute they were drenched in a deluge of rain.

9

Next morning the whole village was talking about the Great Storm.

All those who had been on the Common round the bonfire were soaked to the skin and by the time those who sheltered in the Coach and Horses were able to go home there were floods to wade through. The remains of the fire were quickly extinguished and the torchlight procession to the Haunted Meadow was halted before it began.

'I reckon it were the fireworks what did it! Always got thunder when the guns went off in the war. Storms like that ain't natural.'

'Must have been a curse on that field. You could see the witches running about up there and hear 'em wailin' an' screamin'. Terrible, it was. Wouldn't get me up there to save m' life!'

'Never known a storm like it. Did you see the thunderbolt? Went right across the sky over Galleon's Meadow. If I hadn't seen a thunderbolt before I should have said it had something to do with the place being haunted.'

Benjamin spent his first day in bed for many years, attended by his wife with her usual bottles of medicine. His insistence on staying out in the storm until each barrier to the field had been removed and all the entrances and exits were back to normal had therefore, availed him nothing. He groaned on his pillow and bemoaned his luck.

Sally sat mournfully around the fire downstairs, stroking the cat and looking strangely at the lampshade. She felt a kind of aura about it, as though it were telling her how unwise it had been to dabble with the past, how unforgivable to stretch the truth. She promised God she would be good in future.

Bertie was struggling gallantly to finish off a job that he and Digby had neglected, sneezing copiously and shivering violently, unaware of the strictures that Sally had just imposed upon herself.

Cyrus needed much less provocation than he had suffered the night before to stay in bed and the only difference on this occasion was that he did not insist upon having his meals brought to him. He was too ill to have anything to do with food at all.

The state of debility into which they had all fallen was due more to depression and disappointment at the sorrowful anti-climax to their recent efforts than to the severe soaking they had got from the thunderstorm. Instead of drawing everyone's attention from the annual bonfire on the Common to a more unusual spectacle on the meadow, so that they would associate this in the morning with the sight of a strange new superstructure where there had once been a cowshed, nothing had been seen over Galleon's Meadow except what had been described as a thunderbolt. This in itself was not sufficient evidence to remove the idea of a ghost, and such other stories as had circulated did little to dissipate the fear which existed. Together with the fact that nearly everyone who had been out on Bonfire Night was laid up with cold or pneumonia, it was hardly surprising that nobody went near the field for several days.

It was nearly a week later before anyone mentioned the ruin and, not unexpectedly, it happened in the Coach and Horses. Sam Waterman was recounting, as he did most evenings, his experience of falling into the river near Galleon's Reach. Fred Coman was chiding him for his carelessness in not looking where he was going.

'Well, how can yer, when ye're a pullin' on th' oars? Y'don't row in a boat facin' the way you're goin'.'

'No, but I ha'n't ever rowed into a tree!'

Digby saw his chance to interrupt. 'You've never told us what you saw when you got ashore, have you Sam?'

'What the hell could I see! I'd me eyes covered in mud.'

'Did you notice anything odd in the middle of the field?'

'Didn't go near th' middle o' th' field. Why? What should I ha' seen?'

'Well, I don't know, but I was wondering,' said Digby, taking up his cue. 'I went that way yesterday and noticed something I don't ever remember seeing there before. Looked like the ruins of an old castle. Did you know we had a ruined castle in the village?'

'Wouldn't be surprised,' croaked the old man, drawing smoke from some atrocious tobacco in his ancient pipe. 'Everything in these parts is ruined. What about that road we was a-goin' to repair? That's about the biggest ruin you've ever seen.'

Digby was humiliated enough at having to introduce the ruin himself and felt like the poor comedian who has to explain his jokes. He did not need to be reminded about the failure to his earlier enterprise, so he returned to the attack.

'I'm sure I've been across the meadow before and I don't ever remember seeing any ruins. You must have been that way in your youth, Sam? Was there ever a castle there then?'

'Now, now,' said Sam, enjoying the flattery of the joke, 'I'm not *that* old!'

But he neither confirmed nor denied the idea, for in truth he did not remember, and when in doubt about anything

Sam was wise enough not to talk about it.

Digby looked at Fred for encouragement, but he did not remember either. 'Can't think as there could have been, for I'm sure there'd have been some old wives' tale about it. Are you sure it *was* a ruin and not a crumbling cowshed?'

'Now that's a funny thing you should have mentioned a cowshed,' said Digby, hopeful of keeping up some interest, 'for I thought there was a cowshed on the meadow when I was up there once before. But there was no sign of it yesterday. Only broken stones and rubble, like a ruin. I must ask Cyrus about it when I see him.'

'Reckon he probably built it himself, to amuse the cattle! He's capable of it.'

Fred's remark came so close to their secret that Digby felt shivers in his spine and had no option but to change the subject.

When Cyrus did arrive that evening the mood of the company had already deteriorated. Instead of jostling up to the bar with his usual fluster he walked straight over to Digby and took him to one side.

'Read this. It came this morning.' He thrust into Digby's hand a letter bearing the County crest and headed: 'Highways Department.'

It was obvious the message was a grim one.

'A bypass, eh? . . . And no more work to be authorized on repairs to the minor road through Little Missington. The "minor road" indeed! What a damn cheek! After all the hours we've put into it.'

Cyrus tapped him kindly on the shoulder. 'Never mind, Ben. We may have the last laugh yet. If all those visitors we've been expecting come to Little Missington to see the castle they'll ignore the bypass and use our road. We can put back the toll-gates and make ourselves a fortune!'

'I don't know about that, Cyrus. Judging by the response we've had in the village so far, I doubt whether anyone

97

will ever come to see the ruin. It might just as well have been . . . a cowshed!'

They softened their sorrows with several 'snifters', as Cyrus called them, and then went over to join the others.

'There's nothing for it, lads, but we'll have to get digging again. The County Council have washed their hands of us and decided to build a new road to bypass the village. The one we've got won't be used much, so we'd better put it back the way we found it.'

There was a note of abandon in Digby's voice such as they had seldom heard before. It was the plea of a man defeated.

* * *

Winters in Little Missington were no worse, meteorologically, than those in other parts of the county but the one which they now faced had all the prospects of being the most bleak and uncomfortable in living memory. Their main communication with the outside world was virtually cut off and the demand for increased rates from the County Council loomed over them. Enthusiasm for their 'do-it-yourself' campaign had waned and even the stalwarts, led by Bertie Woodfellow, found it difficult to sustain their efforts now that they were officially relegated to a backwater position in the county.

Bertie and Digby showed occasional glimpses of their public spirit by trying to organise dances and jumble sales for the Road Relief Fund, but receipts rarely exceeded expenses and they were not a success.

Digby valiantly did the football pools with a view to donating his winnings to the common cause, but failed to find the correct combination of results and never actually won anything. Cyrus occasionally put money on the horses, with the same idea as Digby, but his judgement of a good horse was based on experience of its ability to pull a plough and he failed to pick one fast enough to win a race.

There was nothing for it, as winter closed in, but to grin and bear it, and Little Missington dug in, like the squirrels and badgers, to hibernate until the Spring.

* * *

The morning of the tenth of March was a fine example of England under the influence of cold, dry air from the Continent. It was bright and clear, with frost on the hedges, and distant landmarks looked close enough to touch. It made a pleasant change from the dull damp days which had passed.

Digby went off to work with a colourful scarf round his neck and Sally put on her slacks and a thick woollen jersey, as if she were bent on skiing. Her mother did not approve of this attire but Bertie had bought her the jersey as a Christmas present and she had worn it on every suitable occasion since. Even her mother had to admit this was a suitable occasion.

Returning from a brisk walk to the butcher's, on an errand for their lunch, Sally was about to open the garden gate when she heard a whistle. It came from the middle of the road and as she turned to see who it was a young man dismounted from a bicycle.

He was a tall lean figure, in his early twenties, wearing a blue-grey uniform, and even before he spoke Sally realized he was an American.

'Hi.'

Sally answered, and surprised herself by saying 'Hi' as if she had said it before.

'You live here?'

'Yes.' She nearly said 'Yeah'.

'You must be English?'

'Why, yes, I am.'

'Thought for a minute you might be American, seeing those dinky slacks you're wearing. Say, they're smart. And that sweater sure looks something! Don't often see girls round here as cute as that.'

'Thanks'. She didn't tell him who had given her the sweater.

'I'm an American. Daresay you guessed! Come from Baltimore. Joe Buckman's the name. What's yours?'

'Sally, Sally Digby.'

'Hiya, Sal. Pleased to know you.'

'Sally please, not Sal.'

'Oh sorry, kid — what's Sal? Is that a bad name?'

'No, but it sounds a bit like an old boat. I don't like it.'

'Well if you don't like it, I won't use it. That's good enough for me.'

'Thanks. Did you want something when you whistled just now?'

'Oh, yeah!' (She had rather hoped it was a wolf-whistle, but asked the question in order to change the conversation.) 'Where am I?'

'You're in Little Missington.'

'Little Miss'n'ton, eh? That's a cute name for a place. Are there lots of little misses in Miss'n'ton?'

'Where are you heading for?' Sally felt she ought to ignore the crack about little misses, though it rather appealed to her.

'Nowhere in particular. Just drifting. I like mooching around. It's a helluva place you've got here, this countryside of Old England. Beautiful, on a day like this. Don't care much for it when it's raining, which it usually is. But when it's fine, it sure is beautiful.'

'Have you come very far?'

'From Baltimore. Oh, you mean, just now. Yeah, it sure seemed a long way, tho' I guess it's only about ten miles.

100

I'm at the United States Air Force Base at Swivenhall. Ever been there?'

'No.'

'Well, you'll have to come with me one night to one of our balls. Sister, when we have a ball, do we have a ball!'

'I must go in now. Mother will be waiting for me.' Sally closed the gate between them.

'Oh, I'm sorry kid! I didn't mean to be "fast". I forgot that here you need to be introduced before you ask for a date.'

'It's not that, but I must go.'

'Couldn't I see you again sometime?'

'Maybe.'

'I'll come back this way tomorrow, same time.' Joe mounted his bicycle to go, but stepped off it again. 'Is there some sort of monument here I could be looking for, that would give you an alibi?'

Sally's mind clicked quickly to the dungeon she had dug with Bertie and almost without thinking she said 'Yes. The ruined castle on Galleon's Meadow. It's up that way. I'll tell you about it tomorrow.'

The airman rode away and Sally watched him from the doorway. There, in a foreign uniform, unaware of the distinction he was about to bring upon himself, went the first visitor to her father's monument.

* * *

Next morning Sally was out early on her errands and Mrs Digby was puzzled to know why she made three or four separate journeys to the shops and back when normally she would have carried everything in one. But her mother was too busy with her daily cleaning of the cottage to interrogate.

Sally was standing in the doorway, deliberating on another excuse for shopping when Corporal Joseph

Buckman rode into view. Speeding down the hill from the direction of the village, he bumped along the road as if he were riding a bronco instead of a bicycle, but he didn't actually fall off until he reached the cottage.

'Hi'.

'Hi, Joe. Are you all right?' Sally rushed through the gate, but Joe was picking himself up.

'Say, that's a helluva road back there! I didn't come that way yesterday but I figured when I got home last night that that ought to be the quickest way. How wrong can a guy get!'

'You should come when it's raining.'

Joe did not see the joke. He just stared at Sally. She was looking even more attractive than the day before and had tied her hair in a pony-tail.

'Gee, I hope I'm not late. It's not polite to keep a pretty girl waiting ... Mind if I tell you you're pretty?'

'Not a bit. But you've just had a fall. You're probably seeing things.'

'I'll say I'm seeing things! Never dreamed I'd see anyone as pretty as you in these parts. And, say — what about that ruin you told me to look at yesterday. Now *that* sure is somethin'! I haven't seen anything like that since I came to England.'

Sally was delighted. She had thought of little else but the American since yesterday and now here he was again, gushing and flattering as before but noticeably shyer and more awkward. This she took to be distinctly in her favour. Almost subconsciously, her feminine instincts roused, she proceeded to capitalize the gain.

'Joe,' she said, 'you ought to go again on Sunday. That's when the pilgrimage takes place. I'll go with you, if you like.'

She didn't notice, and neither did he, but just as he had lost some of the self-assurance he had displayed the previous day, so she had become more brash and less reserved than when they first met.

'You bet I'd like! I'm a sucker for processions. But what do you have to *be* to join a "pilgrimage"? Can't say as I've ever been a pilgrim before.'

'Don't you worry, you'll be all right. We can just watch.'

Sally watched the American and as she did so a mischievous thought occurred to her. 'I suppose *all* Americans are pilgrims, really, . . . children of the Pilgrim Fathers.'

Joe laughed. But he blushed a little, too, at the sentiment. He could not regard himself as a very devout descendant of the *Mayflower* voyagers. Yet he had always boasted that one of his forefathers had come over on the *Mayflower*. Sally could not have known that, surely? Or could she have got some 'dope' on him during the past twenty-four hours?

'I guess folks don't have to quit your country nowadays if they hold different beliefs, like they had to when our ancestors sailed in the *Mayflower*. My dad's very proud of the fact that one of our family came over with the Pilgrim Fathers. He says I'm the first member of the family to go back the other way.'

'Are you really descended from a Pilgrim Father, Joe?'

'So my dad says, and I guess I ought to believe him.'

'Joe, that's wonderful, being able to trace your family back as far as that. I was only joking when I said all Americans must be descended from the Pilgrim Fathers. I suppose many must come from Red Indian stock; and there were the Spaniards, and Portuguese. . .'

But Sally had got carried away. Which was how it appeared to her mother as she looked out of her bedroom window. She could just recognize the back of her daughter drifting into the distance across the Common, escorted by a man in uniform pushing a bicycle. At least she now knew the reason for Sally's strange behaviour with the shopping.

Benjamin was furious when he heard about it. In the first place he did not like Americans, and secondly he *did* like Bertie.

'What's wrong with a decent, down-to-earth, good-looking, hard-working Englishman? What the devil does she want with a dreamy, drawling, goddam Yank? It's all this modern wireless stuff she listens to. Nothing but crazy kids with their poppycock ''pop'' . . . and she swoons at the first American she meets! How did she come to meet him, anyway?'

'I don't know, but I think he came to call for her this morning. I'm sure she was expecting him by the way she kept going backwards and forwards for the groceries. Do you think we ought to stop her, Ben? She's a bit young for that sort of thing yet, and you never know, do you, where it might lead to and what these Americans might take for granted. I mean, he might be a nice chap and all that, but he's a long way from home. . .'

'He'll not take our Sal for anything, that's for sure!'

'What's that, Dad? What did you say?'

'Sally! Where have you been? Your mother has just been telling me. . .'

'Well, if she has, you know then, don't you!'

'Don't be cheeky to your father, young lady. You're not old enough to answer back like that.'

'And you're not old enough to be going around with Americans.'

'How old do I have to be for that, then? And why should it be all right to go out with English boys and not one from America?'

Sally had a lot to learn, and Benjamin was in the right mood to start off with a few lessons. Her mother intervened, however. She thought it would be better if they had a little chat together on the facts of life before Benjamin gave her any more reasons for discriminating between nationalities.

Anxious to avoid the embarrassment of revealing what she already knew (and perhaps a little more than even her mother knew) Sally protested that she was only fraternizing in the common cause.

'Mr Buckman is very interested in the ruins he saw on Galleon's Meadow and he asked me to tell him what I knew about them.'

'You jolly well didn't, I hope,' said her father, slower on the uptake than when his temper was steady.

'I jolly well did, you know,' said his daughter, beginning to see smoother water ahead.

'Well, what the devil were you thinking of?'

'Calm down a bit, dad! Calm down! I told him exactly what you've wanted everyone to know about the ruin. That it arose in mysterious circumstances one night in a very bad storm and that previously it had been hidden for hundreds of years by a cowshed.'

Digby was loath to subside. He was used to her slipping out of awkward situations by telling plausible irrelevancies and he fancied she was in the midst of one now. Sensing this, Sally went on to recount the yarn she had spun to her corporal friend about the pilgrimage on Sundays.

'Oh you didn't tell such lies!' her mother scolded.

'It needn't be a lie,' said Sally, raising her eyebrows with unusual sophistication. 'It depends whether daddy will help me get a party together so that Mr Buckman won't be disappointed.'

Digby stared at her. And he began to see the cunning of it.

'You mean, you're not "taken" by the American, he's been "taken in" by you?'

'I'm not sure that I know what you mean. He's a very *nice* American.'

Sally had that same look in her eyes as when she produced the handmade lampshade and Digby was still too inexperienced a teenager's father to see through it. He simply accepted her coyness as a sign of agreement and patted her tenderly on the pony-tail.

* * *

They had less difficulty getting together a procession to walk across the Common than they had had in getting volunteers to dig up the road. Especially as they described the occasion as a pageant and announced that it was for the special benefit of a distinguished visitor from the New World.

The idea, they explained, was to highlight and dramatize their new-found and only relic of local history: the ruins of an ancient castle. By parading through the village in old-style costumes and re-enacting some of the battles that must have been fought in the shadow of the castle, they would bring fame and fortune to the village and undo some of the isolation it had suffered since the collapse of their highway. Who better than an American to promote their aspirations?

By now, most of the inhabitants of Little Missington were past knowing what their true aspirations were, but the persuasions of a Digby were not to be lightly cast aside and early on Saturday afternoon a small crowd gathered on the Common in front of Rose Cottage to rehearse their part in the proceedings.

No one had much conception of what the villagers had worn in bygone years but, time being only relative, anything in the family wardrobe not in current use was regarded as 'historical' and worn for the occasion.

Sally and her father began by grouping together those who were dressed in a similar fashion and attributing to them a task which seemed appropriate to their attire.

Those in high stockings and breeches were designated 'Archers', and constrained to tighten their jackets with broad belts and wear soft hats with large green feathers in them. Bows and arrows were to be borrowed from the neighbouring archery club by one of the members who lived in Little Missington and who was to be given charge of the unit.

Men in plus-fours or wellington boots were asked to wear caps and carry rifles or shot guns, but advised not to load them.

Wearers of leather jackets were conscripted for the 'catapult crew', issued with large slings of elastic, and told to collect stones as ammunition on the way to the 'battlefield.'

Women were separated simply into those who carried shawls and those who did not. The shawl bearers were asked to bring bowls and bandages and formed into a brigade for tending the wounded. Those without, who were mostly the young ones, were expected to carry baskets and dispense fruit to their menfolk on the way to battle. They were also besought to wear bonnets.

All the women were instructed to follow their men as far as the moat and to engage in country dancing while the battle scenes were being staged. This was to be Vera Digby's contribution to the programme, accepted without much enthusiasm, but suggested by her husband as a practical way of keeping the ladies occupied while the men were in action.

Bertie had been invited to help with the production but, resenting the presence of the American, declined on the grounds that he was not artistically qualified and preferred to play his part as one of the actors. There was no time to argue and Bertie was swiftly drafted into battle. He had found some material in the 'junk-trunk' at home which looked like a loin cloth and compromised with modesty and the elements by wrapping it across one shoulder and tucking it into a track suit. The result was distinctly heterogeneous

107

but, once a dustbin lid had been added for a shield and a large spear produced from a wall in the Coach and Horses, the effect was indicative of an ancient warrior. Two or three youths who had turned up without any distinctive garments were stripped to the waist and fell in behind Bertie to be his slaves.

By sundown a routine had been worked out for the parade and a series of tableaux conceived for performance round the castle ruins.

They had come a long way from Sally's original idea of a pilgrimage but it showed a sound understanding of human nature that Digby realized how much easier it was to secure the services of volunteers for a practical stunt, with an organized procession, than to persuade the public at large to patronize an event without the feeling of participation.

The 'old warriors' of Little Missington slept well that night after their vigorous exertions in the open air and a few even dreamed of the days they were trying to depict in the pageant. Bertie dreamed of himself cutting down an American with a tomahawk and Sally woke with a start imagining herself being dragged round a cave by a hairy creature in a leopard skin loin cloth.

It was Benjamin, however, who had the most realistic and prophetic dream of all. He saw Cyrus on a horse charging the castle ruins as if they were a windmill.

10

Bertie was up earlier than usual on Sunday morning. He met Cecil Coman on his way to round up the cows for milking.

'Sissy' was six-foot-two and broad at the shoulders. He did not take a dog on his round up. Any cow that strayed was likely to be lifted back into line — and he had been known to make the attempt. There was not much grey matter in his head and he was belligerent at heart, but Bertie found his ignorance and toughness useful at times. This was such an occasion.

'Where are you grazing the cows after milking this morning, Sissy?' he asked.

'In the field,' he answered.

'Which field?' Bertie persisted.

'Same one as I'm goin' to fetch 'em from.'

Bertie saw that it would be better to follow him on foot than to pursue the questioning.

'Don't often see you up at this hour!' Something had clicked in the lad's mind and Bertie felt that perhaps young Coman was the more awake of the two.

'I want you to help me put the wind up a Yankee.'

Cecil stared at him in silence. Bertie tried to explain.

'There's a pageant on in the village this afternoon — a sort of procession, like, and there's an American airman coming to see it. Well, if you do as I ask you we can make sure he doesn't forget his visit to Little Missington — and that he won't be in a hurry to come again.'

'An American, eh? Is he a cowboy?'

'I don't know . . . but we could soon find out. If you do what I ask. . .'

'How big is he?'

'I don't know. I've never seen him. But you won't have to fight him.'

'Oh. I could slug him if you want me to.'

'No, I don't. In fact, I don't even want you to meet him. Now, listen to me . . .'

They went on to the meadow where the cows were grazing and drove them back to the sheds at Galleon's Farm. There the buckets were clean and ready to be filled. Ignoring Bertie, who stood in the doorway and watched, Cecil drew up a stool and began to work away at the bulging udders. It was in every other sense a mechanical operation, for he paid no attention to what he doing, least of all to the cow, but instead of the usual vacant expression on his face there was a broad grin. As the cow fidgeted and puffed, Sissy chuckled, and went on milking.

Bertie slipped quietly away, satisfied that he had secured an accomplice.

* * *

Sally had risen early, too, but with a different sentiment on her mind. Helping her mother prepare the breakfast she asked if she might invite the American to tea on their return from the 'pilgrimage.'

'Pilgrimage indeed! I don't know where you get such ideas. You ought to be ashamed of yourself. I thought you would have grown out of make-believe at your age.'

'Well Daddy hasn't, has he?'

'Your father is nothing to go by. He'll never grow up.'

'It's all in the good of the cause, you know, Mummy.'

'What cause?'

'Our future! If we don't get people from outside the village to take an interest in us, there soon won't be a village! There'll be no work and no wages and we'll end up like the Dodos.'

'Who on earth has been teaching you such rubbish? There's been folk living here for hundreds of years and times have been much worse than they are now. I don't see the sense in making all this fuss about attracting visitors and ancient monuments. Last year it was all modern roads, and look where that got us. We're worse off now than ever we were. You leave well alone, that's my motto, or you never know where it may lead you.'

Benjamin arrived at the breakfast table to be greeted by a wall of silence. 'Has Sally burned the toast again?' he asked, hoping to provoke an explanation.

Vera glared at him. 'No, but she'll be burning her fingers if she's not careful. She wants to have a visitor for tea.'

Digby looked at his wife and then at Sally, whose hands were on her hips and nose in the air. In the circumstances he thought it better not to take sides. He changed the subject.

'As soon as I've had breakfast I'll go up and tell Cyrus what we're doing this afternoon.'

Sally whispered something in her father's ear. Vera sensed what was being said.

'I think it would be nicer if she asked Bertie to tea, don't you?'

Ben winked at Sally. 'Why don't we have them both to tea?'

Sally shrugged her shoulders and felt that perhaps two loaves were better than no bread.

* * *

111

Digby arrived at The Willows to find Cyrus polishing a suit of armour. It had stood in the hall for many years and gave The Willows an air of antiquity, like the mock-Tudor of its architecture. Cyrus never claimed it as an heirloom, for he had bought it in a jumble sale soon after he was married, but he caressed it now as though it had protected him through many a joust. Seeing his dream materialize, Digby's reactions were a little unchivalrous. 'What on earth are you doing?'

'Don't know that I'll tell you,' said Cyrus in offended tone, 'you haven't told me what you're doing this afternoon.'

'That's just what I've come to see you about.'

'Ah, but news travels faster today than it used to.'

'Who told you? We only planned it yesterday.'

'I only heard about it yesterday.'

There was a ring of triumph in Cyrus's voice which told Digby he was more excited at his intelligence gathering success than he was annoyed at being left out of the proceedings. For indeed it was evident to Digby that Cyrus had no intention of being left out of the proceedings.

'Don't suppose you've groomed the horse yet, have you?' said Digby with a thrust that pierced the Galleon armour.

'What horse? Don't know what you mean.'

'Well, you're not thinking of walking to the ruin with that on, are you?'

Cyrus recognized that he had been rumbled and the glint in Digby's eyes made him realize the joke was already won. They roared with laughter and went into the drawing room for a glass of port.

* * *

Corporal Buckman was playing chess in the games room at Swivenhall. His concentration was lacking and a surprised opponent took his castle.

'Guess that's just about ruined it for you, Joe?'

Joe came to life and grinned. 'You sure said a mouthful there, bud! Did you ever see a *real* ruined castle? I'll take you somewhere this afternoon that'll slay you. A real Anglo-Saxon ruin and somethin' called a "pilgrimage".'

Sally's 'pilgrims' were busy collecting their bits and pieces. Last minute trimmings were being added, and old cupboards and trunks and chests-of-drawers turned out for the missing garments which someone remembered they had but didn't know where.

In the Coach and Horses Digby was facing some of his detractors.

'Don't care much for this pageant idea of yours, Ben. Seems sort o' silly, like, dressin' up at this time o' year. It's all right at Christmas, indoors by the fire where you can keep yourself warm, but March is no time for messin' about on the Common.'

'Neither were November!' said a voice which had clearly not forgotten Guy Fawkes Night and the Great Storm.

Digby looked solemnly at the froth on his pint of beer. 'It's not my idea,' he said, 'it's the young 'uns. They thought of it. And they're acting it, so I don't see how we can complain. It's a way of showing their respect for the past, and I shouldn't wonder if it didn't turn out to be a good investment for the future. Do you know who's coming to see it? A descendant of one of the Pilgrim Fathers.'

'I don't hold with all these visitations,' moaned Jack Thatcher. 'It weren't natural the way that ruin appeared out of an old cowshed and it ain't right to expect a Pilgrim Father to appear out o' nowhere on the day we have a procession.'

* * *

113

Joe arrived early in the afternoon and Sally was startled to see him ride up on a tandem with another airman at the rear.

'Hi there, Miss Digby,' he called out, in a mixture of familiarity and formal address. 'Let me introduce a buddy of mine, Sammy Wainright. Sammy, meet Sally. You've heard me talk about her plenty, well there she is, pretty as ever!' Then, quietly to Sally , 'Hope you don't mind me bringing Sammy along. He's interested in ancient customs and I thought you might like an extra spectator.'

Sally instinctively resented the second American but was anxious not to offend Joe. She smiled a welcome and said, 'Pleased to meet you.'

Sammy was delighted and said, 'Pleased to meet you' back in a kind of innocent mimicry which he adopted without malice.

Giving his body a jerk, which looked like a compromise between a bow and a curtsey, Sammy held out his arm for a handshake. Sally obliged and then turned to repeat the convention with Joe.

'I see you've stretched the bike a bit,' she said, trying to be jocular.

'Sure! How do you like it? It's a helluva lot easier gettin' over those bumps with three wheels and three hundred pounds on board than it was with just me and a bicycle. Sammy, you don't know what it was like the first time I rode into this town — felt just like I was back at a rodeo.'

Joe was pleased to have a companion with him. It gave him enough self-confidence to behave buoyantly in front of Sally and to talk freely instead of defensively as he had done at their previous meeting. Sally had not noticed this yet, nor the fact that much of Joe's excitement was the thrill of showing her off to another man, but she had already taken a strong dislike to Sammy. Although she would never have admitted it, she inwardly regarded herself as Joe's

114

property and did not react well to Sammy's attempts at stealing her attention. His flashing eyes and slick expressions irritated her and she felt overpowered and embarrassed by his presence. Joe, on the other hand, despite his boisterous nature, showed a humility and charm which appealed to her. Besides, having two American escorts made her feel conspicuous. Whereas one would have raised her prestige in the village, she felt the pair were likely to be a blot on her reputation.

So the more Sammy tried to impress her the more remote and typically English she became, and the further she retreated the more desperately Sammy tried to get her back.

'Say, Joe, why don't we ask Miss Digby to come and visit us on the camp one of these days? She'd be a wow up there among the boys.'

'Why don't you bring "the boys" down here, Mr Wainwright?' she retorted. 'I'm sure they'd be a "wow" among the girls.'

Not noticing the tone of sarcasm in her voice, he seized on what he thought was an opening. 'Are there many gals in this town?'

'You'll see a few this afternoon, if you look carefully, though you may not recognize them by their costume.'

'Oh, I never did use that method for telling sex...'

Sammy was not allowed to continue. Joe had been told the English regarded that as a dirty word. He apologized for his friend.

'It's all right, Joe,' said Sally. 'I've heard the word before and I know what it means. We're not so frightened of using it today ... the word I mean, of course!'

Joe blushed and Sally laughed a little shyly at her mischief. Sammy thought she was marvellous and practically fell upon her in admiration. But she saw lechery in his eyes and withdrew to a safer distance.

Joe tried to change the subject. 'What time does it start?

115

. . . the pilgrimage I mean.' He blushed deeper than ever and Sally felt sorry for leading him into such ambiguity. Then she decided it was Sammy's fault for introducing the subject and hated him more than ever.

Sensing his stock was at low ebb, Sammy made one last effort to gain some glory. 'Can we participate in this pilgrimage, Miss Digby? Joe and me would sure like to show some respect to our English ancestors.'

'Then I think you had better follow quietly behind the procession and see what goes on. There's quite a ritual and I'm afraid you're not really dressed for a part.'

Sammy looked at his uniform and thought of the extra care he had taken to smarten himself up before meeting this delightful English girl that Joe had talked so much about. While he was still puzzling over what it was she regarded as misplaced or incorrect in his attire, the first of the pilgrims appeared on the Common.

There was a famous picture called the *Laughing Cavalier* that Sammy Wainright had once seen reproduced in a magazine. Digby had seen it, too, on the walls of half a dozen cottages, and the impersonation he now made of it was little short of remarkable. Where he had obtained all the laces and trimmings, and how he had assembled them without his daughter knowing, was almost as surprising as the likeness he conveyed to Franz Hals' portrait. Sally caught her breath and choked back a spontaneous laugh; one that should have been on her father's face not hers.

Joe looked at Sammy, and Sammy at Sally. In fact Sammy never stopped looking at Sally, and this was just another excuse.

'I never did dig what that guy was laffin' at when he had his picture painted! Guess I can ask him now, or when the show's over.'

Joe saw a look of discomfort on Sally's face.

'Say, Sammy, that's not being very reverent. That old

116

gentlemen's playing a serious part in this pilgrimage and it's not for you and me to make fun of him.'

'That old gentleman,' said Sally, 'is my father.'

Neither Joe nor Sammy had a lot more to say that afternoon, even after she had introduced them to her father. He greeted them with an incongruous 'Howdee?', and then made off to round up his brethen.

Doffing his enormous hat and bowing whenever he spoke to anybody or passed an onlooker, Digby thought to himself that if he had to choose between the Americans he would rather have Joe as a son-in-law than Sammy. On the other hand, if he had any real choice in the matter, he would rather not have either of them.

Bertie, who was still Benjamin's favourite, appeared at the rendezvous on time but, apart from exchanging greetings, kept well out of Sally's way. Not so remote that he could not see her, but far enough to avoid meeting her companions.

Three hundred yards of common land stretched between the river and the road in one direction and separated the inhabited part of the village from fields in the other. No longer much used for pasture, it was a place where people gathered on Sundays to preach and pray, or simply fish and play. Had the roads not been as already described, it would have been a paradise for motorists on which to park and picnic.

On this particular Sunday, however, it was the starting point of a strange ceremonial, hurriedly conceived and totally under-rehearsed, to which many came who still wondered what it was all about, regarding it only as a welcome change from their usual routine on that day of the week.

If choregraphy was lacking, colour and commotion were not, and the sheer size of the assembly was impressive, even to the visitors. It far exceeded any congregation the

Salvation Army had ever mustered there, and they were a popular attraction on the Common on most Sundays when the weather was fine.

A roll of drums brought the 'pilgrims' to order and they scrambled into line behind each other as starlings do at night, jostling for position with friends and sweethearts. Benjamin strode to the front, raising his hat high in the air for all to see and, thrusting it out at arm's length like a flag bearer at the head of his cavalry, he led the procession up towards the castle.

Along the riverside they walked to the fields beyond the Common, over stiles and tracks and five-barred gates, till they came in sight of Galleon's Reach. Once in view of the 'ruin' excitement rose, for most of the party had never seen it before. They knew of it only as a rumour, following fearful accounts of witches and supernatural forces that had thrived in a cowshed.

Joe and Sammy found themselves absorbed within the procession as stragglers fell back and others fell over. Sally required all her agility of conversation to prevent them overhearing some of the villagers, whose remarks would have betrayed the novelty of the occasion. 'Have you noticed,' she chattered, 'how the Catapult Men are picking their ammunition as they go along? That's how it must have been done once upon a time. The fields are littered with flints; some may even have been flung in prehistoric battles.'

Sammy simply swallowed her innocent stories and Joe marvelled again at her imagination. Neither had heard of the Catapult Men and Sally's delightful invention conjured up a cross between a Trojan Warrior and William Tell. They knew that catapults had been used in war before cannons, and they had seen films of ancient battles which Sally had not, but the association of such a primitive weapon with the men of Little Missington was one that had not occurred to them.

'Gee, that's romantic, isn't it? Think of all the history we're taking in at this place. War must have been quite jolly in those days. No wonder we can't get it out of our systems.'

Sam went ambling on, but Joe was silent and Sally took him by the arm in case he had any doubt about her attention.

Joe was still brooding over the *faux pas* he had made earlier in the afternoon. 'I guess your family must have been Cavaliers at the time of your Civil War.'

'I doubt if my family goes back that far,' said Sally with sudden modesty.

'But surely, Miss Digby, if Joe here has ancestors as old as the Pilgrim Fathers, and both of us, I know, have great grandfathers who fought the Confederates in the American Civil War. . .'

Luckily at that moment a bugle call rang out across the meadow. The procession stopped, as if signalled to do so, and all the chatter which had accompanied them on the march, ceased.

Some recalled the last time they had heard a similar sound and Digby recognised it immediately. It was certainly not in the programme.

Straight ahead of them, on one of the ramparts, they could see something glistening in the sun and as they stared, transfixed, the clarion called again. This time the drummer, who had marshalled them together at the start of their journey and cursed his encumbrance thereafter, struck back with a vigorous beat. Digby raised his hat, repeated the gesture of sweeping it forward, and the procession moved on.

Joe and Sammy were stunned.

'That guy up there with a horse and a trumpet — is that a ghoul?'

Sally laughed. 'That's Mr Galleon, Chairman of our

Parish Council.'

'Is he the sheriff? Or is he so unpopular he needs a suit of armour?'

Cyrus was having some difficulty with the horse again. He was not riding it this time, for it would not take his weight and the armour. Consequently there was no danger of him falling off, but the horse did not like the feel of steel against its flanks and it probably felt offended at being draped in flags and bunting and having a hood on its head. As the front of the procession drew nigh it reared nervously, neighed loudly and knocked Cyrus flat on his back. A muffled cheer from sections of the crowd went up, but Cyrus did not hear it.

Digby turned to face his followers. Spreading his arms widely, as if telling a fisherman's yarn or doing his physical jerks, he bade them disperse to take up their stations for the tableaux. People rushed in all directions, shouting instructions and answering back. Belongings were dropped and trodden on and tempers frayed. The scene was more like market day in Myrtlesham than Holy Day in Little Missington.

Unfamiliar with castle layout, and this castle in particular, the performers had little idea where to take up their positions. The remains of towers and battlements were so alike in their eroded state as to confuse all but those who had put them there. Digby realised he should have labelled them.

Cyrus was shouting for help as he rolled into the dungeon and Bertie was too busy looking for 'Sissy' Coman to be of much use to anybody. To the accompaniment of flutes and fiddles, groups of women were starting their country dances where archers, pikesmen and musketeers were all seeking to pitch their battlefield. Arrows, pikes and shot were flying in all directions and two of the women in shawls were already tending the wounded.

Suddenly the most fearful screams broke out all over the field. Looking up from the entrance to the dungeon, where Joe and Sammy were helping her rescue Cyrus, Sally was horrified to see a bull charging madly from victim to victim, snorting and roaring ferociously with a spear sticking out of his flesh where some gallant villager had seized his moment as a matador before fleeing to the river.

Without waiting to warn anyone, Sally pushed the two Americans into the pit and jumped in after them, throwing Cyrus to the ground for a second time just as he was about to pull himself clear. Several terrible moments followed while people scrambled for cover, some climbing trees and others jumping into the river. None of the gunmen stood their ground and, with one exception just mentioned, those with inferior weapons panicked without a fight. Some threw themselves prostrate, as they had learned to do when bombs were falling, and others took to their heels and chanced their speed. Garments and implements fell everywhere and the solitary drum came to rest on a gate post as its carrier vaulted the obstruction.

Digby had clambered up the superstructure of his ruin and was surveying the scene from behind a parapet, shouting to his men to keep calm and protect the women.

Young master Coman was crouching behind a palisade, holding a long chain in one hand and a club in the other. The expression on his face was one of startled curiosity, as if he were unable to believe the havoc he had created. Not even the Sorcerer's Apprentice would have looked more concerned.

Hero of the hour was Bertie. Ripping the cloak off one of the women as she raced by with her bandages flying, he opened it out with theatrical flourish and braced himself against the charge of the bull.

No Spaniard would have grudged him the gratitude he earned that afternoon. Not once did he parry the bull but many times, nipping smartly to one side as he thrust the cloak over the animal's eyes and turning swiftly to face it as it came again. Whether the creature tired of its efforts, or was mesmerized by Bertie's movements is a matter for conjecture, but finally the beast came to rest within a yard of its captor. Had the arena been Madrid or Barcelona the crowd would have been on its feet applauding and the womenfolk hysterical with pride.

As it was, the audience had fled and the only witnesses to the scene were Benjamin on the ramparts and Cecil Coman in the role of the ringmaster.

Bertie was paralysed with fear when he contemplated what he had done and would need to do next, but Sissy awoke to his duty at the crucial moment and came forward with his noose and chain, smartly staking the animal to a spike in the portcullis.

Digby cheered from on high, and Sally and Cyrus and Sammy and Joe came up from their hideout to see what had happened.

* * *

The question that nobody asked at tea was how the bull had got there, but the courage of Timber the Toreador was much talked about and a chorus of 'He's a jolly Woodfellow' rendered by his followers. Benjamin thought it a pity the lad was not with them at tea to celebrate his valour, but Mrs Digby had set for five and with Sammy's unexpected arrival she was relieved that he had declined the invitation.

He was, in fact, at the Comans' taking hell out of the cowman.

11

Reactions in Little Missington to what had happened that Sunday were hostile and unfriendly, and recriminations rife, but the interest created at the American Air Base by Joe and Sammy's account of the proceedings, topped any topic of conversation for a long time.

'Boy, can those English pile on the history! You should have seen them . . .'

'You think we've got hep: you want to see these boys when there's a cow in the field.'

'What's dull about a dungeon, when you're sharing it with a knight in armour and a dainty damsel?'

They were so full of the story that they wrote home about it, printed it in their magazines, and told it to their girlfriends. It was not only the colour and spectacle of the pageantry that appealed to them but the action and drama of its climax. 'Bertie' was almost a new word for hero. Everyone at Swivenhall knew who 'Bertie' was and the headlines of the magazine story read: BERTIE BEATS BULL AS PILGRIMS PANIC.

Bertie was invited to visit the camp as their guest of honour, but he declined.

He had already confessed to Benjamin that it was his idea in the first place to have the bull in the meadow so as to frighten the American, but he had asked for it to be tethered on the far side of the field where he intended directing the spectators once the battle scenes began. As it happened, Sissy flapped when he saw Cyrus arrive early with his horse and armour and tried to hold the bull off in a neighbouring field. Hearing the muskets firing, and the fiddles and flutes, the animal broke from its bonds and rushed on to the meadow.

The sequel, he fancied, was common knowledge.

Digby advised him solemnly to 'sit on the story' until the rumpus subsided.

* * *

Sally was torn between her admiration for Bertie's bravery and a growing affection for Joe. Her father reminded her that of all the men in the field it was only Bertie who had stood his ground against the bull.

'But I pushed Joe into the dungeon,' she protested.

'So, was he pushed, or did he jump?' Her father mocked. Sally was not amused. She would not listen to any further account of the incident. Inwardly she respected Bertie's courage but fiercely defended Joe who, she felt, might have done something equally brave if he had had the chance. She wished she had just pushed Sammy in — and left him there! Joe was an airman and must be brave, too — perhaps braver than Bertie if it came to the test. Perversely, she hoped one day he would be able to prove it.

Meanwhile, Bertie's coolness towards her continued, or appeared to continue by virtue of the guilty conscience which kept him away for the rest of the week. Only Benjamin knew the reason why.

It was Friday evening when they next saw Joe. He came on his own this time and having been introduced to the Digby household felt confident in calling on them without a prior engagement.

He leant his bicycle against the garden gate and walked

up a narrow path to the front door of the cottage. Unhappily for Joe, the Digbys rarely used this door, which led directly on to the living-room, and in her latest rearrangement of furniture Vera had placed an armchair across it on the inside. Confusion resulted as he rapped a second time upon the knocker.

Had he peered in through the window, as they did out of it, he would have seen Benjamin pulling a table in one direction and Vera pushing the settee in another, while Sally struggled to move chairs into the space between. Finally Sally reached the door as her mother and father scrambled to look settled and, after one last obstacle with the bolt, managed to open it.

'Gee, I didn't mean to put you to all that bother,' said Joe, not knowing the half of it, and only guessing at what had been going on. 'I always seem to drop in the hard way. Guess I should have figured it out and come in the way I went out last Sunday.'

'Oh, I'm sorry, Joe. You were right, this *is* the front door, only Daddy always brings visitors in the back way, so it's sort of gone out of use.'

'It's my fault really, you see . . .'

'No, no, Vera you mustn't make the lad feel uncomfortable. It *was* my fault, as Sally said. After all, I helped build the house in the first place. What we didn't know in those days was that porches would ever be popular with the working classes. They were almost a symbol of the well-to-do and an unnecessary obstacle to overcome on a dark night. Times have changed, of course, and so have fashions. Now, take that picture over there, for example . . .'

But Vera was having none of Boadicea this evening and she quickly steered Joe into a fireside chair and asked if she could get him a cup of tea.

'Coffee, Mum.'

125

'Oh, he won't want coffee at this time of day. It's much too early for coffee. You'll not be going to bed just yet, will you?'

Joe smiled and said he'd love a cup of tea.

Sally drew the pouffe up to his chair and sat down beside him, protesting that he need not have had tea if he would have preferred coffee. Joe said he did not mind a bit, to which Sally argued that he ought not to be drinking tea just because it was easier to make, and Joe said he was interested to learn that it was easier to make for he had always found coffee easy to make. Whereupon Sally said, there, she knew he would rather have had coffee and, by the time he had extricated himself the second time, Vera was back with the pot on a tray.

Had it been Bertie who was visiting the Digbys there is little doubt that Benjamin would have found some pretext for leaving the room, and if Vera had not automatically continued with the housework he would have suggested they went for a walk together or did some similar vanishing trick. But Joe had not yet earned that status and neither Benjamin nor Vera were inclined to leave him and Sally alone, no matter what they might have been able to do elsewhere.

Sally sensed their resistance and resented it.

Joe merely thought how polite they were and went on talking.

It was not until he got up to leave, an hour or so later, that he confessed the reason for his coming. Looking awkwardly at Mrs Digby, and trying hard to take Sally to one side, he gave up all hope of a good-night kiss and offered a handshake all round. Slipping her arm round his waist, Sally gave him the cue he wanted.

'Come and see us again, Joe, any time,' she said. 'I know Mummy and Daddy won't mind. Will you?'

'No, of course not,' said Vera.

'Come when you like, my boy,' Digby found himself

saying, and could have bitten his tongue.

'Thanks a lot. I sure appreciate your hospitality. I really came tonight to ask Sally if she would do me the great honour of being my partner at a ball we're having on the camp a week tomorrow. That is,' he added hastily, turning towards Sally, 'if your Ma and Pa give their permission.'

Sally did not wait for her parents' reaction. 'I'd love to, Joe. But what do I have to wear? And how will I get there? And what time does it start?'

Her eyes were wide and bright with excitement and Joe felt the thrill of giving pleasure overtake the joy of getting her agreement. Digby thought she must have expected the invitation to have had quite so many questions ready, but her mother only observed the signs of independence she was displaying which left a gulf between them and reminded her that Sally was no longer a child.

Joe got his kiss after all. It was a brisk one, on the cheek, in full view of her parents, and it surprised even Sally. She waited until he had answered her questions, including a few she thought of at the last moment while he was talking, then gripped him firmly by the forearms, raised herself on tiptoe, and pecked.

It seemed to give him an extra dimple and to fix his expression in a permanent smile. Immediately he got back to camp he looked in a mirror to reassure himself. It was the first time he had ever been kissed.

* * *

Two days later it was Sunday again and the Salvation Army was assembling on the Common in front of Digby's cottage. They had heard of the so-called 'pilgrimage' the previous week and were outraged at the pagan rituals which had been reported. Determined to march against the forces of evil, they gathered under the big tree by the river and sang

127

hymns between sermons and calls to action.

It was a brilliantly fine day, with the full flush of Spring everywhere. April showers had yet to wash the dry air which had blown away the winter and although the sun's warmth was limited by its low angle in the sky it nevertheless brought cheer and encouragement wherever it shone.

Sally was sorry that Joe had to be on duty that day and, as she had seen nothing of Bertie since the brief glimpse of a week ago, she felt disinclined to look for him as an escort. It was a rare occasion, therefore, on which she set out for a walk with her mother and father in the early afternoon.

They had not gone far into the village when they met a group of Americans cycling towards them. The unusual spectacle of strangers in their midst was almost overlooked as a result of their recent familiarity with the uniform. Sally looked instinctively to see if Joe was among them but it was not until a second party appeared ahead of them that they realized something out of the ordinary was happening.

'You don't think they're looking for *you*, do you, Sal? I mean these Americans do talk and old Joe might have. . .'

'Daddy, do you mind!'

'Ben, don't tease the girl. Take no notice, Sally.'

'Of Daddy, or the Americans?'

'Both.'

Digby wondered who else in the village had been entertaining Americans besides himself, and a similar thought occurred to Sally who began to think there might be other girls from Little Missington at the ball next Saturday.

Vera was beginning to fear they had been invaded and looked anxiously at Benjamin and her daughter.

The next bunch of cyclists stopped and asked them the way to the 'pilgrimage'.

The Digbys hastened back to the Common and saw to their amazement a ring of foreign uniforms surrounding the red bonnets and peaked caps of the Salvationists. No less surprised were the Salvationists themselves. Within an hour there was an outer ring of villagers surrounding the Americans, and the congregation was bigger than anyone could remember.

Digby had done some quick thinking. It was clear that the Americans had come to see a repetition of last week's parade and as there was no time to re-muster the players for another performance of the pageant, he had to make do with an urgent call to his followers to meet him on the Common as soon as they could get there. It was vital, he said, that these visitors should not be disappointed and that something should be done to sustain their interest in the village. Dashing back to the cottage Digby changed hurriedly into his Laughing Cavalier attire and reappeared on the Common swinging a handbell. In the first silence conceded by the Salvation Army Band he began to shout:

'*Oyez, Oyez, Oyez!* Harken all ye men of Little Missington and those beyond the seas ... At four-thirty of the clock ... this same afternoon ... there will leave from the Common ... a party of free men ... and women ... of the village ... to see, and inspect ... the now famous ruins of our erstwhile castle ... All those wishing to join the party ... should gather here in good time. *Oyez Oyez Oyez!*'

Mrs Digby and Sally were purple with embarrassment and the Salvationists crimson with anger, but Benjamin strode backwards towards the cottage swinging his handbell and drawing a thread of Americans behind him as if he were the Pied Piper and they the children of Hamelin.

At four-thirty he began his conducted tour, following the same route he took the week before. More out of curiosity than sympathetic support, some villagers went with him who had not been there previously and others, who could never resist a procession, joined in again for the fun of it.

Unlike the last time, when Sammy and Joe were restrained from fraternizing with the locals, none of the Americans present on this occasion were prevented from rubbing shoulders with the villagers. With their well-known capacity for breaking conventions, they soon overcame the lack of formal introductions, and many were on the friendliest terms with their escorts by the time they reached the ruins.

Despite Digby's anxieties in this respect, it did not matter to them that some of the local inhabitants were seeing the ruin for the first time, or that they knew so little about its origin. This was a common characteristic among Europeans who were notoriously blasé about their history and historical possessions. To these boys, who had such a relatively recent past to be proud of, almost any relic they came across on this side of the Atlantic was exciting.

Hence the sight of Digby's structure on the skyline as they reached the meadow stirred their imaginations, and after Digby had shown them round in meticulous detail, describing vividly the manner in which it had come to light, they went away impressed beyond all bounds.

With a few embellishments of their own to dramatize it, the story was retold in the next edition of the camp magazine under the headline: A MARVEL AT LITTLE MISSINGTON.

By the following Sunday the villagers were a little better prepared. The more enterprising of them were waiting on the Common for the first arrivals and quickly introduced themselves as guides.

The route to the ruins became dotted with little groups instead of one procession and all afternoon a steady traffic moved to and fro across the fields.

Back in the village, wives and daughters were busy

130

preparing teas, and had baked heavily in anticipation of the menfolk being able to coax their companions back at the end of the tour. It was the beginning of the tourist trade, for nobody would believe that the Digbys had entertained their visitors for nothing and although they were careful to create the same impression of benevolence, it was obvious that most of them were charging handsomely for services rendered.

The Digbys, however, were unaware of the extent of their promotion, for they were spending the day quietly at home after Sally's dawn return from the Swivenhall ball.

12

Sally's description of the Swivenhall Ball was that of a chromium plated party.

If for a brief moment beforehand she had imagined herself going to a ball in the Victorian or Viennese sense, with chandeliers and crinolines and chaperones, this was certainly not her expectation after being collected in a jeep and bounced several miles across open countryside with Joe her only companion. His apologies for the draughty vehicle, and excuses for the rugged road were a consolation, but they only emphasised the improbability of her fantasy.

It was a cold night when she left the cottage and an anxious mother and father to step for the first time into another world. The gaily decorated and spacious ballroom at the American base was far removed in space and time from the dance hall at Little Missington. Not only did it represent the culture of a distant hemisphere but it opened for Sally a window on the twentieth century, which she had scarcely seen before.

The first chink through which she saw this different way of living was in the ladies' cloakroom on arrival, described without gender as the powder room. This was larger and more luxurious than any living room she had known in Little Missington and the very fact that she compared it with a living room and not a lavatory demonstrates the impression it created. She wanted to take off her shoes and pad upon the thick piled carpet, sit in the gilded chairs, stare in the full length mirrors and glow in the brilliance of fluorescent lights. She almost forgot to spend a penny, and she did forget that Joe was waiting for her.

A thought which occurred to her as she breathed the scented air and held her hands in a drying machine, was that none of the other girls was speaking with an American accent. She had not yet guessed that they had been brought there as she was, from the nearby towns and villages.

She stepped on a weighing machine, then because she had only English coinage and thought she would need a dime, stepped off again. A breezy voice alongside said, 'Gee honey, I wish I weighed as little as you do. I go a hundred and forty pounds in the altogether.'

Sally smiled. American at last. And how comforting! Pounds instead of stones, dimes instead of pence, powder room instead of ladies. No doubt she would get used to it, but it gave her the thrill and sensation of being in a foreign land, and she loved it.

Joe had looked at his watch several times and greeted a few buddies as they swept into the hall with their partners, but when Sally eventually emerged he forgot about everything and everyone and was immersed in pride. Sally looked lovely. She wore a white dress with two delicate straps across the shoulders and a little crimson bow on one of them. Her handbag and gloves were also white but her shoes were red to match the bow, or vice versa, and the effect was stunning. Her pretty fair hair was pinned up at the back and she passed for many years more than eighteen. So did most of the girls although some were young enough to be still at school, yet it is doubtful if their teachers would have recognized them. None, however, carried herself as daintily or with such charm as Sally and the secret, if such she had, was simply that she had not tried to be anything other than herself.

They met Sammy on their way into the hall and although it was a coincidence Sally thought at first it might have been arranged. The girl he was with made her feel uncomfortable, for she had pink hair in the shape of a bottle on her head and a very low-cut dress that revealed more than Sally — or Joe, for that matter — had ever seen exposed before. Sammy seemed keen to keep her to himself and, like Joe, had no wish to join up in a party. So, to Sally's immense relief, they separated after a brief exchange of pleasantries.

The beat of the band throbbed out from beyond the entrance hall and Sally realized they were still some way from the ballroom. As they walked towards it she saw the most spectacular display of food that had ever been placed before her. Along the entire length of each wall were tables dressed with such a variety of sweetmeats and savouries and sandwiches; cheeses, pastries, pickles, hams, salads, ketchup; salmon, chicken, asparagus; fruit, trifles, and ice-creams — especially ice-creams — that she was almost sick before she had passed them. Behind each table was a pretty serving-maid or a chef, and behind them an array of flowers in every colour of the rainbow and unbelievable arrangements. One end of the room was devoted entirely to soft drinks and coffee, and at the other end there was a liquor bar. The centre piece was a huge goldfish bowl, surrounded by tiers of azaleas, and above it were repeated clusters of electric light bulbs, in narrow tubular shades, hanging from a high ceiling like scattered organ pipes.

The band reached its crescendo as they stepped into the ballroom and, dizzy with emotion, Sally clasped Joe by the hand and drew him closer. 'Joe,' she said, 'thank you for bringing me. It's wonderful!'

They danced and then sat out at one of the tables round the floor. Joe got some Coca-Colas and Sally drank hers as if it were nectar. They danced again and then returned to the table. Sammy and his provocative girlfriend waved across the floor from another table where they sat hand-in-hand and laughing. Joe tried to take his cue from them but found Sally's hands elusive. They met later, however, but out of sight beneath the table top. It was early yet and all but the very slick were still at the preliminaries.

'How often do you have a ball like this, Joe?'

'Can't say exactly, seeing as I've never been to one before, and haven't sort of taken much interest in when they happen. There's usually a dance of some sort on every Saturday, but this is kind of special. That's why I wanted you to come to this one.'

'I'm so glad you asked me.'

'Guess your mother didn't seem too pleased about it, though.'

'Oh, Joe, I'm sure she didn't mind you asking me. It was just that ... well I've never been to a dance with anyone outside the village before. Poor Mum, she doesn't really know what it's like anywhere else and she probably thinks all sorts of awful things about Air Force camps ... and Americans ... and..'

'Yeah, I understand, Sally. But it's not always like that, y'know.'

'Joe, I may not be over twenty-one yet, but I reckon I'm old enough to look after myself. So don't mind what Mummy thinks; I can disillusion her when I get home.'

They talked a lot more, and danced a lot, but drank very little. Glancing occasionally at Sammy's table they could see a row of empty glasses and bottles accumulating on it, but neither of them had any inclination to follow suit.

The intermission came sooner than they expected and everyone, including the band, rushed for the food. Only then did Sally realize how many people were present. As they came in from the dance floor and surrounding tables, and such other places as were used, officially or otherwise, for sitting out, they packed the entrance hall like locusts on a field of corn. When she had first come in it had seemed there must be food for all to feast upon for days. Now it looked as though it ought to be rationed if everyone was to get a share.

Sally need not have worried, for they managed to extract some hearty helpings of all they fancied and made veritable pigs of themselves until the dancing resumed.

By now the amount of alcohol consumed by the weaker elements was beginning to have its effect. The young Romeos without partners; the high-spirited, newly-enlisted, not-long-out-of-High-School crazy kids; the boisterous undisciplined, ill-mannered hooligans, started to show up in little pockets about the room, as conspicuous in the crowd as pimples on a freckled face. Those who could take their liquor and were still sober found the spectacle mildy amusing, in a cynical way. The abstemious and teetotal, who had never experienced the 'kick' of over-indulgence, looked upon them with discomfort as an impediment to their enjoyment.

It was at this stage that Sally first experienced the practice of 'cutting-in' on the dance floor. Until now, she and Joe danced exclusively together, without thought or hindrance of others, but suddenly she noticed a strange hand on the shoulder in front of her. Before she could grasp what was happening, Joe had been brushed aside and she was dancing with another man. Disconcerted, and a little frightened, she glanced back to see where Joe had gone and saw him drifting miserably against the stream towards a side of the floor.

'Hiya, sister! Mind my cutting-in? You're a humdinger! Couldn't let that guy hog you all evening. Pretty ones is scarce: oughta be passed around. How about a date sometime?'

Sally stopped. 'You've just had yours. Now can I go back

to my friend?'

Julian Battenberger blinked and tottered beneath the flickering coloured lights, grinned foolishly, steadied himself, shrugged his shoulders and went off to tap somebody else on the shoulder. Sally found Joe waiting for her and they finished the dance together as though nothing had happened.

After this performance had been repeated a second and then a third time, however, Sally became less attentive to the music and more watchful for signs of intruders. Eventually, when a particularly unpleasant looking character loomed close and loose, she asked Joe if they could go for a walk somewhere to get away from the interruptions.

'Sure, let's go,' he said and took her through a door marked 'STAFF' into a little passage-way which led to the kitchens. Here Sally was fascinated with the gadgets and Joe had to take her on a conducted tour to satisfy her curiosity. The large white refrigerators and washing-up machines were as much an innovation to her as the steam-heated serving counters, glass-fronted ovens and mechanical potato peelers.

Only when they thought they heard somebody coming did she stop asking questions and abandon the sightseeing. Joe was patient but disappointed, for it seemed he was doomed to share her attention with half-canned cronies or cooking utensils.

'We'd better get out of here, Sally, before they pitch us in the guard house. Kitchens are classified ''beyond limits'', that's ''out of bounds'' in your language.'

'OK, Joe, but where now?'

'Any suggestions?'

'Nope! You live here, remember? I've never been here before.'

'What about the hangars?'

'Won't they be cold? I'd rather go somewhere a

137

little warmer.'

'I know, the boiler-house!'

They went out of the kitchen on to a courtyard at the back and tiptoed across the concrete so as not to attract attention. Behind the officers' quarters on the other side they came to a few steps leading down to a breeze block wall. Round this was a door marked DANGER. Sally recoiled, but Joe pushed it open and to her horror a vivid glow split the darkness and a rush of hot air hit her in the face. She grabbed Joe by his coat and let out a little scream, which he quickly stifled by lifting her off the ground and swinging her bodily through the door as he slammed it after them. She gasped, and for a moment choked with the stench of fumes but, recovering, saw the look of concern on Joe's brightly lit face and felt his arms relax. Tightening her grip, she pulled him back and held on, hugging him for all she was worth, and burying her head in his tunic.

He could feel her heart pounding away against him and realized that what he had supposed for one glorious moment to be affection was really an attack of fear. Unwilling to open the door again immediately in case somebody had seen the glow and would spot them coming out, he lifted her head gently and looked keenly into her eyes, kissing her softly on the temple as he held her firmly between his hands.

Sally felt his lips linger an instant and then pull shyly away. She caught up with them as they receded and, to a background of radiant heat from the roaring furnace, drew hard upon the fire that burned between them, sending their blood pressures rising and hormones rushing into circulation. Joe almost lit up with excitement and she, herself, melted in the heat of the moment.

When she opened her eyes she could see beads of perspiration standing on Joe's forehead and knew that for one reason or the other it was now too hot for them to stay.

Letting go her clasp, she took him roughly by the wrist and with the other hand pulled the door open. They almost fell out against the wall and stood panting in the cool night air. He tried to kiss her again, but she refused.

'No more, Joe. Not just now. You see what it says on that door, don't you?'

Joe smiled but saw no danger.

It was better, she thought, that one of them should be strong than that they should go too far through mutual innocence or weakness.

Reluctantly, but ready to do anything to preserve their friendship, Joe led her back to the ballroom, and was about to go boldly through the main doors where they had entered, when he remembered something. 'Sh! How stupid can y' get? We can't go back that way without a pass-out ticket, and they weren't issued the way we came out!'

'Can't we go back the way we came?'

'Yeah, if the door's still open. Let's try.'

But it was shut, and the bolt had dropped on the inside so that it was locked as well.

'I've got a cloakroom ticket, Joe. Won't that prove we've been in already?'

'Daresay it would, but some guys spoiled that by giving their pass-outs to other guys who hadn't paid to go in and getting back in using their cloak-tickets. Then it came out in orders that cloaks were not a substitute for pass-outs. So they'd got wise to it. Guess if we tried it now they'd clap us in the jailhouse!'

Neither of them knew whether to laugh or cry, but a decision was spared when the door onto the courtyard suddenly opened and two figures loomed out. It was Sally who recognized them first, and the hair-do that did it.

'Sammy!' she exclaimed, forgetting all reticence. 'Don't shut it! We want to go in.'

'Why, hi there! If it's not my beautiful. Fancy seeing

139

you around. What's it like out here, Joey boy? And, where's the hide-out?'

Joe blushed, but it was too dark to be noticed. 'We got locked out,' he said weakly, 'when we came to get some fresh air.'

'They came for fresh air, d'ye hear that, honey? Tell 'em what we've come for, baby!'

But Joe dragged Sally smartly inside, leaving Sammy to steer his girlfriend into the darkness, and whatever else besides.

The band seemed very loud when they returned to it and the ballroom was hot and full of smoke. Not so hot or smokey as it had been in the boilerhouse but more unpleasant than when they left it. They decided to have another Coke and Joe asked if Sally would like a rum in it to counteract the cold.

'I'd rather that than ice,' she said.

* * *

The last dance came when they were just beginning to warm up again to a festive spirit. How much was due to the spirit that went into the Coca Cola and how much to the rhythm of the music did not matter; what did was that they saw the ball out on a happy note. They stood for the National Anthem, which Sally and a few others heard for the first time, expecting the *Stars and Stripes Forever* instead of the *Star Spangled Banner*. Then there were cheers for the band and cheers for the organizer and finally cheers for the guests, which left them all breathless. The doors were thrown open and currents of cool air flowed inwards against streams of dancers moving out. Sally collected her coat, a scarf and a pair of shoes, and meantime Joe nodded goodnights to a number of people he had not noticed all evening. The lights in the ballroom

140

went out, the entrance hall emptied and the party was over.

* * *

The jeep was waiting where they had left it, in a bay by the Squadron Office, and Sally was glad to get into it to rest her feet. It seemed more comfortable than when she had ridden in it the first time. Joe too, found the seat less hard for he was lighter altogether now that the evening had passed off with such success. They drove out of the camp singing happily together.

It was four miles out of Swivenhall where they broke down. No other vehicle had passed them on the road since they left the camp and nothing was likely to be going in the direction of Little Missington at that hour of night. The situation was extremely bleak.

Joe tinkered with the engine for a minute or two and then tried swinging the handle, but Sally knew the old story about running out of petrol and was not surprised when she saw the gauge reading zero.

So! She would soon know whether Joe was really the nice, kind innocent boy she had believed him to be. She turned up the collar of her coat, as if to ward off any similar thoughts, and waited for Joe to make the next move.

Joe was disturbed by the silence. Not only had the engine stopped purring and the noises of the camp trailed out of range but Sally had not said a word, either in comfort or concern.

'Say...Sally! Do you know what? We must be out of gasoline!'

The fact that he did not call it petrol did not make the slightest difference.

'I know. Fancy that!'

Her voice, when it came, was as cold as the wind that

141

blew it to him.

'Gee, Sally, you don't think...? Oh, hey there, hold on! You don't think I did this on purpose, do you?'

'How many miles is it to the village?'

'About eight.'

'And back to camp?'

'About four, I guess.'

'Either way it's a long walk!'

'Sally, please! I didn't know it would do this, honest I didn't. I had the tank filled this afternoon specially. Some lousy twister must have milked it, or driven it somewhere, while we were at the dance. Oh, kid, please believe me.'

Sally did not like his expressions but felt there was sincerity in his voice. 'Well, what can we do? Push?'

'You just stay there and don't move. I'll take the can back to camp and fill her up.'

'And how long do you suppose that would take? You'd be an hour at least getting there and another getting back. I'm not sitting here all that time on my own in the middle of the night. If you're going to walk you'll have to take me with you.'

She got down from the jeep and without another word led the way back along the road to Swivenhall. Joe kept pace and tried to take hold of her arm, but she strode faster and kept her elbows swinging.

'Sweetie, please! Stop a minute while we get this straightened out. I'm as sore as you are about what has happened, but it was an accident. I wouldn't have had this happen for all the oil in Texas. You made this the most wonderful night of my life and do you think I'd want to spoil it? Do you think I'd have risked that? I'm just not that kind of guy!'

Plausible enough, she thought, but what would his actions have to say? Like Felix, she kept on walking.

Joe was hopelessly out of his depth and floundering

badly. What on earth could he do now? For the first time that night he wished that Sammy was with them. He, surely, must have met this situation before.

Sally was trying not to be frightened. Her assessment of Joe made her feel that he was on the level. (She even used one of his own expressions to define it.) But facts were more significant than fancies. That was something her father had always taught her. Mother's advice about talking to strangers and gypsies in the wood was old-fashioned, but she appreciated the moral and realized this was the stiffest test she had ever faced alone. Yet why alone? For surely this was the point: she was not alone, Joe was with her, and he would take care of her.

'Joe, I think I believe you . . . I want to believe you . . . I've no reason really not to, except that . . . well, it's a corny situation you must admit. Anyway, I give you the benefit of the doubt. . . . But Joe if you did try to take advantage of me, that would be the end of our friendship, you know that, don't you?'

Joe was desperately hurt that she should even have thought this possible, but he was so relieved at her change of attitude he just smiled and said nothing.

Sally stopped for an instant and as Joe waited to see what she would do next she put her arm firmly into his and gripped him by the hand. 'Come on,' she urged, 'we must keep going.'

They had gone about three-quarters of a mile when she stopped again.

'Joe,' she said, 'aren't we being rather silly? Wouldn't it be much more sensible to walk the other way. By the time we have reached the camp and collected more petrol, then got back to the jeep, we could be home at the cottage.'

After such a promising opening, the rest of her remarks were an anti-climax. This was feminine capriciousness at its worst. How unchivalrous it would sound of him to

143

remind her that by going first to Little Missington he would then be faced with the journey back on foot. In the circumstances he deemed it best to agree without comment and put it all down to the price one paid for courtship.

* * *

There was no moon, and clouds obscured the stars. Trees were still bare and the hedgerows thin of foliage. Birds were asleep and only the sound of frogs and insects answered their footsteps. Sally was cold and uncomfortable and hated the atmosphere that had come between them. She wanted more than anything else to lie down and go to sleep.

Such a thought as sleep had to be pushed to the very back of Joe's mind, for the prospect of him getting any at all that night was remote.

Mile after weary mile they walked, speaking little to each other, but inwardly to themselves. The first hour seemed an age but the second one endless. When they were barely half way home, Sally felt she could go no further.

'I'm sorry Joe,' she said, 'we should have walked the way you wanted. We'd have been there by now, wouldn't we?'

'Maybe, but I've been thinking it over. Perhaps your idea was best. We might not have got any gasoline at that time of night without a goddam fuss and you'd have had to stay on the camp till morning. That might have looked worse, don't you think?'

Sally was too tired to care. She could see a patch of grassland in front of them and without a thought for the damp, lay down on it.

'Precious, are you all right?'

Through the gloom she could see Joe's eyes peering anxiously at her and felt the warmth of his breath as he stooped over her. In a flash she was asleep.

Sleep is a timeless voyage and when she awoke she had no idea how long she had slept, nor what indeed had been going on around her. Luckily she had not dreamed and there was no confusion between anything she had seen in her imagination and what had really taken place.

Joe was still there and he seemed to have moved little since she fell asleep. Her coat was still buttoned round her neck and it remained very dark.

What a silly thing to do, she thought, and what a mockery it made of all her caution earlier on. Or did it? No. Perhaps it was as well that she had made herself clear in the beginning.

Poor Joe, he was anything but clear about it all. First she had thrown her arms around him in the boilerhouse and kissed him like a vacuum cleaner, then brushed him off when he had tried to return the compliment. After that it was all on again until the jeep ran out of gas, when the shutters went up with a whoosh! Now she was flat on her back in the middle of a field, fast asleep and totally defenceless. What *was* a guy to do about a girl like that?

'Joe,' he heard her say, 'how long have I been asleep?'

'No time at all.' He bent closer and held his face very near to hers. 'Dearest', he began, but she raised her head and kissed him, checking whatever he was going to say.

Before he could recover to make any kind of follow-up she had wriggled clear and was standing up beside him. 'Come on,' she called, 'we mustn't dither.'

And while Joe was working out what 'dither' meant she had grabbed his arm and they were under way again.

Even a moment's sleep was enough to revive her and the rush of mental exercise which followed served to lubricate the senses. Sally was wide awake now and her step became brisker.

Joe, too, had responded to his better treatment and the brighter outlook led to them recovering much of their earlier ease of conversation.

A far off bird gave the first sign of morning and soon its calls were reinforced to a chorus. Dogs barked in the distance and the cock's crow woke the farmyard. The sky to the east grew light and a gentle breeze licked their faces. Landmarks became visible and Sally recognized the outskirts of Little Missington.

They stopped finally on the last bridge before home and held each other very close, looking back on the way they had come.

'You can't go all that way back without sleep,' she said. 'You must come in for a while and lie down on the couch.'

'But... your Ma and Pa ... what will they say if they find me there when they get up?'

'I shall be very surprised if we do not find them up already.'

13

The Digbys went late to bed after Sally had left for the Ball and lay talking into the early hours of the morning. Vera was certain something dreadful would happen and said Benjamin ought to have stopped her going. Benjamin said it was up to a mother to influence her daughter and if she had not told her the facts of life by now, so that the girl could protect herself, it was a pity and she should have done. Vera said it ought never to come to that for it was a parent's responsibility to keep temptation out of the way of their children. Benjamin wished he could go to sleep.

'He looks a nice boy, I know, but you said yourself you should never trust an American.'

'I was talking about American politicians.'

'No you weren't, you were talking about keeping English girls to the English.'

'That was to encourage young Bertie.'

'Well, I still don't think we should have let her go all that way with a stranger. And a foreigner, too!'

'Look, love, she's gone now and there's nothing more we can do until she gets home. After that we must see she doesn't go again.'

'But that might be too late.'

'Oh, Vera, for goodness sake!'

'I knew when she was little you'd be no good as a father, once she grew up.'

'Who let her bring him here to tea in the first place?'

And so it went on. Several times Vera got up and went to the window. Each time Digby hoped he would fall asleep before she got back.

When he heard the church clock strike four, however, and Sally had still not returned he began to share his wife's doubts about the wisdom of the expedition. Determined not to betray his own anxiety, he refused to get up and make a cup of tea when Vera suggested it but gladly drank a cup when she produced one at five o'clock. With the first light of dawn about half past five they were both up and dressed and pacing about the cottage arguing as to whether they should go and look for her in the lorry or get the policeman to telephone the camp.

Benjamin was in fact crossing the yard on his way to the lorry when they returned.

'And what time do you call this to come home? You know, young man, we keep different hours in this country to those you may be used to. Go inside quickly, Sally, and see your mother: she's been up all night looking for you.'

'Oh, Daddy, don't be like that, please. It's not very nice for Joe after he's brought me all the way home, is it?'

'Mr Digby, I sure am sorry, and I wouldn't like you to think...'

'I don't think anything, my boy, I'm just referring to an indisputable fact. It's nearly breakfast time and that's not the time I like to see my daughter come home.'

'But Daddy, you haven't heard what happened to us. We'd have been home hours ago, only the jeep broke down.'

Digby was not the sort to hit a man when he was down, and this was hardly the moment for seeing the funny side of things, so that his retort was more involuntary than intended.

'Not very reliable, the jeep, is it? Always said I'd rather

have an English truck.'

'Daddy! Joe's got to go all that way back again. Don't you think he ought to have a rest first, and lie on the couch or somewhere until he's had some sleep?'

Vera caught the tail-end of Sally's plea as she came out to see where Benjamin had got to.

'What's the matter? Is he hurt? Are you all right? He's not drunk, is he? Ben, what have they done?'

'They've walked home, that's what they've done.'

'Oh, how silly! Why didn't they ask? We could have lent them the lorry. You poor dear, you must be crippled. Come inside at once and sit down. Both of you.'

Inside, the argument raged anew and the inquest on the jeep found it guilty of many things except running out of petrol. Sally thought that was much too inflammable an excuse in the present atmosphere. Joe was desperately uncomfortable and whenever he tried to speak for Sally she seemed to interrupt him. When Vera asked if he would like a wash she said it was sleep he needed. Digby said *he* did too, but Vera said he had had more than she had and the confusion increased so that no one knew whose side the others would be on from one minute to the next.

Joe tried again to break through. 'It's been very good of you, but now if you don't mind I'd better be hittin' the road back, or else I may not make it before some other guy stumbles on that truck and tries to tow it away.'

'Ben, we can't let him walk all that way back after he's been good enough to bring Sally home. Couldn't you take him there in the lorry? You were going to get it out to look for them, weren't you?'

Digby thought of all the contradictions his wife had uttered over many years and fancied there had never been a bigger *volte-face* than this. Ten minutes ago she was eager to stop Sally having any more to do with the fellow and now she was fixing him up with a chauffeur!

149

'Go on up to bed then, Sally, I'll get the lorry out.'

'That sure is good of you, sir, but I couldn't let you do that.'

'Then you must stay here and snatch some sleep on the sofa.' Vera's tone was positive and forceful and Joe felt unable to refuse this time without causing offence.

Benjamin watched her puffing up the cushions and shook his head, but before he could say anything to upset the arrangement Sally had bestowed on him a big kiss and said, 'Thank you, dear Daddy!' in a way which put an end to all further resistance.

Her mother looked surprised that the reward should have gone to her father but Sally was quick to repair the omission. Turning to Joe she said in a whisper they could all hear. 'I told you not to be frightened of them, didn't I?' They're darling parents, aren't they? Both of them.' There was a quick exit and in no time at all she was asleep on her bed upstairs.

Vera concealed her emotion by fussing over the improvisation of a bed on the sofa and Joe was made to stretch out while blankets were tucked around him and the curtains drawn to keep daylight from his face. This done, she returned to the kitchen where Benjamin was already busying himself at the stove, preparing an early breakfast and brooding over the duplicity of his daughter.

'I don't know what she sees in him that Bertie couldn't improve upon!'

'Ben, he's quite a nice lad really. Very sensitive and thoughtful.'

'It wasn't very thoughtful keeping her out all night, was it?'

'Well, you know, it could have been a lot worse. He might have wanted her to stay at the camp all night. That's what I was worried about.'

Digby pondered, and Vera went slowly up in his

estimation. Whatever fate he had envisaged overtaking Sally in those sleepless hours of the morning that which is reputedly worse than death was not in his mind. An accident, maybe, or drunkenness; elopement, or corruption of spiritual virtue — but not downright seduction. His wife's remark revealed a romantic disposition which had been lost to him for many years. He opened his eyes in astonishment and saw the truth of an old saying that one's children make one young again.

Their differences dissolved in reminiscence, they ate their breakfast between yawns of fatigue and nostalgia, and wondered why it was that age must rob them of the innocence which youth enjoys. To see no evil was easy enough, if one never went further than one's own doorstep. To hear no evil required a positive defence against the regular gossip of all-comers. To think and speak no evil was regarded as a sign of the simple and self-righteous, indicative of no imagination, and a matter of suspicion or disbelief. In no sense, therefore, could the Digbys be described as innocents.

Benjamin helped with the washing-up and the preparations for lunch, which were normally Sally's duties on a Sunday morning. Vera smiled at the sight of him in the kitchen, for not since Sally was a babe had he automatically assisted in this way, without a prod or protest. She warmed considerably towards him and unashamedly copied Sally's example by kissing him suddenly on the cheek. It was a pleasant reversal of the usual situation to find mother and father embracing in the parlour while daughter and escort slept soundly in adjacent rooms.

* * *

Joe woke with the offer of a cup of tea. He wondered where he was, how he got there and what the time was. The voice

151

which spoke to him might have been speaking in a foreign language, and the wallpaper bore no resemblance to the background he was accustomed to when waking.

'Come along, young man, it's time to be up if you want to get back to camp before lunch.'

'Gee, but those roses look pretty. . .'

Sally took longer to stir after she was called, but the recollection of Joe being left downstairs brought her quickly to her feet and she soon dressed and descended. It was the first time in her life she had entertained a man to breakfast and the novelty was no less exciting for the fact that it was already approaching noon.

In the event they sat and stared across the table like two travellers in a railway compartment who knew each other and yet were embarrassed to speak for fear of sharing their conversation with other passengers. Luckily, they found refuge in their toast and boiled eggs and studied each mouthful as though it were contaminated, reserving their pleasantries for moments when they were left alone.

* * *

'Now then, my lad, are you ready? The truck's waiting and I've slung a rope in the back so we can tow the jeep when we find it.'

'Daddy, can I come too?'

'Yes, and so can your mother. We're all going, How's that for an escort, Mr Buckman?'

'I'd be delighted if you'd call me Joe, sir.'

'Yes. Well, are we ready then?'

And so they departed. Mr and Mrs Digby in the cabin and Joe and Sally in the back. As they approached the stretch of road described by Sally as the breakdown spot, Benjamin lifted the flap separating driver from payload and called out for directions. Sally and Joe stared through the

152

opening and scanned the countryside but it all looked very different from the night before.

Seeing a duckpond in the distance Sally called out, 'I'm sure it wasn't as far as this for I remember taking that corner in the jeep.' Joe looked surprised and a little hurt but she added. 'I thought how dangerous it would have been for the ducks if we had been going too fast to straighten out.'

Her father took the hint and slowed down, stopping altogether at the next convenient place to turn. They went back a couple of miles until Sally could say she remembered a haystack they had passed on foot and they knew they had reversed too far. The jeep had obviously come to rest somewhere between the haystack and the duckpond, but there was no sign of it on the road.

'You didn't drive in anywhere, I suppose?' shouted Digby.

'Where would they have driven to out here?' his wife asked without following the implication.

'No we didn't'.

'All right, I only asked. It probably sank in the dew this morning, or maybe the fairies have borrowed it.'

Sally knew that her father had begun to disbelieve their story and saw the look of bewilderment and misery on Joe's face.

'Really Mr Digby, it *was* there when we left it, only I can't think what can have happened to it since. No one uses this road that I know of so it should be still there.'

'Don't worry, my boy, there may be another duckpond. We'll go on a bit further and see if Sally was mistaken about that one.'

But they had reached the camp before they found another pond.

Joe was clearly agitated when he got down from the lorry at the camp gates. He wanted to thank the Digbys for bringing him back and then be left alone to sort out the problem of a missing jeep, for which he would be held responsible. On the other hand, he did not want them to go with the inference hanging over Sally's head that they had made up the story about a breakdown in order to account for their late return from the dance. Since by nature he was ready to put other people's feelings before his own, there was only one course he could take and that meant keeping the Digbys occupied while he checked up on what was known about the vehicle he had lost. In the moment of crisis and indecision a solution was thrust upon him.

Coming out through the gates, as he approached them, was Sammy Wainwright. Sally, who had also got down from the lorry but was standing alongside the cabin, went cold when she saw that he still had with him the girl they had met the night before.

Sammy had seen them too, and was quick on the draw.

'Say, doll, look there's Joey and Sweetie-Pie! Hi there, Joe. Just back from another pass-out? No need to slip in the back way this time, bud, the party's over! We quit hours ago: expected to see you back in quarters. Don't know where you've been, mind, but bet you didn't kip as good as we did. Seein' as you weren't usin' it, we kinda commandeered your bunk so that Maisie could sleep in a bed of her own. She's a good girl, y'know. Does what mother tells her.'

With a thrust and a tug from Maisie, they disappeared, shrieking with laughter. Joe had been trying to fend them off with all manner of facial expressions, keeping his back to the lorry so that the Digbys would not see, while Sally stood on the running board shouting through the cabin window, valiantly trying to distract her parents' attention.

It would have registered less suspicion if they had ignored Sammy altogether and pointed him out as a drunk. But the damage was done and Digby was now certain there

154

had been a conspiracy to conceal something from him.

'I suppose you don't happen to remember the number of the jeep we've been looking for?'

Sally and Joe looked awkwardly at each other, for not only did the question come as a surprise but the answer would not come at all.

'It had an American number . . .'

'Yeah, that's right, it was an American.'

'But what number?'

'Gosh, I don't remember.'

'Daddy, why do you ask? Can you see something? Where do you see a jeep?'

'That's just it, my girl, where indeed? Maybe I do see something, something I ought to have seen a lot earlier. I'm not sure that you've been telling me the truth. Just you come up here, young lady, and we'll talk about this on the way home.'

'Oh, sir, you can't do that, really, you mustn't! I mean, Sally and me . . . we weren't . . . that is, we haven't . . . we *have* told you the truth, sir!'

'Mummy, you believe us, don't you?'

It was an old trick, trying to split the alliance, but it did not work. Vera kept silent, with tears in her eyes and a very dry throat. Benjamin's temperature was rising.

Just then, Sammy re-appeared. 'Joe, excuse me! Joe, what happened to that truck you had last night? Could I use it for an hour to get Maisie home? Seems like we've missed the bus into town.'

Joe took hold of Sammy and for a moment Sally thought he was going to choke him. It was probably the first time she had seen Sammy without a grin on his face. There was a stunning silence and then Joe poured over him a torrent of what was on his mind. He had borrowed the jeep without asking permission from the Squadron Office after it closed on Saturday and meant to return it before it would be

155

noticed on Monday morning. He had run out of gas and left it on a quiet country road while he walked the rest of the way to Little Missington. When he returned to retrieve it a few minutes ago it was gone. Disappeared. *Kaput*! Nobody could have known it was there; it had no gas in it to be driven away, and yet it had vanished. As a result Sally's mother and father thought they had been told a pack of lies, and he had no means of proving the contrary. In short, he was finished, done for, through! They would never allow her to see him again and she would be in disgrace for something she had never done. It was a nightmare! Then, on top of everything, he, Sammy, had come along and put his big clumsy foot in it, making the whole business look ten times worse.

Sammy's grin returned and, walking over to the lorry, he left Joe gasping at what he might say next. Opening the cabin door, he beamed up at the Digbys, and bade them a big welcome to the United States Air Force Base at Swivenhall. Apologizing for not recognizing them sooner, he said he had been carried away with the exuberance of a fine day, and hoped they would not be misled into thinking he was suffering from an overindulgence in that wicked liquid alcohol. Whatever the impression he had given of himself, however, was unimportant compared with the good name of his friend Corporal Joseph Buckman. Joe's father was a very big shot in the City of Baltimore and he had a great family tradition to uphold. Joe had been brought up 'real good' and 'classy'. He didn't act like the other guys because he didn't think like them. Joe's thoughts were pure and decent, like a good Christian's, not primitive and jazzy like the 'bums' he had to mix with. They hadn't any need to worry about their daughter so long as she was with Joe, and they could take it from him, Sammy Wainright, from personal experience, that Joe wouldn't let another guy get his claws

156

on her while he was around.

He might have continued in this vein for much longer had not their attention shifted to a breakdown vehicle passing through the gates with a mud splattered jeep on tow behind.

Joe let out a cry of recognition and Sally impulsively ran towards it shouting, 'There it is, there it is, that's our jeep!'

Hearing the commotion, someone appeared at the guardhouse door as the powered and powerless vehicles came to a halt outside. There was a brief discussion with the driver who was about to drive on when Joe decided he had better own up.

Questions and formalities followed which were infinitely less embarrassing to him than the fact that the entire Digby family had been asked to accompany him to the guardhouse. His statement that he had borrowed the vehicle with intent to return it occasioned much dry humour, but the confession of running out of gasoline and walking on to Little Missington produced gusts of laughter.

Only when he realized that the evidence for the prosecution would corroborate his story to the Digbys did he relax and accept the situation philosophically.

Benjamin was not slow to grasp the significance of the charge, however, and saw that the proof of Joe's honesty in one connection would lead to conviction for larceny in another. He urged him to submit a plea of mitigation on the grounds that his action had been taken in consideration for his guest, and testified as the girl's father that he believed Joe had acted in the best interests of his daughter, for which he and her mother were particularly grateful.

This went down rather well with the Duty Officer who decided not to put the Corporal under close arrest but to release him pending a report to the Squadron Commander. He was, therefore, free to leave, which he did immediately.

Sammy had already left. He disengaged himself from

the party the moment the law appeared and was thumbing his way to Myrtlesham with Maisie.

Apologizing profusely to the Digbys for causing them so much trouble, Joe asked them up to the bar for a drink before they returned. Speaking on behalf of his family, without the slightest consultation, Benjamin accepted the invitation.

It was long past lunch time when they left the camp and each in their way was under the influence enough for it not to matter. Benjamin, who had been drinking bourbons and ginger, was sober enough to give Sally the keys and ask her to drive them home, but once in the passenger seat went quickly to sleep. Vera, who had stuck to familiar gin and it, was equally sleepy but dreamed of the various luxuries she had seen, imagining they were installed already in her cottage, only to be horribly miserable and depressed when she woke to find they were not. Sally, resuming where she had left off the night before, drank only cordials and Coca Cola, and her intoxication derived from a spirit much stronger than alcohol, called youth. She was head over heels in love with Joe and more than a hand-across-the-sea to twentieth century living.

14

For the next few weeks discontent reigned in the Digby
household. Benjamin was mad at his complicity in the
betrayal of Bertie; Sally was sad at the way Joe had been
humiliated by a jeep; and Vera was thoroughly dissatisfied
with everything about the cottage, which she now
considered drab and old-fashioned.

Rose Cottage was no longer the happy homestead it had
once been, where only petty squabbles and domestic banter
rippled the smooth waters of contented family life.

Digby's consumption of ale in the Coach and Horses
rose as the pressure on his patience grew. Ironically, word
went around he was in the money now that he and his
daughter were 'in' with the Americans. A similar aspersion
was cast upon many villagers who appeared to be drawing
from the inexhaustible well of American wealth. Others
were not slow to follow in devising ways of extracting
money from their visitors.

Sunday tea parties were proving a success and with the
onset of a spell of good weather they were often held in
the garden so that the term Tea Garden became as popular
in the village as the drawing room had been in middle-
class surburban society.

Copper kettles began to appear over gateways and the
announcement of home made cakes became a familiar sight
on tree trunks and flagpoles. The letters T E A and S were

painted on the tiles of sloping roofs and W E L C O M E on mats and window panes.

Little Missington was waking up and the dawn of a new enterprise brought warmth to its people after their long dark winter.

This, however, was not the dawn that dwelled in Corporal Buckman's memory. Confined to his camp as a punishment for abandoning rather than borrowing the jeep, he saw a hundred times the image of Sally that Sunday morning, silhouetted against a crimson sky, her head held demurely to one side, waiting to be kissed. It recorded an instant only, like the single frame of a cine-film, but was studied and cherished in every detail, and relived again and again, while the rest of the reel ran on and faded.

Seeing red of another sort, but suffering from similar fixations, was Bertie Woodfellow. He had watched Sally and Joe leaving together in the jeep on their way to the Swivenhall Ball and, although he knew nothing of the sequel to that event, every reminder of it roused his indignation to the pitch of fury. He raged first at the fickleness of women, then at the affrontery of his rival, and finally turned to vent his anger on the bull which had failed to do what was expected of it when Joe was at its mercy.

Joe's absence from Little Missington in the four weeks following the ball left Bertie a clear field, but clear fields were unlucky to Bertie and he preferred being in the ring to being crowded out of the arena.

Digby did his best to get his daughter back to the village way of life, but the more he tried the more he drove her into her mother's camp. With two ladies in the household forever criticizing what he looked upon as truly British, and clamouring for labour-saving gadgets which he regarded as tools of laziness, he felt the time had come to have another man about the house.

His offer to take on Bertie as a partner in the business

met with less enthusiasm from Bertie than it might have done a few weeks earlier. Most young men would have jumped at the idea, and Bertie's father certainly would have done had such an offer been made to him when he was alive, but Bertie was suspicious of Digby's motive. It looked as if he was being bought off as compensation for losing Sally to the American. In any case, the prospect of working on Sally's doorstep while relations between them were strained did not appeal to Bertie and he resolved to turn the offer down.

It was only when Digby confessed the trouble he was having at home and appealed to the lad for support, as man to man, that Bertie was persuaded to change his mind. Indignation and pride were not to take precedence over patriotism and loyalty. The youth who had rallied to Digby's side in the cause of local independence and conspired with him in the construction of an ancient monument, could hardly fail to respond to the call of duty when a matter of Britain's honour was at stake. It was one thing to have American aircraft here for our protection, but someone had to. protect us from the protector!

Sally and her mother, who again had not been consulted, were surprised to find Benjamin painting AND WOODFELLOW after DIGBY on the traders' sign at the side of their cottage. Digby's explanation was nothing if not ingratiating. One thing he had learned from the Americans, he told them, was the need to think and act big about business. He had already expanded from erecting barns and cottages to making coffins, and diversified from builder to undertaker, but his was still a one man family business. He would never be able to afford the modern amenities his wife and daughter were asking for, he told them, unless he brought in some new blood with fresh ideas.

Sally agreed that he had gone to the right place for those!

Ignoring the sarcasm, Digby continued. 'Since we

haven't got a son in the family to carry on the business when I am gone, it's about time we took someone in to help me out.'

Vera felt this might be an aspersion on her fertility rather than a hint of her husband's infirmity and went away to shed a tear. Sally wished she had been born a boy, or not at all. Digby went back to the Coach and Horses.

* * *

The Officer Commanding the USAF base at Swivenhall was not a man to fraternize with the natives and he had never heard of Little Missington until the case of Corporal Buckman came before him. Joe's defence had referred not only to the Digby's but to what the camp magazine had described as: A Marvel at Little Missington. Colonel Simon A L Peters, therefore, decided he had better take a look at the place and see for himself what it was all about.

Needless to say he did not get as far as the village at his first attempt. The usual state of the roads led him along minor routes by mistake and he came to the inevitable halt not far from The Willows, where the owner was spraying his fruit trees.

Cyrus greeted the Colonel, whose nationality and rank he identified from the uniform, in a typically matter-of-fact manner. 'Just dropped in from the New World, I daresay?'

Colonel Peters asked plaintively where he was.

'In the Old World,' said Cyrus and went on spraying.

The Colonel turned to go but Cyrus called him back. 'Need any help?'

'D'you know where Little Miss'nt'n is?'

Cyrus began by telling him he was there already, then asked which part of it the Colonel wanted and, without waiting for the answer enquired if he intended going by foot or helicopter.

Displaying more patience than he was renowned for at base, Colonel Peters explained that he had abandoned his car in a mud heap; would need a horse to pull it out; was looking for a man called Digby, and some sort of monument which everyone on the camp was crazy about. If it were remotely accessible, which he now doubted, he wanted to take a look at the thing. Could Cyrus help him?

Cyrus put aside the spray and led a bewildered colonel into The Willows. Seizing his opportunity to get one up on those in the village who were making capital out of their visitors, he drew a couple of tankards of home-brewed ale and sent a message round to the stables for a horse to be led to the derelict car. He then regaled the Colonel with so much history of the neighbourhood, and his own ancestry in particular, that it was hard to tell whether the ale or Cyrus caused the more confusion in the officer's mind.

Eventually he persuaded Colonel Peters to return as his guest for the next pilgrimage which he said would take place in three weeks' time, on the first Sunday in the month. Sally, herself, could not have done better on the spur of the moment.

News that Cyrus had 'captured' the Commander of the American Forces spread from the Coach and Horses during the evening and renewed activity for various commercial enterprises designed to cash in on the occasion.

Benjamin and Bertie found themselves suddenly in demand for notice boards, turning many a simple cottage into a GUEST HOUSE or a TEA SHOPPE. Bed and Breakfast cards appeared at windows and someone with a gate-plaque forbidding hawkers and circulars added a footnote that it was OK for Yankees. One cottage, which had long been known as The Laurels, displayed its owner's limited knowledge of the American film world by changing overnight to 'The Laurels and Hardies.'

163

Bertie was as busy on such jobs as a plumber after the thaw, and while he was attending to these tit bits of the trade his senior partner was out and about seeing to it that the next 'pilgrimage' would be more successful than the first. A certain amount of recasting was necessary among the actors, and improvements were called for in the costumes, but it was chiefly in production and choreography that more had still to be done. Here it was that Digby was fortunate in gaining the support of the village schoolmaster, George Henry Whackett.

George was a reserved man, of very high principles, who had looked upon earlier events in Digby's career with horror and apprehension. One thing he had always striven to teach his pupils was the unwisdom of undertaking tasks that were too big for them. In his own words, 'never bite off more than you can chew.' This, he felt, was what Digby had done, albeit encouraged by his fellow councillors, in tackling the matter of road repairs. He had the satisfaction of saying 'I told you so!' when the enterprise failed.

This had certainly not endeared him to Digby, who regarded his attitude as hostile and 'crusty', but the moment had now come to put aside all prejudice and seek a reconciliation. Whackett was not only an historian, insofar as he taught history at the village school, but he also wrote and produced an annual play which made him virtually a dramatist as well. The combination was exactly what Digby wanted.

It is doubtful if Digby would have persuaded Mr Whackett to foresake his insularity without the unexpected, unsolicited intervention of Katherine.

Kathy was George's daughter, the same age as Sally but not at the moment a friend of hers. She had 'gone steady' for a while with Jim Brewer, who adored her, but was now involved in a struggle for Bertie's affection, knowing Sally to have abandoned him.

The way to a man's heart is not always through his stomach, and Kathy saw a way to Bertie's, through her father's participation in the pilgrimage. Jim had told her what his father had overheard in the Coach and Horses and she worked on the principle that if she could arrange matters to please Digby that would somehow rebound to her credit with Digby's newly appointed partner.

George Whackett was no less susceptible to his daughter's flattery than Digby had been to Sally's. A few deft strokes of the hand through his greying hair; some gentle kisses on his whisker stubs; and those incandescent smiles, reserved for such occasions, made him ready to listen to anything she said.

'They're talking about you in the village, you know. They say you're the only one who could put on a show like the one they're planning. You ought to do it, you know. It would be a shame if you left it to someone else and they made a mess of it.'

It worked. By the time she had finished there was little resistance left for Digby to overcome.

It took Bertie longer to discover he was in a similarly fortunate position.

* * *

Anxious for a good turn-out to impress the Colonel, Cyrus gave his official blessing to the pilgrimage and other members of the Parish Council now felt it their duty to assist.

Apprehensive as always of the Chairman's influence, Digby urged upon him to stay behind the scenes 'in case anything untoward should happen for which the Colonel might hold him responsible.' It was a shrewd argument and had the same effect as telling a husband not to wash up because he might break some crockery. He did not

165

dispute the possibility and remained aloof.

George and Benjamin, therefore, were able to get on with their preparations unmolested, though not, as Kathy had imagined, in dual harness with Bertie assisting, but each in his own way, separated by the length of the village and a wide span of temperament. Two wives would live happier in the same kitchen than two producers with the same play. Benjamin knew this and once George had agreed to take charge of the production he was left alone with it. Ben and Bertie had plenty to do in the building line and 'every man to his last' was the order of the day.

* * *

Sunday the second of May opened with a clear sky and the thin morning mist lifted early to reveal another transformation scene. The Common at Little Missington looked gayer and more inhabited than it had done for centuries. Not since the Middle Ages had there been a maypole there and George Whackett's resurrection of it was the centre-piece, surrounded by a ring of tents from which there hung a hundred flags. The maypole and the tents had been erected by the firm of 'Digby and Woodfellow' and the bunting borrowed from the church collection by Syd Stubbles — under protest.

It was 'sacred-ledge' he said, that anything blessed by the church should be associated with something as pagan as the pilgrimage. But if Cyrus said it was all right, then *he* would have to answer for it when he came before the heavenly council.

Beyond the tents were stalls for the Pilgrim Merchants, on which their various wares were displayed, like Puddlethorpe on Market Day. Signposts and notices were everywhere and there was the atmosphere of a fairground without the hurdy-gurdy.

All morning a buzz of activity spread through the village as last minute touches were put to props and costumes, and extra attention given to under-rehearsed items on the programme. George had amended the original concept of a procession of 'pilgrims' to a pageant of 'Little Missington through the Ages'. Or, as Cyrus sourly put it, 'through the eyes of Mr Whackett.'

Colonel Peters arrived at The Willows on foot shortly after mid-day. He left his car in a field by the last navigable stretch of made-up road and took a compass bearing on it so that he would know where to look for it on the way back. Cyrus greeted him facetiously by saying he would have had an avenue of willows planted to lead him there but it was the wrong time of year to plant them. Colonel Peters responded by saying he could not bear the thought of so much weeping on his account, and the meeting got off to a good start. A bottle of extra dry sherry kept the humour going and a vintage Pommard with the side of beef made it distinctly jovial. Mrs Galleon asked about the Colonel's family and admired his walletful of snapshots. Cyrus asked about his antecedents and matched him generation by generation until the Colonel ran out of forebears, conceding pedigree supremacy to his host. Stories about the war were swopped, without particular reference to which war, and a common interest in muskets led to a perilous exhibition of arms which threatened the safety of them all. Mrs Galleon retrieved the situation by remembering the Americans were also farmers and getting the Colonel so excited about his livestock 'back home' that Cyrus had to admit he had fewer chickens than the Colonel had heads of cattle.

It was remarkable that they remembered the 'pilgrimage' and even more so that they arrived in time to see it begin. Cyrus insisted his guest should be taken in style and drove him down in a pony-trap. Luckily the pony had made the journey before and was not concerned with the confusion of signals conveyed to it through the bridle. Colonel Peters was also happily muddled by the wine and port which followed, and noticed little of the discomfort in his mode of transport. He kept thinking, however, how much steadier it was in the cockpit of his aircraft and how strange it was that they kept taking off and landing quite so often.

The Salvation Army Band was approaching the Common as the pony brought them into view of it.

To the strains of 'Onward Christian Soldiers', skirmishing broke out between the leading ranks of advancing Salvationists and the rearward elements of 'ancient warriors'. Clashes of steel and brass occurred as shield struck cymbal and pikesman poked at trumpeter. Robbed of their pitch by George Whackett's pageant, General Booth's disciples were roused to battle and the spirit of crusade shifted suddenly from supporters of one procession to those of another.

Colonel Peters was impressed with the vigour of the opening scene, and Cyrus was dumbfounded at the measure of support the schoolmaster had achieved. It soon became clear, however when he saw the drum and tuba floating in the river that any co-operation the Salvation Army had given to the occasion was entirely unintentional.

The rout of the band was followed swiftly by a start to the scheduled programme and while ranks were reassembling and debris was removed, dancing began around the maypole.

Ribbons floated prettily in many patterns as boys and girls weaved in and out, and changed direction. The pole swayed dangerously as boys pulled harder than the girls, but somehow they managed to counteract each other; the pole wobbled but remained upright and George Whackett breathed again.

Cyrus and the Colonel had now tethered the pony to a

tree at the top of the Common and were walking among the tents and stalls, which Cyrus called the 'sideshow'. Colonel Peters was surprised to find a 'hot dog stall' in such an English setting, but his attention was drawn more to the terrifying butcher who attended it. Patrick O'Hachetty was dressed to kill, as only a man from the slaughterhouse would know. Blood was smeared all over his blue striped apron and a newly skinned carcase hung steaming and dripping from a hook on the beam behind him. In his hand he held a knife that was long enough to be a sword, and on the block of blood-stained wood in front of him he was making sausages. Cyrus shuddered and the Colonel smiled, but they both made a mental note to join the vegetarians.

After the dancing there was a brief display of tumbling by the Junior School in pixie outfits, and then the procession moved off towards the ruin, following a route now marked and described as 'The Pilgrims Way.'

On Galleon's Meadow, where the ruin stood, Cyrus introduced his guest to 'The Laughing Cavalier', and Digby delighted them both by stepping back to bow and falling over a boulder which had been brought up to roll at the castle during the big siege scene to follow. With a glance at the laughing Colonel, Benjamin uttered a crisp medieval oath, and beat it.

Tableau after tableau followed, and slowly 'Through the Ages' they were taken, from the Early Britons pitching flints at passing animals, to Anglo-Saxons pelting stones at Roman sentries; outlawed archers aiming arrows at the ruling barons, to ranks of soldiers firing gunshot at beleaguered garrisons.

With no bull to bring proceedings to an abrupt end, the pageant lingered on and Cyrus lost interest before they reached the present century. Steering the Colonel to a corner of the field where he thought they might sit out and smoke another cigar, he was confronted with a huge notice saying RETURN BY BUS — ONE SHILLING.

Cyrus was curious to know how this could be, since the arrow on the board pointed clearly towards the river. Leading his guest to the water's edge he was astonished to see a red painted punt with Sam Waterman wedged up in the stern with a ten foot pole.

It was an enterprise ahead of its time and showed that there was no monopoly on new ideas when it came to making money. Sam's waterbus was slow, and hard to propel, but it gave comfort to many tired feet and grew in popularity as the evening wore on. It would probably have carried more on each voyage if the costumes being worn that day had been designed with pockets for the carrying of coins.

15

Bertie did not return by waterbus from the pilgrimage. He was waylaid by Kathy as he stepped from the battlements, shivering in the evening breeze, with only a loin cloth to protect him. Kathy offered him her shawl but he demanded more. Much to his surprise, he got it.

Digby went home, sore in mind and body at the indignity he had suffered before the visiting Colonel, but saddest of all at the sight of Bertie and Sally estranged on the site of their own creation.

Sally had grieved all day at the absence of Joe and would have sooner dressed as a sorrowing woman in widows' weeds than the gay-hearted girl in bonnet and blouse. Outwardly she looked fine and played her part well, pretending to feed and flirt with the ill-sorted warriors, bar one in a loin cloth whom she carefully avoided, but inwardly her heart was beating for the prisoner from Baltimore.

Aware of her evasiveness, Bertie took pains to be seen with as many young nursemaids, Nell Gwyns and widows as possible, seeking their favours and flaunting his manly physique. His choice, however, was not indiscriminate and the effect he had on the opposite sex was not always reciprocated. One young lady, for example, aptly appearing as a witch had more than her costume to blame for getting the cold shoulder. The truth was that Bertie would rather have walked with Sally than stay behind with any of the other girls, yet while Sally's affections were fixed on the American he was determined to show her that two could play at infidelity.

Kathy was not among his favourites but she was a well-built girl, invariably smart, and by no means unattractive. Once she had removed her shawl and exposed the flesh on her shoulders, Bertie wondered why he had taken so long to recognize her beauty. For her part, Kathy had long been impressed by Bertie's virtues and his Spartan appearance confronting her now did much to heighten the attraction.

'A shawl's not what I want round my shoulders,' he told her bluntly, casting her offer aside. 'If you want to keep me warm you'll have to come a lot closer.'

He had never lain flesh to flesh with a woman before and the effect on his nervous system was quite disturbing. Kathy seemed calm but provocative and the heat generated in one small corner of the castle ruins was enough to dry the underlying ground to powder. Sally's experience in the boilerhouse at Swivenhall had been temperate compared with this!

George Whackett was too drunk with his own success to notice his daughter's absence from home that evening, but Mrs Whackett was a bundle of nerves waiting for Kathy to return.

'George you must have seen her somewhere before you left.'

'Yes, she was here at breakfast, wasn't she?'

'Oh, for goodness sake, you went out together after lunch.'

'Did we?'

* * *

172

'Am I more attractive than Sally?'

It was a silly thing to say and Kathy knew it the moment she asked. Bertie remembered why she had never been among his favourites: she was a greedy girl!

'I haven't asked you about Jim Brewer, so why bring Sally into it?'

'I'm sorry. I just wondered, that's all.'

'Well don't.'

'All right.'

'We'd better be going.'

'I could stay here all night.'

'Well, *you* can if you like; I've got work to do tomorrow.'

Benjamin was out in the yard before his partner arrived in the morning. Bertie was not late, but it made him feel that way when he saw the Boss pottering around as he walked in.

'Good morning.'

'Hullo, my boy. What happened to you last night? I thought you might have looked in for a drink.'

'No sir, to tell you the truth I was too tired.'

'I suppose it was all that close-quarters, armed-combat stuff you were doing? Must have been very exhausting.'

Neither was quite sure how to interpret the other's expression.

* * *

Bertie allowed some time to pass after accepting the partnership before behaving in any way like a new broom. Apart from suggesting they called themselves Funeral Directors instead of Undertakers, he was quite content to think of Digby as the Boss and himself as the Boy. The sight of his name on the board, however, and the sound of being called a partner reminded him he had now a responsibility to contribute something to the business and

173

the opportunity to do this came when the weather broke and outdoor work became impracticable. Looking around the sheds at the back of the cottage for something to do, he came upon the junk that Digby had collected during his brief excursion into the rag and bone trade.

'You can clean that lot out, if you like lad, and build yourself a bench. I put it there for a rainy day, so you could say this is it.'

Unlike the front line soldiers, Bertie's wartime experience had not been entirely destructive. Endless drilling, parades and inspections had taught him a methodical, military approach to problem solving. Faced with the assortment of domestic debris that folk in the village had discarded, he set about arranging it first by size and then according to its intended use. At one extreme were high-backed chairs and chests of drawers which Digby had somehow managed to lift into his hand cart, while at the other extreme were tiny bottles of ink and perfume, miniature toys and costume jewellery. In between there were firescreens, bedpans, jugs and vases; bonnets, braces, rugs and cushions; brushes, curlers, wigs and waistcoats; collars, cufflinks, stays and gaiters; tablecloths, curtains, handbags, picture frames and walking sticks.

Bertie lingered in admiration at items which conjured up a reminder of his childhood and in wonder at those which gave him a glimpse of the past he had never known. Checking the inclination to dwell, he pressed on through a pile of leather-bound books, lace-up boots and embroidered lingerie; a stack of faded pillow cases, frilly blouses and worn-out overalls; to a mound of kitchen utensils, fishing tackle, workshop tools and sewing materials.

The instinct for self-preservation is present in all of us, but the desire to preserve everything, including other people's rejects, is less common. It was, however, a failing of the Woodfellow family which Bertie unwittingly inherited. The thought of destroying some of these articles was so painful to him that he could not bring himself to do so. Even those in need of repair were reprieved.

When Digby returned home that night he found that instead of making himself a bench, Bertie had built shelves along the shed walls and filled them with pots, caskets, books, tankards, ornaments and bric-à-brac. On the floor, beneath the shelves, he had stacked a range of large solid articles, like furniture, machinery and picture frames. Hanging from the walls were tapestries, draperies and costumes in a glorious mix of colours.

'My heart, you've been busy, boy! You'd make a good shopkeeper ... if folk'd only buy rubbish!'

'I reckoned,' said Bertie, apologetically, 'if something were rare enough there'd be somebody rash enough to buy it.'

It was the beginning of a backward glance from which there would be no looking back. The start of a new era in the annals of Little Missington. The first glimpse of a future built firmly on its past. For Little Missington it was the founding of a fortune!

Like most original thought, Bertie's inspiration was not immediately understood. Benjamin was sceptical but anxious not to discourage his partner by openly objecting. Sally and her mother were decidedly hostile and said they wanted nothing to do with a load of old rubbish that should have been burned or buried years ago. Give them something new, they said, like they'd seen at Swivenhall.

'Take no notice, lad,' said Digby, 'It's not everyone who recognizes beauty when they see it.'

'Beauty my foot,' retorted Vera, 'you wouldn't know the difference between ... beauty ... and the beast!'

'Which did I marry, then?' asked Digby.

* * *

'I thought you appreciated works of art, and things like that,' Bertie grumbled when Sally brought the subject up.

'So I do, when they *are* works of art, and in the right place, but I don't see why you should turn our house into a museum!'

Bertie was on the point of dismantling the exhibition when his first customer arrived. Her name was Angela, and she was a cypher clerk at the American Air Base who had read about the ruin in their camp magazine and was on her way to 'do' it, as she did all the sights wherever she went. Seeing a sign over Digby's shed inscribed ANTIQUES FOR SALE she dismounted from her bicycle and came to look for a souvenir to send back to her mother in the States.

'Excuse me!' she drawled, taking Bertie and Sally by surprise, 'do you sell souverneers?'

'What's a souvenir?' asked Bertie.

'Gee, but you're cute! Fancy asking what a souverneer is in this country. Why England's full of souverneers. Don't you have any?'

'Why don't you come in and look round?'

Bertie looked at Angela and felt a momentary sympathy with Joe. If this was a typical American female, no wonder Joe had fallen for Sally. There were many bespectacled girls he knew who could make themselves appealing to men, but Angela not only wore frames that were unsuited to her eyes but revelled in specimens that were unsightly to everyone else's. Physical imperfections were not her fault but Bertie felt she could have helped a little by hiding them. A tight fitting sweater and nylon trousers were not the happiest of choice for such a figure.

176

'Thanks, I will. Mind if I park my velocipede?'

As she walked to the shed, after propping her bicycle against the gate, Bertie noticed that all her muscles were in violent agitation; those at one end causing her bottom to rise and fall as if each buttock were a counter-balance to the other; those near the other cheeks working away at her jaws on a piece of chewing-gum.

Sally noticed the look of fascination on Bertie's face and mistook it for one of affection. She left him to handle the transaction alone. He heard the door slam as she went back into the cottage.

'That your sister?'

'Well, I don't know as you could say that . . .'

'Gee, you don't know anything, do you?'

But he sold her a snuff box and a jewel case and so much 'atmosphere' that she promised to come back again and said she would tell her friends about the place, and anyone else she met. It was not until after she had gone that Bertie wondered if she had bought the snuff box as a powder compact for her mum.

The joke was enough to restore him to good favour with Mrs Digby and to speaking terms with Sally, but he had a long way to go yet to win Sally back from his rival. 'Just because you've met one unattractive American is no reason to think they're all cannibals.'

The idea of anyone wanting to eat Angela was so repulsive to Bertie that he changed the subject.

'When does your corporal friend come out of prison?'

'He's *not* in prison!'

Sally's response made her mother jump. 'You don't suppose the poor boy has been locked up all this time, do you? What would he do about a change of clothing?'

'Oh Mummy, don't be silly; he's not in chains! He's just confined to camp, that's all.'

'It sounds much the same to me.'

'I've heard they wear arrows on their tunics so you can recognize them when they escape.'

'Now you come to mention it, I remember . . .'

'Mummy! They were his corporal's stripes! Bertie Woodfellow, if I hear any more of your wickedness I'll . . .'

Before she could finish her sentence, Bertie was on his way back to the shed with a grin as broad as a bandage.

* * *

The antique shop was soon as much a talking point in the village as Sam's waterbus, and both did excellent business. Once it was known that the Americans liked sending things home to relations, every cupboard, trunk and attic in the place was emptied of contents that had lain idle for years. Things for which no further use had been imagined now went on display, and where sheds were not available for showrooms, stalls were soon erected. Back gardens in which afternoon teas were served on Sundays now took on the appearance of bazaars.

The market in antiquity brought work for Bertie who found himself commissioned to promote his own opposition. Not only was he asked to make shelves and set up stalls out of boxes, planks and trestle tables, but he was pressed to make signs and fix brackets to publicize his competitors. ANTIQUES, GIFTS and SOUVENIRS were the three most popular signs but one individual in the village had read Charles Dickens and wanted to call his 'The Old Curiosity Shop.' On being told he would be charged by the letter, he settled for 'Shoppe'.

Meanwhile Angela Cotton had kept her word and paid a second visit with a smart companion called Pru. Bertie was at work on a new bench, which he now badly needed, when they called. Sally met them at the gate and immediately realized Bertie would be impressed by Pru.

Seeing this as somehow likely to put Joe in a better light, she hurried off to fetch him.

While she was gone the two girls went into the shop and browsed among the relics, arguing from time to time about the name of this and the use for that, picking up and fondling each item they came to as though they were archaeologists unearthing treasures that had been buried for centuries.

They had just inquisitively pulled to pieces an eighteenth century commode, and were struggling to reassemble it, when Digby burst in, looking for an extension ladder which used to hang along the inside wall of the shed. Unable to see it there because of Bertie's rearrangements, and forgetting the shed was no longer a retreat where he could express himself without restraint, he uttered a loud oath and strode angrily toward the tapestry which covered the wall.

Angela, who had heard the word before, was embarrassed and looked the other way, but Pru who had not was unabashed. 'Excuse me, sir,' she said, 'we haven't seen one of these before. What do you put in it?'

The last time Digby had blushed was when he bumped into his daughter in the nude while dashing between bathroom and bedroom to find a towel. This time he had no extremity to conceal but was equally lost for words. Fortunately for him Bertie arrived on the scene in time to distract attention. Pru's reaction to Bertie was immediate. She flashed him a look of bewitching friendliness, then pretended to be absorbed with something else. Bertie felt as though he had been hit in the stomach and went suddenly weak and breathless. From the corner of her eye Pru saw him watching her and jerked her head to one side as fisherman flick at their lines to secure a catch. Bertie knew he had been well and truly hooked.

Sally was not perturbed, for this is what she had predicted

179

and secretly hoped for, but Benjamin was shocked and could hardly contain his displeasure.

'The trouble with young people today,' he muttered to Vera when they were alone that evening, 'is that they can't settle anywhere for five minutes without wanting a change.'

✳ ✳ ✳

Such a remark would have earned a hollow laugh from Joe who was still sweating it out in confinement at Swivenhall and had remained substantially in one place for considerably longer than five minutes.

Not so his thoughts, however, for they were constantly on the move and frequently in Little Missington. Visions of the Digbys turning their backs on him and barring their doors to a convicted man tortured him more than the disgusting diet and restricted routine to which he was subjected. Sally, he was sure, would shy at the prospect of ever associating with him again, and to spare her the shame of being seen with one who was now sharing a billet with the criminal classes he resolved to get himself posted, and spent five days with an atlas looking for remote and unlikely places in which to be exiled.

So great was his conviction (in both senses of the word) that his morale fell to a staggering low and without Sammy to sustain and redirect him he began to dread the day of freedom when he would be released.

How often time can race us to that moment in the future which we await with apprehension! That visit to the dentist when a tooth is aching and relief lies painfully beyond the chair; that meeting with a new employer when the flush of welcome fades and the first sign of authority appears; those painful hours of pregnancy that are the prelude to every new display of life.

No sooner was Joe purged of his misdemeanour and out

of his sentence than he was back on a bicycle speeding for Little Missington. Savouring the landmarks and bouncing joyfully upon the saddle he forgot the swamps and caves and deserts he had planned to go to and found himself in sight of Digby's cottage . . . and a shock for which he was not prepared.

Over the gate on which he had once leaned with Sally, and fixed to the fence on which he had previously propped his bicycle, he saw the notice saying DIGBY AND WOODFELLOW (PARTNERS). Below it, with an arrow leading to the woodshed, the other which said simply ANTIQUES FOR SALE. Unsure if the one were meant to refer to the other, Joe had just remembered that Woodfellow was the name of Sally's former boyfriend when Bertie himself walked out of the shed; with Pru.

Now, whatever Joe's reluctance in the past to date a female, and until he met Sally he had never done so, he had not escaped the notice of his more precocious fellow countrywoman. Seeing him now hurriedly trying to remount his bicycle, Pru called him back.

'Hi! Joe Buckman! Fancy you finding this hideout. Come and get a load of this. It's fabulous!'

Joe had already taken in far more than his mind could carry and there were tears in his eyes when he turned to go. Pru's recognition put an end to his escape.

Hearing Joe's name trumpeted across the yard, Sally came running from the cottage and collided with Bertie who was anxiously steering one American away from the other.

What followed was observed by Benjamin and Vera from their backroom window, with bewilderment and sorrow. Joe stood beside the gate, holding his bicycle, while Sally ran and threw her arms around his neck. Beaten by a short head to the same idea, Pru reversed directions rapidly and bumped deliberately into Bertie who, to score off Sally, seized and kissed her. Pleasantly surprised, she hugged and clung to him, calling to Joe to 'get a load of this as well!' Joe was too embarrassed and overcome even to acknowledge her, and so awkward in his excitement that he let go of the bicycle at a critical part of the clinch with Sally and it rolled gently in a broad arc, under the influence of gravity, until it struck Bertie a sharp blow on his bottom and toppled over at his feet.

'Gee, Ber-tee, you sure pack a kick in them kisses. Gimme another!'

At which point Benjamin felt it was time to be introduced.

16

'We missed you, Joe.'
  'You did?'
  'Well I did, anyway.'
  'And I missed you, Sal. Sorry, Sally.'
  Half sitting half lying, they found a cutting in the river bank, concealing them from any but the closest passer-by, and were sharing the enjoyment of reunion on a warm, fine evening at the start of summer.
  Absent-mindedly, Joe drew from his pocket a packet of chewing gum and offered some to Sally. She recoiled instinctively.
  'Why do you eat that stuff?'
  'Oh, Gee, I forgot!'
  He threw the packet in the river and apologised. Then he tried to explain that the idea was not to eat it but to chew it. Hence the name, chewing gum.
  'I can't see the sense in that,' she persisted. 'What satisfaction can you get out of teasing the appetite? It's like ... well, giving a baby a dummy when it wants a drink.'
  Joe looked at the water and reflected. Babies, he thought, ... dummies ... drink: he looked at Sally and saw the associations. Putting his arms affectionately round her, he pursed his lips, and drank.

* * *

183

Downstream, on another stretch of the river bank, unaware of the close proximity of their respective rivals, Bertie and Pru were fishing. Unlike their neighbours, they were sitting some distance apart, and only the curvaceous loops of their tackle had so far become entwined.

Watching a fisherman unravel his twisted line is like eavesdropping on a private conversation, and Pru exercised that virtue after which she was named by keeping silent. It enabled her to study her companion's display of digital dexterity without distracting him and encouraged her to marvel at his youthful manliness and painstakingly resolute country character.

'How come you don't date your boss's daughter?' she asked suddenly as he reached the last inch or two of gut above the hooks. 'She's cute.'

Bertie's concentration faltered and he pricked himself on the hook.

'They don't mix. Work and pleasure, I mean,' he answered, sucking the blood from his finger.

Pru looked back at the water. 'So you have thawt about it? If you think she'd be a pleasure then you *must* have thawt about it.'

'I think about a lot of things. Don't you?'

It was a trick he had learned from Sally. When you don't want to pursue a subject, and can't think of a way to change it, ask a question; it puts the ball in your opponent's court.

Prudence hit it back.

'Sure!' she said, 'but some things more than others.'

By the way she cast her glance at Bertie he had little doubt of what she meant. He only wished she were as good at casting her fishing line. Taking the tackle, which he had now straightened, in one hand and a triple-jointed tapered rod in the other, he stood up, drew breath and gave her a splendid demonstration of the angler's art. She followed the flight with admiring eyes, permitting her imagination to run on beyond the point at which the hooks and sinker struck the water and then to swell out in all directions, like the ripples spilling from the splash.

'Berr-tee,' she sighed, taking hold of his ankle and slipping her hand in the top of his socks. 'Do you ever think of me in terms of pleasure?'

He let the rod go, for it was pointless to ignore the feeling that this bait was being taken above the water if not below it, and the more he speculated on the kind of catch he might have in store the more he liked the prospect of securing it.

When he next looked at the water it seemed much darker and more disturbed than when he had last noticed it, reflecting no doubt his state of mind. But what had happened to his float? He leapt abruptly to his feet. There, among the shadows and a smudge of weeds, a red-tipped quill was dancing sadly, striving unsuccessfully to signal that the line beneath it was in tension.

Bertie grabbed the rod which had lain at his feet and flicked it vigorously to one side, expecting a weight on the far end to counteract his pull. Unfortunately, there was no fish on the other end and so no equal and opposite force to resist him. The ground, being wet and slippery, offered no friction underfoot and he fell unceremoniously backwards on to a tray of worms.

Pru gently picked him up and sought to soothe his damaged pride. 'Wow, that sure was some fish! I guess I haven't seen a guy jump like that since my old man touched a live wire in our bathroom!'

Bertie's first reaction was to see if the bait had gone from the hooks. It would be less humiliating to find that a fish had got away than to realize that he had struck too soon or, even worse, without a 'bite'. He wound the loops of loosely lying line on to the reel and hauled the hooks in to the palm of his hand to inspect them. Then he shuddered and dropped to his knees.

It is strange that a man who can handle slugs and maggots, worms and other wriggly things without qualm or nausea can get a chill in his spine when his skin comes into contact with something unexpected.

Bertie stared down at the shape of what he had jettisoned and wondered what kind of a creature it was that had changed places with his bait. There could be no supposing it had swallowed it.

Pru looked cautiously over his shoulder, expecting to find him grappling with a poisonous snake or prehistoric reptile, but was horrified to see him shrinking from a strip of chewing gum. She stepped over the scattered pieces of tin and tackle and unwrapped from the lower spike of that featherless quill, whose excited bobbing on the water had caused Bertie to humble himself on the mudbank, a piece of coloured paper with the stark inscription RUM-TUM FOR GUM, CHUM. It meant about as much to Bertie as commodes had meant to Pru, but he was less restrained than she had been in owning to his ignorance.

Digby, meantime, had been looking after the partnership alone. It was Bertie's half-day, so Ben was in the shop browsing over the relics of his rag and bone collection, taking them down from the shelves where Bertie had carefully placed them, dusting them, and putting them back, wondering why anyone should want to buy such rubbish, when Angela walked in.

'Hi there, Mr Digby. What's new?'

Benjamin had grown to like Angela. She was plain and loud and awkward, but homely and straightforward, so that he felt at ease with her. She, for her part, referred to Digby as a 'pet' and sang his praises as the local sage to whom all visitors should go before they put a second foot in Little Missington.

'What's new, you ask? Not much, I'd say. Just look

around! There's not a piece in this old shed that's less than five score years, I'll wager. We don't have what's new in Little Missington. What we've got we've had for generations.'

Angela watched his eyes and was mesmerized. They seemed to draw her into the thick burly brows beneath which they moved and she was trapped like flotsam in the reeds.

'You take that river, now,' he went on, as if he sensed the simile, 'that's ancient, if you like! There weren't 'ny villagers around when that began. That's prehistoric. I've heard it said you can dip your hand in there and touch some of the same drops o' water as were there when Adam took the apple.'

'Is that so? Gee, that's marvellous!'

* * *

Angela walked to the water's edge before resuming her journey to the camp. She felt drawn to those drops that had been touched by Adam. In the gathering twilight first Sally and Joe went by without seeing her, clasping each other's hands behind their backs and tilting their heads so they touched at the temples; then Bertie and Pru emerged from the gloom and also passed her without being aware of it. They were so close together that from where Angela stood they appeared as one body with two pairs of legs and one head. The image sickened her, for she had developed a secret crush on Bertie since their first meeting in Digby's workshed. Overhead a bat banked sharply on the skyline, screeched, and swooped blindly on its prey. Unable to copy it, Angela picked up a pebble and flung it into the river.

Bertie turned when he heard the splash. He was quickly redirected. 'That was a fish,' he said, 'they always bite better at night.'

187

'So do I,' said the far side of the face, and the four legs moved on.

* * *

Digby had another customer before he shut up shop for the night. His name was Billy Gosling and he lived in a lonely part of the village in what used to be a tied cottage but was now rented out at half-a-crown a week by the Parish Council. Billy's days of labouring on the farm were finished so his income was limited to an old-age pension, but his family had grown up and his expenditure was small. Asthmatic and arthritic, he was tethered to his home and rarely ventured out.

There were those in the village who said he hoarded like a miser.

'Well I'll be blowed,' said Digby, 'if it ain't old Goosey! What brings you to this part o' the village? I reckon it's many a day since you saw my backyard. Never you mind, Billy, it's good to see you. How are you?'

Digby was conscious of the old man's wheezing and spluttering after so strenuous a journey, so he kept the conversation to himself till Billy could answer him.

'Here, have a seat, old chap, you're just about all in. Won't you come inside to the cottage and have a tot o' rum, or summat? I'm just packing up for the night. I'll close the shutters, then we can go in.'

'No, not yet, Ben! I came to see you on business, and . . . and . . . then I'll take a nip, if the offer still goes.'

Ben was reminded that the last time they had met was when he was going round with his rag and bone cart and had called at the Gosling's cottage offering cash for their 'old containers'. Billy had pulled out a copper kettle, a bronze warming pan and a brass fender with ornamental corner boxes, and Digby had paid him a pound for the lot and been blessed for his generosity. Now the old man had come to purchase them back.

'Y'see, Ben, at the time we b'aint needin' them. And I never thought we ever should again. But since they cowboys have been comin' round on the Sabbath and droppin' in for cups o' tea and payin' for them, like, well, it's not that I think it matters, but Jessie says we ought to do it proper for them and let them see the kettle boilin' on the hob like we used to do.'

Digby longed to asked the old man what his wife's reason was for wanting the warming pan back, but he resold the lot for thirty bob and found that again he had done them a favour.

Billy was not the first of the villagers to buy from Digby's store to augment their own supply of antiques for sale, but he was the first to buy back what had once been his. Such was the market now for what had recently been valueless that Billy was soon followed by many more who had once been glad to rid themselves of junk and now came eagerly to buy it back.

It was not their craze for collecting things which brought about this sudden boom in bric-à-brac, but the demand exerted on them by their visitors from Swivenhall. Jessie Gosling, if she had been correctly quoted by her husband, was being disingenuous in asking for her kettle back, 'to boil the water proper, like', because she knew that if she used a brightly polished copper kettle on the hob instead of a cast-iron version in the kitchen, she would probably be able to sell it and make more on that transaction than by selling teas for the proverbial month of Sundays.

It was evident to all who entertained them, whether they did so freely or for profit, that Little Missington's visitors from America liked her souvenirs as much as her scenery. Whereas they came originally to see the ruin and the pageantry that Digby staged, they returned repeatedly in search of presents to send back home, 'from the Old World to the New'. A regular Sunday sport developed of looking for older and quainter articles to send their ever more bewildered relatives in the States. It was a game that had its forfeits, and the penalties they paid were closets with no water; back rooms and barns with draughts and no heating; low beams and worn steps on which heads were bumped and ankles sprained.

It was a game in which the village revelled. To vie with one another in the stock they had to offer, villagers were quite prepared to buy from one another as well as from Digby. The trade in antiques which had first accompanied now overtook the trade in teas, and Digby found the competition stimulated sales and boosted prices. In a month many of his shelves were cleared and the kitty stood at several times what he had paid for the junk when he collected it. Added to this profit was Bertie's contribution from the sale of plaques and notices and the charge he made for fixing them.

The Digby and Woodfellow partnership prospered and Bertie was able to buy himself a second set of fishing tackle so that when Pru went with him to the river her hands would be occupied with a rod of her own.

Sally had meantime struck up a closer bond with Angela, whose infatuation with the English had appealed to her. When it dawned on her that the infatuation was with Bertie she was even more delighted and did her best to foster it. Despite her lack of interest in Bertie, now that Joe had won her favours, Sally felt a certain jealousy at seeing Pru so swiftly take her place. Her pride would have preferred that someone much less pretty should succeed her.

Angela was still unsure of Sally's motives, and instinctively regarded her as hostile but, with the native cunning of a bold Red Indian, led her deeper into unfamiliar country, encouraging her whenever possible to

190

visit Swivenhall. This was what Sally often spoke of doing, threatening with mischief more than malice to watch Joe on parade or catch him with his buddies. She had to confess that she still knew little about his working life and less about the background to it. Swivenhall, in her book, was the modern Mecca of everything mechanical, the bright light of artificial illumination, the land of lotus-eating luxury, the place of make-believe. Once, like Cinderella in her jeep-shaped pumpkin, Joe had transported her there; once in her father's lorry she had seen it by the light of day; now in her imagination she was taken there whenever Angela came round and talked about it.

So it happened that one morning when Bertie was busy in the workshed making a new sign for TEAS & OLDE TIT BITS, Angela appeared on her bicycle with a message for Sally, from Joe. It said he was sorry but he would not be able to ride to the village that afternoon as promised on account of a boil having 'gotten into his bottom'. Sally felt sure the transmission of the message had gained something in the telling, for it was not a written message, but the gist was evidently correct. Angela, with sweetness overflowing, offered Sally her 'velocipede' and suggested she might like to go in to Swivenhall herself to visit Joe. The idea appealed to her and, catching Mrs Digby unprepared, she got her mother's consent before her father heard of it and by the time he did she was already half way there.

Bertie had just burned the 'O' in a smooth piece of timber and was shaping up to do the 'L' when he looked at Angela and sensed the guile behind her generosity.

'What are you going to do while Sally's away with your bicycle? She'll be hours getting there and back.' He knew the answer but hoped the question might induce her to offer an alternative.

'If you need any help, I could scratch out some letters

with that soldering iron while you're smoothing down the next piece of pinewood.'

Bertie was about to decline the offer when Mrs Digby put her head round the door, asking for Benjamin. 'He's out on a call at present, Mrs Digby. Should be back in half an hour.'

'Thank you Bertie, I only wanted to tell him where Sally had gone. It was good of Angela to lend her a bicycle, and I couldn't help hearing what she said when I came in. I wish sometimes Sally was as thoughtful and helpful to other people. I've been trying to get her to do that lettering for you for ages. I'm sure it's a job a woman could do while you are getting on with other things.'

For the first time, Bertie wondered if he'd like her for a mother-in-law. Angela adored her.

When Digby returned he was surprised to find his partner working with an assistant and inclined to attribute the increased output to her efficiency. Closer reading of Bertie's expression persuaded him that Angela's presence was responsible only indirectly and that Bertie's vigorous approach to the batch of work in hand was in order to get it finished as quickly as possible: a not unlaudable endeavour, but one surpassing even Bertie's usual enthusiasm. Sally meantime had stormed the gates of Swivenhall and been shown her corporal's quarters by a fascinated sergeant who leered and said she could stay and talk to Joe, so long as she kept out of his bed and got out of the camp by midnight. Joe was so embarrassed he turned over in his bed and rolled on to the offending tumour.

'Gee, I never thawt I'd have a visitor! It sure is swell of you to come and see me.'

Sally wondered if she dare risk the pun and say it was he who was swollen, but she lost her nerve and desisted. Once the sergeant had left them she began to feel more at ease until, out of the blue, in walked Pru.

192

'Say, honey, I just heard about your . . . What bit you?'

'Oh gosh! Pru, I wish you hadn't come. It's nice to see you, but you know it's out of bounds.'

Sally was now uncomfortable again.

'That's OK brother, Sergeant Blue-eyes said I could. "There's a dame in there already," he said, "and with what he's got on his fanny it won't matter how many women he has to vamp him!"'

Sally blushed but only pretended she understood. Pru took her kindly by the hand. 'Don't mind him, sweetie, he's a loudmouth! No one cares a cuss what he says. I saw you talking to him at the gate so I came around to make sure he didn't maul you . . . Oh, yeah, I came to see Joe as well, but I might have left that until after dark if you hadn't given me the cue just now.'

Sally would not have been keen to stay long in the same room with Pru at any time and to share Joe's bedroom with her was a particular torment. What made it so much worse was that having taken the only chair by the bedside, she was obliged to see Pru sit herself on the end of Joe's bed, and considerably nearer the top end than seemed casual. In the circumstances, therefore, Sally's visit was not overdrawn and, for duration at least, would not have offended the hospital rules of a most conscientious sister.

Joe objected when Sally got up to go.

'It sure was good of you to come and see me. D'you have to go back right now?'

'It's a long way, Joe, and, besides, Angela might be wanting her bike back.'

'But she *offered* it, you said. You didn't just take it, as I did the jeep?'

'Yes Joe, I know, but suppose she wants to get somewhere while I'm away?'

'Bertie'll take care o' that, I guess.'

It was an unfortunate remark and Sally wished she could

have smothered it. The reference to Bertie was enough to set Pru's imagination working.

'Say, I've got an idea,' she said. 'Why don't I keep you company and pedal into Li'l Miss'n'ton with you? I could do with some more souv'neers from your ol' man's store.' Then, turning to Joe and putting her hands on his chin, 'C'n I dig something out for you, honey, like an old bed pan, maybe?'

Joe did not want a souvenir, and Sally did not want Pru's company, but the two girls cycled out of the camp soon afterwards and returned together to Little Missington in almost total silence.

The arrival of Pru in the workshed was a shock to Angela, and an immense relief to Bertie. Slipping her arm through Bertie's, she turned sweetly to Angela and congratulated her on what she had been doing. 'Sweetie-pie, you should have been a blacksmith!' Then, stretching up in search of a kiss from Bertie, she added: 'Now you've gotten yourself an assistant, what say you and I take the rest of the afternoon off?'

Angela did not stay long after Pru and Bertie left. She thanked Sally for the safe return of her bicycle, hoped she would make better use of it another time, and rode quickly off in the direction of Swivenhall.

Not until she had been gone for some time did Sally notice that it was Pru's bicycle she had taken.

17

It was dark when Bertie and Prudence returned to Rose Cottage to collect Pru's bicycle. The lights in the cottage were out and it was difficult to see clearly in the dark. Pru was sure she had left the bicycle leaning on the water butt, which they remembered was near the door to Bertie's workshop. Groping together, they found the water butt, but not the bicycle. Thinking someone might have put it in the shed, Bertie unlocked the door and stepped inside. More groping led him to the bench where he found and lit an oil lamp. This threw light upon the shed, but shed none upon the missing bike.

Pru began to see herself sleeping on the floor, on a bed of straw.

Bertie then remembered where he and Sally used to put their bicycles when they expected to return late from a dance and did not want to disturb her mother and father. He imagined Sally had remembered it too and placed Pru's bike there to save her from waking the family. Swinging the lamp to cast its light across the courtyard, he could see the outline of handlebars between the palings and a large tree by the gate.

'There it is,' said Bertie, and Pru put aside her thoughts of a night in the workshed.

The lamp went out and Bertie groped again for his goodnight kiss. Pru obligingly steered his fingers to her waist and no further illumination was needed.

Steering the bicycle round a tree and through the gate was less exciting but no less successful, and Pru mounted it with a modicum of help from Bertie. Once in the saddle, however, she realized they had made a mistake.

'Sweetie,' she whispered, 'this seat could take a horse: I guess it must be Angie's!'

They searched again, but in vain. If this was indeed Angie's bike, and Pru was convinced it was, there were two possible explanations for it being where they had found it. One was that Angie had taken Pru's by mistake, and the other that she was still around and would soon be needing it. The saddle on Pru's bike was so small that Pru thought it would have done Angie an injury before she got it out of the village, so she was sure that Angie was still around. Not wishing to bump into her in the dark, Bertie suggested they put the bike back against the tree and said he would take Pru home in his partner's limousine. It sounded rather grand at first but when she found this was a hearse she shuddered and demurred.

Bertie assured her it would be all right, that there was no resident corpse, and that he would not be punished for taking it, as Joe had been for borrowing a jeep. Since her idea of a night in the workshed was now dead, Pru relented.

* * *

Digby's reaction in the morning, when Bertie told him of the journey was restrained. 'I don't mind you taking it in daylight, but it's bad for business if you drive it after dark.' Bertie was contrite, if uncomprehending, but he pleaded it was preferable to keeping Prudence out all night.

'She had to be in by midnight or they would have put her on a charge.'

Digby was not familiar with the jargon of the services,

nor the servicing of electric batteries, but he grinned and chuckled as another thought crossed his mind.

'I suppose she didn't suffer a fate *worse* than death?'

Bertie blushed but did not answer.

* * *

Sally was in a fighting mood when she saw Bertie with her father. 'Where did you and Miss Peabody spend the night? If she'd come back for her bicycle she would have seen that Angie took the wrong one by mistake and that I had put Angie's out for her, where I knew you would know where to look for it. As it is still there, you're not going to tell me, are you, that she walked back to camp.'

'No,' said Bertie, 'I drove her there.'

'In that case you had better drive back and take the bicycle with you this time.'

Bertie looked awkwardly at her father and asked his permission to use the vehicle a second time.

Benjamin's mood had improved. 'Of course, my boy, I told you, any time so long as it's daylight and there isn't a body inside!'

Bertie shuddered at the thought and backed the limousine into the yard. As he stepped out to open the gate Sally jumped up into the passenger seat.

'You don't mind if I come with you, I suppose? I should like to visit a friend of mine . . . in bed.'

Their conversation on the way to Swivenhall was cautious and infrequent, but on the way back, after Sally had spent half an hour with Joe, and Bertie had failed to find either Prudence or Angela, it became slanted and hostile.

'If a man has boils on his bottom it means he must sit around too much!'

'In that case, I'm surprised you haven't got boils on the

back of your head because that's where you're talking from!'

'You mind your tongue don't burn a hole in your throat, young lady!'

Sally responded by putting out her tongue in a most unladylike manner. Bertie drove on.

'Is that a Yankee habit, like chewing gum?'

'I don't know what you mean.'

'You didn't use such vulgar expressions before you met that American boy.'

'Talking of vulgar expressions, that just about fits your American girl friend!'

'I find her rather attractive.'

'You would! And doesn't she know it!'

'Well, she's entitled to.'

'Oh! And is she entitled to walk into your bedroom whenever she pleases?'

'She's never been to my bedroom.'

'Well, she walked into Joe's while I was there so she's that sort of person.'

'Oh, I see, it was all right for you to be in Joe's bedroom but vulgar for Pru to be there. That's feminine logic, if you like!'

'I didn't sit on his bed.'

'Daresay you'd rather have slept in it!'

'Now who's being vulgar?'

'Sorry. I thought you still liked a bedtime story.'

'You'd rather stay up all night, of course, and drive home in the morning!'

'Hey! If anyone's been out all night on this road it was you, remember, so I'd be careful what you say. I haven't forgotten the night you went off in a jeep, too proud to know anyone from the village, and came back in the morning with some corny yarn about running out of petrol.'

'We *did* run out of petrol!'

'Then so have I!' Bertie turned off the ignition and folded his arms.

'Turn that key the other way at once and take me home!'

'Not until you've shown me how you dealt with the situation when it happened before.'

'I wouldn't dream of it.'

'Perhaps you dreamed of it then?'

'Bertie Woodfellow, I hate you!'

This was the first time Bertie and Sally had confronted each other in private since they stopped going out together, and it was evident their feelings had far from cooled down. In fact, the temperature inside Digby's limousine was rising above that of the water in the radiator and no amount of re-circulation between the occupants could stop it boiling over.

Red-faced and trembling with indignation, Sally jumped out on to the courtyard when they got back to the cottage and slammed the door. Bertie 'put the buggie to bed' and went quickly in search of her father.

Benjamin was in the shop, surveying the shelves and filling gaps in their collection made by the recent rush in sales.

'Mr Digby, I think it would be better if you found another partner.'

Digby pretended he had misunderstood and said that whatever the views he may have expressed about his wife in fun, he was really rather fond of her.

Deflated, Bertie tried again. 'It's not that I'm ungrateful, but I think it would be better if I left.'

Digby put his hand on his partner's shoulder and bade him sit down.

'Now, lad, just you sit there and take a grip on yourself. Whatever has happened can't be so bad as can't be put right between the two of us. Now then, what's happened?

Have you had an accident?'

'No, sir,'

'Then you've lost something?'

'No. Well not exactly.'

'What do you mean, "not exactly"? Has something been stolen?'

'You could say that, I suppose.'

'Well, for goodness sake, lad, don't talk in riddles. What is it? What have we lost?'

'It's difficult to explain.'

Digby realised he was leaning over Bertie like a schoolmaster, and sat down on the form beside him.

'Well, what say we start at the beginning? You went off this morning to take that Yankee girl's bike back. Then what happened?'

'She wasn't there.'

'You mean we've lost Angela?'

Bertie did his best to explain. He had been unable to find Angela or Pru but had bumped into a fellow called Sam who said he was a friend of theirs. So he had left the bike with Sam and brought Sally home.

'Sally? What was *she* doing there?'

'I took her with me.'

'Oh, I see. Well, that's all right, then. Angie's got her bike back and you . . .'

Ben's hopes were dashed before he could finish the sentence.

'No, you don't see, I'm afraid. Sally and me are all washed up. That's why I can't go on working on her doorstep.'

Digby began a lecture on the tragedy of letting a woman's infidelity wreck a young man's future. 'You've a promising career if you stay in the business. What will you do if you give it up?'

Bertie confessed he had not thought about it yet. All he

knew was that if the morning had been anything to go by the sooner he and Sally got away from each other the better it would be for both of them.

'I suppose I could rent a barn off Mr Coman and build a workshop down there.'

Digby grew serious as he saw the consequences of the breach. 'You realize that if you did that and set up on your own like, you and I would be in competition, cutting each other's throats?'

Bertie did not get the chance to answer, for as Digby dramatized the point by drawing a large sixteenth century sword from his sheath and waving it across his face, the shop door opened and a customer walked in. Converting the gesture into one of salutation, Digby offered the sword for sale and Bertie accepted the opportunity to retreat.

'That's not what I've come for, Ben,' said Reggie Ploughman, one of the hands from Cyrus Galleon's farm. 'I were lookin' for another o' them firescreens, like what I bought back off o' you the last time I was here. We give that one to the wife's sister's girl what's just been married, and now we could do with another one for ourselves, to hide up the hole in the chimney.'

Digby was familiar with the pretence that purchases were for someone in the family when in fact they were being sold to visitors. He looked swiftly round the shelves at his depleted stock and realized that he had nothing suitable to offer in its place.

'Well, I don't reckon it'd matter much if it weren't exactly an antique, so long as it looks like one. There's a right lot o' timber in your yard, Ben, what'd look a lot better beneath my chimney stack than beneath the sods in Mr Harper's cemetery. I'll call again when you've had time to knock one or two up along with the "boxes". Daresay some folk might be right glad o' one o' them screens when they get to where they're a-goin'!'

Bertie had slipped back on hearing Reggie's voice, and he and Digby looked at each other in amazement. It was not the blasphemy, or the thought of misappropriating the timbers that surprised them, nor even the deceit that he was proposing to perpetrate upon his purchasers; but the scope which this opened up for establishing a new and lucrative business caught their imagination. The prospect seemed to cross their minds together and all thought of abandoning the partnership was now forgotten.

18

With six in the family, all living at home, there was no room to spare for Bertie at the Comans'. Nearby, however, in Anvil Lane, Bob Blackett had an empty washhouse attached to his cottage and this he was prepared to lease to Bertie for the equivalent of eight ounces of 'baccy' a week. Situated in a remote part of the village, next to an old forge, it offered Bertie seclusion and the opportunity to add metalwork to his skill as a carpenter.

It also suited Digby to have Bertie working off the premises for, although he felt no impropriety in building cottages and coffins side by side, he thought there might be an outcry if it became known that he was mixing a trade in genuine antiques with one in modern reproductions. With Bertie now working from another bench, and the village well aware of his estrangement from Sally, it would be possible he thought for a steady stream of skilfully produced 'carpentered copies' to find their way on to his shelves alongside the few remaining articles of ancient origin without any suspicion being aroused. Few of the purchasers bothered to ask the age of the articles they bought, or would have known how to assess it for themselves, and the quality of Bertie's craftmanship meant that the customer had little cause for complaint.

Before long, therefore, shelves began to sag again in many a shed and showroom, and Sunday visitors from

Swivenhall went back with their trophies as pleased with themselves as ever. The shop at Digby's again became a warehouse from which villagers renewed their stocks when their own collections ran low. It did not occur to them to question how it was that Digby's stocks never seemed to run out.

Even before the introduction of replicas, Digby had found the new enterprise more lucrative than either of his other occupations. This was just as well, for the death rate in Little Missington had been so low in recent years that had he been obliged to depend for his living on burying the dead, he might have been in danger of going under himself. Instead he was in the happy position of putting back into circulation scores of unsuspected treasures, buried for generations in their owner's ignorance and, by the wealth they generated, he revived many a family which had long been poor.

Riches, however, are relative and some of the villagers were barely better off than if they had given up their glass of ale or pouch of tobacco but, because he had yet to acquire such habits, Bertie amassed what seemed to be a fortune. His partnership with Digby carried with it a share in the business and, with overheads low and custom increasing, business was booming.

The idea of saving for a rainy day in an English climate seemed absurd to Bertie so his response to the new-found wealth he had acquired was to spend it. First he wanted to give some to his widowed mother, who had to be reassured that he had not stolen it. Next he bought himself a suit, a watch and a fountain pen. Later, when Digby declared a bonus, he purchased a rowing boat and told Pru they could use it to go fishing. Then, as trade in the village expanded, and the demand grew for more stock, Bertie realised he would need to employ an assistant.

This was the opportunity for which Gordon Tyler had

been waiting and although it meant that his apprenticeship would be served on a programme of mass production rather than a comprehensive introduction to a craft, he learned much and earned a steady wage. His father, who had worked for Digby on many a job, was pleased to see him following in the family footsteps and glad of his contribution to the family purse. It was never certain whether his father was called 'Old Slatey' because of his skill in the laying of roofs or his habit of living on loans, but Young Slatey was a prudent lad and Bertie feared that if he let him too soon into the secret of what they were doing he might slip off to the anvil and forge himself a coin or two. He, therefore, stuck to the story that what they were doing was repairs and restorations.

* * *

Sally's reaction to Bertie's departure from the cottage was to profess good riddance and pretend that she did not care. Secretly, however, she missed him and the fact that he was not around to be compared unfavourably with Joe meant that she remembered less of his shortcomings and more of his redeeming features.

Not for the first time as a father, Benjamin had found it expedient to tell his daughter half a truth. He told her that Bertie wanted to stand on his own feet and was setting up a rival business with a view to buying himself back into partnership once he had proved he was capable of working on his own. Told in this way Sally felt a flush of admiration for Bertie's courage and initiative, but on reflection she saw it as a proof of his dedication to the past. In contrast, her own aspirations for the future were based increasingly on the visions she had glimpsed in one brief evening of American hospitality. It did not please her to be deployed in the shop now that Bertie was no longer there.

Surrounded by relics and (although she did not know it) replicas of relics, representing several generations in taste and culture, she hated the fustiness of the place and the gloom which hung over it. Every polished piece of brass she would have exchanged for chrome, and every silver candlestick for a tube of fluorescent light.

Benjamin did not tell her the true nature of Bertie's business. He considered it would spoil her skill in salesmanship if she knew that some of the goods she was being called upon to sell, which looked as old as fossils, were in fact as fresh as new-laid eggs, and he felt sure it would strain her sense of loyalty to expect her to keep the truth from Joe once he recovered from his boils.

Cut off from both past and current boy friends, Sally consoled herself with the thought that when Joe made his next visit to the village she would have him to herself. Bertie could do what he liked with Miss Peabody, she did not care, and what the eye did not see the heart would not rage about. With great determination she put both men from her mind and applied herself to a shed full of antiques and the new experience of shop-assisting.

The first thing she did was to rearrange the goods on display. Items of glass, porcelain and chinaware were washed and neatly placed on mats and coloured cloth. Chairs, tables, cabinets and chests were given a new polish and positioned against a background of tapestries and carpets. Paintings and mirrors in their gilded frames were dusted, draped and artistically re-hung. The old shed which had once been filled with winter logs and fishing tackle now had style and the look of a lady's influence.

It was while attending to these transformations that Sally received a visit from Gordon Tyler. She did not know that he had gone to work for Bertie and her first reaction was to treat him as a customer. This illusion he dispelled by telling her he had a cart load of goods to deliver from

Mr Woodfellow. Thinking this might be a practical joke of Bertie's to arouse her curiosity, she assumed indifference and went on with her tidying. After a few minutes, fidgeting from one foot to the other, Tyler asked her where he should put the boxes.

'Wait a minute,' she replied, 'I'm busy.'

'And so am I,' said Tyler, 'I've got ten more o' these to deliver and I hain't got all day to do it in!'

Unused to such bluntness, Sally flicked her duster a little too hard and a glass vase with green pythons wrapped round its stem, crashed to the floor and shattered.

'There, now look what you've made me do!'

'Never mind, Miss,' said the lad, undaunted, 'if we can't repair it we'll make you another one what'll look just as good.'

The revelations which followed this incident gave Sally a bigger shock than the sight of broken glass at her feet. Not because they were more surprising than many of the recent discoveries she had made, but because these had taken her so long to rumble.

Bertie was not expecting a visitor when she called. It was no less of a shock to him to discover that his apprentice was delivering a dozen identical articles to twelve different addresses instead of a set of twelve different objects to each. Without waiting for Sally to finish, he leapt over the bench and tore into the village as fast as his bicycle could carry him.

The boxes which Tyler had delivered to Sally contained carefully packed jewel cases, with initials carved ornately in heart shaped recesses cut in the lids. Inside each case was a neatly fitting tray with small lips at each end for lifting in and out. The interiors were lined with red baize and there were studs around the base to stop the case from scratching whatever it stood upon. Closer scrutiny of the consignment showed that the same initials appeared on all the cases, that every tray had the beading on one side damaged, and that the base stud in one corner of all cases was missing. Sally also noticed that in each case a piece of red baize had curled up and come away from the wood, exposing a mottled green, mould-like underside as if the whole object had been abandoned in a damp place for many years.

On the work bench in front of her, over which Bertie had just vaulted, she caught sight of another such jewelcase. Above it, on a shelf were six more and beside it were pieces of wood cut to the same size, a stencil of the initials she had seen on the lids; chisels, gluepot, wire brush, sandpaper, paints and polish. Something about the one on the bench suggested it was authentic and genuinely old; everything about the others confirmed that they were copies.

Looking further afield, she found another shelf with rows of wrought-iron candlesticks and beneath that a box full of unworn horseshoes. In other parts of the workshop she came upon a pile of oakwood plaques inscribed with verses from the Book of Psalms, a stack of pinewood pipe-racks for screwing to the wall, a collection of needlework boxes on Queen Anne-shaped legs, a column of shallow fruit bowls placed one above the other, a tier of rectangular tea trays, painted on top and felted underneath, a sack of cedarwood joss sticks, and a tub full of birchwood biscuit barrels.

Fascinated by what she saw, Sally explored deeper into the old washhouse and came upon the large copper boiler in which the late Mrs Blackett had cast the weekly wash. Brought up on stories of hidden bodies and buried treasure, she raised the lid expecting to see a human skeleton, real or replicate, or a horde of jewels, removed from their cases like pearls from their oysters, but instead she found an assortment of antiques waiting their turn to be copied. Closing the lid with a sense of disappointment, she stepped back to survey the scene in its entirety, only just beginning to grasp the significance of it all. It was then that she noticed a number of items out of keeping with all else that she had seen.

On the shelf under the bench there was an electric drill and soldering iron, an electric kettle and toaster, a portable radio and a telephone. So this was what her father had meant when he said they were having a new kind of electricity installed at the cottage!

To Sally's credit, her choice of friends had never been determined by their financial circumstances. It was not the money that Bertie was now earning which mattered but the discovery of what he was doing with it gave her much to think about. Far from being imprisoned in the past, as she had imagined him to be judging from his flair for antiquity, Bertie was obviously alive to the benefits of modern science and not afraid to invest his capital in them. This was a very different Bertie from the one she had known so recently. It seemed as if Pru had been good for him after all.

* * *

By the time Bertie caught up with young Tyler he had delivered three more of his consignments, but luckily none of them had been opened and they were all recovered before anyone had noticed the contents.

Sally did not wait for Bertie to return to the workshop but left a note for him which amounted to a statement of her price for silence. 'I will keep your secret,' it said, 'so long as you keep Pru away from my Joe.'

Human nature being what it is, the effect of Sally's undertaking did more to disturb Bertie than to reassure him. No longer could he regard his friendship with Pru as a purely personal pursuit. From now on it would be part of the pay-off to prevent a scandal and the disgrace he would suffer if it became known that his products were counterfeit.

In fairness to Bertie, none of the goods he made was being sold as a period piece or at an unreasonable price: at least not by him. What happened when they took their place in a window beneath an 'Antiques' sign and were sought after by Sunday souvenir hunters was out of his control. Yet he knew he was taking advantage of the demand for anything old, and of the villagers' inexperience and innocence in dealing with things they had until now treated as rubbish. To that extent it troubled his conscience, but not his pocket.

As time went by another aspect of Sally's note stuck fast in Bertie's throat. It was the presumptuous use of the possessive pronoun. '*My* Joe', he muttered every time he thought of it. '*My* Joe, indeed!'

He had to admit he was still fond of Sally and it was not his fault that she had fallen for this American. On the other hand it was her fault that he had taken up with Pru. Much as he liked 'the Peabody Popsie', he would not have been unfaithful to Sally had she not first deserted him. The irony of it now was that in asking him to remain unfaithul, so as to remove a source of rivalry from her path, she was in fact drawing Bertie back to her and upsetting her rival in a quite unintentional way.

While Sally was priding herself on the strength of her position with Joe, Pru was paying another visit to Joe's bedside. This time, however, he was in a Sick Bay at the camp hospital and Pru was obliged to sit at the side of the bed.

'Gee, honey, who'd have thawt all those little bacteria would have wanted to settle . . . where you've got 'em! I sure hope if they ever get in my bloodstream they'll choose a different place to rear their little ones.'

Joe was grateful for her attention but embarrassed by her cheerfulness.

'Guess where I'll be tonight when some pretty little nurse is squirting in your last shot of penicillin for the day? In little old Bertie's boat, pretendin' to catch fish. Won't that be a wow! Don't you wish you'd be there too?'

Joe wished he could be anywhere but where he was.

'I tell you what, honey: if I should catch anything, I'll see that you get it for breakfast.'

He rang for the nurse and asked for a bowl.

* * *

Among those in the village besides Digby who had cause to thank Bertie for starting the antique business was Christopher Hopper and Gertrude, his wife.

Life at the malthouse had been very slow and ordinary for many years, with its annual peak of activity soon after the hops had been gathered, but for much of the year it stood idle. The Hoppers had managed to make a living out of it but to supplement their income they had let out space for storage, and Christopher had supervised the village dances. With the arrival of visitors to look over 'the ruins' or to follow the Sunday pilgrimage, they were not slow to open their doors for the sale of TEAS. The frothy smell of malt, which seemed never to escape, made theirs a popular port of call.

In no sense, however, were the Hoppers a happy family. Chris was a tense man with great energy but little patience, and easily flustered. His wife was a busybody with quick hands and a sharp tongue. They were devoted to each other insofar as each was the centre of the other's life, yet there was no real affection between them. Allan, their son, was the result of their first experience of sharing a bed and although they had not taken to different rooms thereafter, they were never again able to submit to each other without painstaking precautions which created a severe strain on their nervous systems.

Despite the unexpectedness of motherhood, Gertrude had been a good parent and a conscientious housewife. Without many of the labour-saving devices she would have liked to have, she managed to keep the house clean and tidy and was forever nagging her husband for wearing muddy boots in the kitchen and resting dirty clothes on the cushion covers. It was such strictures as these which added to Christopher's tensions and drove him as often from the house as through it.

In retaliation, Christopher often criticized his wife's reluctance to rid herself of anything that was not immediately consumable. The back shed, spare bedroom and loft were littered with unwanted paraphernalia which, in his opinion, should have provided fuel for his ovens or been fed to his compost.

It came as a surprise, therefore, when the tea trade turned to a craze for antiques and the Hoppers found they had in their midst a source of revenue such as few others in the village, apart from Digby, could produce. Gertrude's tendency to hoard had been vindicated.

The day after Bertie left the Digbys for Bob Blackett's washhouse, Christopher called at Rose Cottage with a proposition. Glad as they had been of the money, he said, and ready as they still were to entertain their visitors from overseas, it was not altogether convenient to serve teas in the malthouse. Gertie had been telling him this for some time, he said, but as she had always been rather a discontented woman he had made allowances. Now it had come to the point, he said, that either they would have to give up the teas on Sundays or close down the malthouse.

Digby, whose taste for the end product of which hops was a constituent, regarded the alternative as unthinkable.

'Unless,' and Mr Hopper thumped an eighteenth century writing table, 'unless you can build us an extension.'

Digby fell off the post he was leaning on. Of all potential customers, he would have rated Chris the least likely to commission anything approaching a worthwhile building job. Once, in the past ten years, he had called Digby to the malthouse to repair a hole in the roof, but Digby never imagined the Hoppers would ever have more done to the place than was necessary to stop it falling down.

Realizing that Chris Hopper was quite serious, Digby arranged to go round to the malthouse to measure up and estimate the cost of the project. On the way there it was explained to him that what was wanted was a new outhouse to serve as 'a kind of old world teashop-cum antique shop'. Mrs Hopper had euphemistically described it as 'a sun lounge for Sunday visitors'.

Digby, who had been delighted at the prospect of getting back to his main trade after sundry distractions, saw that what he was being asked to do was not so different from what Bertie was doing in his converted washhouse. They were both employed in producing artificial antiquity and as such would be accessories to the act of selling the buyer short by at least a hundred years.

Two or three days after he started work at the malthouse, Digby was approached by Gertie Hopper when her husband was out of earshot.

'The trouble with Hoppy is that he's too conservative. Can't get him to see that he's out of date. It's taken me years to get him round to the sun lounge idea. I've been at him about it ever since that marvellous summer we had when Allan was born.'

Amused to hear her calling her husband by his nickname, but thinking she was about to run down his character, Digby tried to escape. Gertrude obstructed his exit.

213

'Afore you go, there's somethin' I want you to do for me. Without him knowin', that is.'

Digby was trapped and could only wait for his orders. What Gertie wanted was a washing machine and an electric cooker, only they must not be visible to her visitors or they would spoil the atmosphere.

Mingling in Digby's mind with the impression of great respect for Gertie Hopper was the fear that Vera Digby might get to hear of the idea.

'It's got to be a secret then,' said Digby, 'from everyone?'

'That it has!' said Gertie, and Digby was reassured.

'Ah, but where can we put them,' he asked, suddenly thinking, 'so's they can be used but not be seen?'

Mrs Hopper had it all worked out. The cooker would fit in one compartment of their huge wall oven in the living-room, and the washing machine would go inside the copper boiler in the kitchen. All that Digby had to do was to transport the equipment under cover of some building materials and fit them into position when her husband was not at home.

On his way back from Myrtlesham with two of the most modern domestic appliances wedged in a corner of his lorry, surrounded by bags of cement, bricks and old boards, Digby ran into Christopher Hopper.

It was a gentle collision. Hoppy was backing his vehicle out of the malthouse yard as Digby was slowly turning into it. They got down from their cabins and faced each other in the gateway.

'Ah, just the man I wanted to see,' said Hoppy, and Digby was taken to one side while the two vehicles remained locked together.

'There's something I've been wanting to ask you to do for me, Ben, only I dursn't let Gertie know about it or she'll say it's extravagance. You know that there kitchen range we've got in our living room? Well, there's a lot o' space in that what don't get used, and I've been thinkin' to myself, that would be just the place to hide somethin' you don't want everyone to know about.'

Digby's heart was sinking fast.

'Now I've been looking at some o' them gadgets what the townspeople have been buyin' and, though I don't hold with all of 'em, I reckon we ought not to deprive ourselves of what's good just because it's modern. Only, seein' as people expect us to be old-fashioned, we need to keep up appearances.'

Digby raised his eyebrows, waiting for the crunch.

'What do you want me to do, Chris, buy Gertie a washing machine?'

'Good lord no, man, she'd never use one o' them! What I want you to fix alongside that oven, behind the door what shuts into the wall, is a shortwave radio receiver.'

19

For dereliction of duty while in possession of a jeep, Joe had spent twenty-eight days confined to his camp. For treatment of boils on his bottom the punishment was nearly twice as long. For four weeks he was confined to bed, first in his corporal's quarters and then in the hospital ward, after which he was stranded for three more weeks recuperating, unable to leave the camp on account of being unfit to saddle a bicycle.

Cycling to Little Missington being out of the question, and the loan of a jeep forbidden, Joe's only means of communicating with Sally was the mail. Since her disastrous and quarrelsome journey with Bertie, Sally had made no further expeditions to Swivenhall but she had written regularly and received replies by return of post.

One morning during the fourth week of Joe's confinement, Wilfred Stamp arrived at Digby's cottage with a letter addressed to 'Miss Sally B. Digby'. She was there at the door to accept it.

'What do the 'B' stand for, Miss Sally?' he asked.

'Honey,' she said, and rushed away to open the envelope. Wilfred stood for a moment on the doorstep then went on with his deliveries, murmuring what a nice girl she used to be before she started mixing with Americans.

It was Joe's joke and Sally was rather proud of it.

'Guess I can call you what I like *inside* the envelope,'

he had written in one of his earlier letters, 'but outside it wouldn't do for everyone to know what I think of you. And since I want to call you ''honey'', honey, I guess I'll just have to let the ''B'' do it for me!'

After brooding on what he took to be a snub, Wilfred attached quite a different word to the initial.

It was on page seven of the letter that Sally excitedly started reading aloud to her mother, taking care to censor such words and passages as she thought might offend or be misunderstood.

'. . . and what do you think (sugar)? As if I haven't been idle (bummed around) long enough! Next month I get another ten days off (gash) when the squadron goes on holiday (furlough). Suppose I ought to look up a few more historical relics, seeing as the folks back home keep asking me about them. But, honest, (sweetie), now that I've met you and your folks I just don't want to look any further. . . .'

Sally read the sentence again to herself but seeing that her mother had not registered any disapproval she continued aloud.

'. . . All the same, (angel), if you think I should, please give me some suggestions — about where to go, I mean. And, (honey), don't get me wrong, of course, but if there's any chance of you coming with me to look for such places, that would be just swell.'

Vera inadvertently put some marmalade into her tea cup.

'Mummy, wouldn't it be better if we asked him to stay here with us?'

Her mother swallowed a chunk of orange peel and choked.

'Well, there's no need to get upset about it! I just thought you might prefer that to my going away, that's all.'

With which retort Sally retired to her room and Mrs Digby went in search of Benjamin.

* * *

In Anvil Lane, a few yards from the Blackett's washhouse, Bertie was forging ahead with some early Victorian lamp brackets, and Gordon Tyler was doing penance for his recent carelessness by working the bellows over the furnace. Between the blows of his hammer on the anvil Bertie could hear the ringing of a bell. It came from the workshop.

'Would that be the television, Mr Woodfellow?' Gordon asked.

Bertie explained the difference between telephone and television and went hurriedly to the shelf beneath his workbench where he lifted up the receiver and said 'hallo'.

It was fortunate indeed that there *was* a difference between telephone and television because, unknown to him, the caller at the other end of the line was standing beside an excitable young lady.

'What number is that?'

'Myrtlesham two, eight; who do you want?'

'Is that you, Bertie?'

'Yes, is that Mr Digby?'

'Yes.'

'Sorry, Boss, I didn't recognize your voice.'

'All right, my boy, I didn't recognize yours either.'

Angela was fascinated by the formality of the call and fancied the speakers must have supposed they were calling to each other across a room. She had been accustomed to a quick 'hiya' as a recognition signal and thought it was only the Chinese who procrastinated before getting down to business.

'Bertie, there's a customer here who remembers you and wants to take your photograph. Says she could come down and take it where you are, but I said as you'd not be altogether respectable right now seein' as you're workin' on an old furnace and like as not haven't got much on. Be a good lad and put your shirt on and come up to the cottage as soon as you can.'

'Yeah, but who is it? It's not Pru, is it?'

'Here you are, lad, you talk to her yourself and tell her you're on your way.'

Bertie did, and a few minutes later he was.

* * *

If anyone had told him he would ever hurry himself to meet Angela Cotton, Bertie would have said they needed their head examined. Yet the idea of entertaining her in his breakaway workshop, even with young Tyler as a chaperon, so appalled him that he made for Digby's without a second being wasted.

It was not a charitable sentiment to regard an unattractive person as repulsive, and Bertie could think of many young women in the village who did not appeal to him but from whom he would not have hurried to escape. Angela, however, had an effect on him which normally urged him to rush as far away from her as possible. The fact which compelled him to overcome this inclination was simply that she was the last person he wanted to discover what he was doing at his new address.

Known to himself and Digby as The Forgery, Bob Blackett's washhouse was conveniently inconspicuous beside the smithy, but it became almost as important to keep people away from it, as it had been to keep them out of the meadow when he was working on 'the ruin'. As far as Pru was concerned, he was busy on 'an inside job' and unobtainable during working hours. Their usual rendezvous was on, or under, the village bridge, according to whether it was wet or fine.

The prospect of Angela trying to track him down had never occurred to him for he assumed that by now she had accepted the fact that he and Pru were going steady.

Digby's dilemma when he realized how intent she was upon finding Bertie was solved by the use of the telephone, which he had had installed so that he could talk to his partner without betraying his whereabouts or seeming to be associated with what he was doing.

So, the instrument which had revolutionized communications at the end of the nineteenth century brought Bertie back to his old bench at Digby's cottage and in touch with some events in the New World in the middle of the twentieth century.

'I'm glad you've come, lad,' said Digby as Bertie panted in through the gate. 'Our young friend here's burstin' to tell you the news, and I shouldn't be surprised if you didn't come apart at the seams yourself when you hear it!'

'Hi, Bertie! Oh you beautiful boy, am I glad I met you! Now stay where you are! No, don't move, I must get the shop in, too.'

Bertie recovered his breath while Angela adjusted her camera.

'In two week's time you'll be the talk of Baltimore. And this li'll hamlet you live in will be famous. Maybe folks will come from all over the world and ask to speak to Bertie Woodfellow.'

'OK, so I'm dumb! Now, for Pete's sake, Angie, what's it all about?'

'Don't move! There, hold it! That's great! Wow. Say, Bertie, I sure am grateful!'

'Angie, would you mind telling me what it's all about?' Bertie was raising his voice.

'Sit down, I guess you're excited. I was, I can tell you. When I read my old man's letter, I couldn't believe it. Do you know the first thing I did? I went right out and splashed my face with water, just to make sure I was quite awake.'

Digby passed over the handbowl but Bertie ignored it.

'Do you remember that first night I came to your store?

I asked if you sold souv'neers and you said come in and look round.'

A shiver trickled down Bertie's back as he recalled the invitation.

'D'you know, I nearly didn't buy a thing that night. I was so thrilled at meeting a real English country boy I didn't see a piece you showed me. But I could have listened to your voice all night. You had only to say "how about it?" and I was sold on whatever you offered. You could have filled me up with trash and I would have hugged it!'

Digby slipped quietly away and walked round the garden.

Bertie blushed.

'But you *dear* boy, you didn't take advantage of me, did you? You talked me into taking two of the cutest little boxes I'd ever seen. One was for packing pearls and diamonds and things one dreams about, and the other was for some stuff called snuff which I'd never heard of.'

A sneeze from the bottom of the garden suggested her voice was carrying well.

'I guess I felt sort of stupid when I sent them home, because I knew Mamma hadn't got any jewels, and whatever that snuff stuff was I couldn't imagine Pa ever had any. So I just said put them on the bureau or under the bed and I hope they bring you luck! . . . And, boy, did they do that!'

Bertie's attention had wandered again to the size of her hips and was taking in the shape of her legs when she came to the point.

'According to Pa they were on the bureau when Professor Chippendale went round for a cocktail. Pa is always entertaining someone from the Johns Hopkins, that's our University, by the way, it's a sort of compensation complex for not having been to College himself. Well, evidently, this Professor Chippendale specializes in English history:

221

don't ask me why, unless it's because we don't have enough of our own to go round! When he set eyes on those boxes he just picked them up and hollered!'

'Bertie,' she continued, 'did you know they had once belonged to Lord Nelson? Well I guess you didn't or you wouldn't have sold them to me for a couple of bucks. I ought not to tell you this, because you may be mad at me for making a profit, but the Professor said they were priceless, and he offered Pa a hundred dollars for them. But that's not all. He said they threw a new light on what was known about the Nelson family and someone ought to explore the place where they were found. He asked Pa to get me to post him some pictures and said he'll raise funds to send some students here next summer. Won't that be just wonderful?'

Bertie's patriotic spirit swelled with indignation but before he could express himself Digby returned from the garden and offered to take his photograph with Angela if she would show him how to use her camera. It was as near as Bertie ever came to striking Benjamin.

'Say, that would be super! Could you get the shop sign in too? Then the Professor might get it published in the Baltimore noos-paper.'

Digby positioned them so that Angela's head was captioned with all but the last letter of ANTIQUES, and Bertie was sandwiched between her and the water butt. The shutter had just opened and closed on the scene when Vera Digby came out to confront her husband.

The sight of Bertie and Angela posing together made her forget for a moment what she had come to tell him.

'Well I never,' she said, scowling at Bertie, 'you certainly change your partners more often than young men did in *my* day!'

There was a lot of explaining to do after Angela had left. Bertie had to defend his reputation with Mrs Digby and

Benjamin had to explain his reason for playing along with Angela. Vera remembered what Sally had told her about her letter from Joe and the commotion brought Sally herself out of hiding to repeat her ultimatum.

Digby decided to settle the family squabble first. 'If Sally wants to have the American here to stay, that's all right with me, so long as she doesn't expect us to entertain him.'

The two women retired to the kitchen and Digby turned to Bertie.

'It's all a matter of compromise,' he said, and Bertie thought for a moment he was laying a plot to catch his daughter in an act of impropriety.

'If I'd said he couldn't come, Sally would have sulked and I should never have heard the last of it from her mother. Besides, there's an old saying that the more you see of someone you don't really know, the less you find you want to know about them. Familiarity breeds contempt, they say, and I reckon that's how it will be with Sal. But that's not what I wanted to talk to you about . . .' Digby led his partner to their old workshop.

'I don't mind telling you,' said Digby from the privacy of his shed, 'I'm getting quite fond of that girl, Angie. She were our first customer, remember, and she's what I'd call reliable. When she said she'd come back for more, by Jove she did! And look what she brought *you*! I can't say as I've ever heard you complain about the young lady with the pony-tail! Now, the point really is this: if those boxes she bought *were* worth all that much there might be a few more where they came from.'

Bertie thought he could see a proposition coming for more work at The Forgery, but again he was wrong.

'I daresay we'll not be the only ones to think like that. Once that Professor chap starts writin' in the papers, and sending his students over here to snoop on our historical connections, we'll be overrun with treasure hunters. Look how many came to see the ruin once they wrote about it in their local rag. Mark my words, Bertie, any people who could go rushin' after gold the way those Yankees did won't leave us alone if they think we're sitting on something that's worth having.'

Bertie was impressed and Digby went on to discuss what they ought to do about it.

'Y'know, if we're going to have "that guy Joe" around here next month, we'll have to work fast!'

. . . There may have been a Freudian connection, for he pronounced the word as if to rhyme with the first syllable of 'chastity'.

224

20

August had always been Sally's favourite month. For years it had meant holidays from school and warm summer days when she could wear her pretty cotton frocks and watch the harvest being gathered and lie in the haystacks after the horses had gone home. Last year she had helped Bertie and her father build the ruin on Galleon's Meadow, and that had led to her meeting and making friends with Joe. Now she was going to entertain him for ten glorious days and the amount of energy that went into her preparations was quite out of proportion to the length of his stay.

Her father and Bertie were busy, too.

Sally asked her father's permission to drive into Swivenhall so that she could bring Joe back in the lorry. She wanted to spare him the agony of bumping along those roads on a bicycle. Digby had no wish to make the journey himself and readily agreed. Before leaving Sally put so many cushions in the cabin that she could hardly see out of the nearside window, but ignored Bertie's taunt that she should take the hearse in case he took a turn for the worse.

On setting off she was so excited that she failed to see a notice tied to the tailboard and was unaware of it until one of the sentries pointed it out to her when she drew up at the camp gates. It said:

BLONDE DISPOSAL: KEEP CLEAR

225

She knew that only Bertie would have thought of that. What was more maddening, however, than being laughed at by the sentries was being reminded of Bertie at that moment. She would have liked to have left the notice where it was and to have driven out of the camp with Pru in the back, but that was not what she had come for and she hastened to remove the notice before Joe appeared.

Unlike her last drive back from Swivenhall in the lorry, when Bertie was with her, the journey with Joe was uneventful, except that it conjured up memories of their ill-fated ride in a jeep and the very long walk which followed.

Benjamin was not at home to greet them when they arrived but Vera shook Joe by the hand and said she hoped he would be comfortable. She had made arrangements, she said, for him to sleep in Sally's room, but before Joe could get any wrong ideas about that she made it clear that Sally would be sleeping with her in Digby's place. Her father, said Vera, would be sleeping on a camp-bed in the living-room which they would put up after everyone else had gone upstairs for the night. The matron of a reform school could not have made better provision for the maintenance of propriety.

Sally was embarrassed at the way her mother had explained it all, and Joe was full of apologies for the inconvenience he was causing, but the return of Benjamin in a distinctly good humour put a stop to their discomfort and everyone sat down to tea in the best of spirits.

Joe gave Mrs Digby a bottle of perfume and Benjamin a pipe, but he held back his present for Sally until they were on their own. Conscious that her mother and father were curious to know what it was he had brought their daughter, he changed the subject by taking from his pocket a letter which he said had arrived that morning from Baltimore.

Enclosed with the letter was a cutting from the local newspaper which contained a report on Professor Chippendale's 'discovery', an almost unrecognizable photograph of Bertie and Angela, and a picture of the jewel box with a large ring round the initials: 'H.N.'.

The newspaper article made it clear that the Professor had based his identification of the ownership of the box on those initials together with the fact that they were inlaid in pine on a mahogany lid. Pine and mahogany, according to the Professor, were known to have been Horatio Nelson's favourite woods. Digby thought about this for some time and then remembered that Hector Nightingale's paternal grandmother had been a Hilary and there had always been a pine plantation behind their house. Moreover the Nightingale family had all been carpenters. He made a mental note to see Hector next morning and warn him to be careful what he said when the Professor came over.

After tea Digby took his usual place in the armchair and began to try out his new pipe. Vera and Sally cleared the table and went out to wash up, urging Joe to take the other chair nearer the window and to make himself at home. Paying more regard to the second part of what was said, Joe sat down on the bench seat under the window, leaving the second armchair for Mrs Digby when she returned.

Digby sat drawing at his pipe and twisting his lips into various shapes which Joe hoped were expressions of satisfaction and not of complaint.

When Sally returned she seemed surprised at the silence and asked Joe if he was all right.

'Wouldn't you rather sit in the armchair?' she asked.

'No, I've left that for your mother,' he replied and Sally admired his courtesy.

When Mrs Digby returned, however, she expressed alarm at where Joe was sitting. 'I shouldn't sit there,' she said, 'it gets rather hot by the window.'

227

'Yeah, I guess it is kind o' warm, but I surmised that was because I'm a bit more sensitive around those parts than I used to be.'

Digby noticed it was raining on the other side of the window. 'Excuse me a minute, I've just thought of something that needs attendin' to in the washhouse'.

* * *

'When did you turn the hot water on?' Digby asked his wife after the rain had stopped and Sally had taken Joe for a walk.

'When I did the washin' up, that's when.'

'Well I must have opened the valve on the radiator instead of turning it off. No wonder the lad had a warm reception! Mind you, it would have been worse if he'd seen the radiator before I covered it over.'

* * *

Joe slept badly on his first night at the cottage, despite the trouble Sally and her mother had taken to make him comfortable. In the first place, he had never slept in a four-poster bed with a canopy on top. It gave him claustrophobia and the feather mattress made him sweat. The canopy was a last minute creation designed to give credence to the idea that everything about the cottage was old. It took no account of the size of the room and made little allowance for ventilation. He wondered if there were mosquitoes in the village.

Another reason why Joe found it difficult to sleep was that he knew the privy was downstairs and across the yard and to get there he would have to pass and probably wake his host. The idea of using what was under the bed was simply out of the question.

In all, he was glad when the morning came.

Returning from across the yard, much freshened by the early morning breeze, all set to perform his ablutions at the wash table in his bedroom, he noticed Digby slipping out of a small closet off the landing at the top of the stairs. This had been described to him the night before as 'the study' and was passed over on his conducted tour of the cottage.

In his hurry to escape notice, Digby had left the door ajar and Joe could not resist the temptation as he passed to look inside. Against the far wall there was a low oak chest over which hung what appeared to be the largest cuckoo clock he had ever seen. Behind the door was a neat but roughly made chest-high cabinet over which were mounted, attached to the wall, two chromium plated candlesticks. The odd thing about the candlesticks was that they had large wing nuts at the base and gave the impression of inverted water taps.

There was little other furniture in the room and Joe wondered what it was that Digby studied there.

He was about to resume his walk to the bedroom when he noticed that the cuckoo clock had stopped. Checking the time against his own watch he re-set the hands of the clock and took hold of the pendulum which he concluded had reached the end of its traverse. Instead of mechanical noises accompanying the pull, as when most clocks are rewound, there was a familiar hydraulic flushing sound which started where the cuckoo should have been and finished up at the bottom of the oak chest.

Joe thought perhaps he had not slept so badly after all and that he was still in the middle of a dream.

* * *

Sally's expression at breakfast suggested she had not been

sleeping well either. By the time Joe sat down to join her he had recovered and was raring to go on the first full day of his furlough.

'It sure is good of your Ma and Pa to let me stay here in your home like this. I would probably have gone to some God-awful hotel in the sticks and not spoken to a soul. Where do we go from here, honey? I've got ten days to see the whole of Little Miss'n'ton and I don't want to miss an inch of it.'

Digby's new pipe made rather a lot of smoke.

* * *

They began with a visit to the General Stores in which Frank Morse ran the Post Office and Madeline, his wife, looked after the groceries, haberdashery, perfumes and toiletry, hardware and babyclothes. Over the door a dirty strip of varnished metal announced that they were licenced to sell stamps, and a red box in the wall under the shop window bearing the insignia of Queen Victoria was opened once a day for those who used them.

The shop sign hung from a bracket fixed between the bedroom windows and ever since Sally could remember had said:

OPEN DAILY 10 - 6

To Sally's surprise this had been overpainted and the sign now read:

GENERAL STORES
OPENED 1066

They went inside.

Sally noticed the sign on the grocery counter which used

to say NEW-LAID EGGS now said simply EGGS, and the one by the milk churn which used to say FRESH CREAM now said WHEY. New potatoes were not in season.

Joe bought some stamps and Sally looked to see if they bore the head of Queen Victoria. They did not, but when Joe asked the postmaster if his letter could go express Frank told him, 'That'll be another sixpence ... and Wilfred'll take it to the General when he goes into market this afternoon.' Joe had a vision of Britain in the hands of the army and of this being one of the rebel outposts he had stumbled on.

They moved on to the upper end of the village, passing the Coach and Horses where Ted Brewer was rolling barrels across the yard from a horse-drawn dray.

'I guess it's not so long since coachmen used to drive in there and change their horses. That sure was the way to travel! Maybe it wasn't as fast as an automobile but I bet it was more exciting.'

Sally wondered if he was right. From what she had heard of the old coachmen they probably made the journey to Puddlethorpe in less time than it now took a motorist. Joe seemed to sense her thoughts, for he added, 'I don't want to be rude, honey, but I doubt if folks who sat in those old-fashioned coaches were any more uncomfortable than I was riding through here on the seat of a bicycle.' In that moment Sally felt very close to Joe and it was easy for her to ask him about the condition of his boils.

'Sweetie, it wasn't the pain that hurt so much, though that was bad enough; it was the goddam humiliation of all those females peering inside my pants every few minutes!'

Sally said she understood but thought nurses were pretty indifferent to that sort of thing. 'Yeah, they sure were pretty, but I wouldn't say they were all that indifferent!'

Sally changed the subject.

Beyond the church, just short of the bridge that crossed the river marking the parish boundary, was Sam Waterman's boathouse. Next to the sheds, where Sam had been building boats since his father taught him the trade over fifty years ago, there was a stretch of open land between the road and river on which travellers used to tether their horses and leave their traps while they did business in the village. A stone trough had stood against one of these sheds for as long as Sam could remember and rainwater ran into it from gutters on the boathouse roof. Whenever it dried up Sam would fill it from the river. With the coming of the motor car some drivers, out of force of habit, parked where they once would have tethered and Sam in his enterprising youth saw the advantage of offering them the equivalent to what had been provided for the horse.

He had a petrol pump installed beside the trough and turned the shed adjacent to it into a service station. The service was limited to the repair of punctures and the sale of a few spares, but this was often enough to save the vehicle from having to be towed into Myrtlesham.

At the time it was a bold stroke of business but, for reasons which should now be clear, it was much resented in the village.

All this was being explained to Joe as they approached.

It was something of a let-down when they arrived to find only the trough where Sally had described it. Where Sally had expected a pump she could only see a large plinth on which was inscribed:-

MYRTLESHAM 5 MILES
PUDDLETHORPE 6 MILES

In the rush to conceal things which were alien to the age

232

they were trying to preserve, suggestions had been considered for turning the pump into a tombstone, a totem-pole and a war memorial, but it was Sam's idea to make it look like a milestone.

Joe accepted the absence of a pump as a natural consequence of the lack of traffic. It was, to him, a simple case of the inverse ratio of supply and demand. From the number of vehicles he had seen passing through the village he doubted if enough petrol would be sold to pay for the power needed to pump it from the tank.

Sally was awkwardly trying to apologize, but Joe would not hear of it. 'Don't let that upset you, honey. We don't have petrol pumps in the States either.'

'You don't?' said Sally, momentarily off-guard.

'No sir,' said Joe with a grin, 'We fill 'em up with gasoline!'

Playfully she poked her elbow into his ribs. He responded defensively, ran to the water's edge and leapt into a boat which Sam was just mooring up to a bollard.

'Woa there! What's a-goin' on? What d'you think you're a-doin' of?' Sam let go of the rope and was about to round on his stowaway when Sally came running after him.

'It's all right, Uncle Sam, he was running away from *me*... but he's a friend of mine.'

Sam struggled to recover the rope and perceive the logic.

'Did you say "Uncle Sam"? Well, what do you know? Wait till I tell 'em back home about that!'

Sam recognized the accent but missed the allusion. 'I never did see a Yankee 'less he were runnin' somewhere!' Joe was far too engaged with what he saw inside the boat to be concerned with what was being said of him on the bank. Too long to be a dinghy, and too broad to be a skiff, he guessed it was what they called a rowing boat, but not until he looked at the bows did he think of it as anything more than a river craft. Then the vast upswept curve

233

projecting forward, with a carved and coloured figurehead, reminded him of drawings he had seen of Viking ships. In his imagination he could see Sam stepping ashore from some romantic voyage from across the sea.

'Tell your father there's a good pike just short o' the bridge if he wants it. It came clean out o' the water as I passed it. And tell him, there's another little job I'd like him to do for me, if he would,' he added in a confidential tone.

Sally seized on the word 'another' and the mystery of the missing petrol pump was solved. She knew now what her father and Bertie had been doing in the past two weeks and realized that the preparations for Joe's visit had gone far beyond refurnishing a room or two in their cottage. The pretence of age, to which she had been a party in more than one instance, had captured the imagination of several villagers who had run out of the genuine article and those, like the Morses, who never had any to offer. Acceptance of the ruin had been slow and dubious, and few in the village really believed in its miraculous conception, but the visitors who came to see it were real enough and their interest in buying souvenirs to take home had led to a rich trade in bygones, bric-à-brac and antiques. To keep up supplies when they ran short Bertie's mass produced reproductions had bridged a gap but the latest development, brought about by the need to deceive their 'special visitor', succeeded in going much further. It not only covered up some of the more recent adornments and blemishes of modern society that had crept into the village but it opened up a vast new business in restoration and replacement which 'Digby and Woodfellow' were well equipped and ready to exploit.

Joe was reluctant to leave Sam Waterman's boatyard and by the time Sally succeeded in dragging him away he was getting along well with Sam. What Sam did not know about Viking ships Joe did, and by carefully steering the conversation Sam managed to add much to his knowledge of them.

'So long, Uncle Sam,' said Joe as they left, 'and thanks for the look around.'

'You're welcome!' said Sam, and hurried to his workbench to make a note of what he had learned from Joe. It would come in useful when showing other visitors around the yard on future occasions.

Making their way back to the cottage for lunch, Sally decided to catch up on time lost at the boatyard by taking a short cut through one of the narrow lanes known locally as a loke. Finding himself enclosed by vegetation, and out of sight of even the grazing livestock in neighbouring fields, Joe mistook Sally's motive for one of emotion and drew her to him in a warm embrace. Surprised, but not offended, she offered no resistance yet for the first time in their relationship felt that their outlook on life was not so harmonious. Opening her eyes while their lips were still together she liked him just as much to look at, and the gentleness with which he held her roused her more than had he squeezed, but the readiness with which he had swallowed one deception after another, and the greed with which he liked to wallow in the past, made her doubt the bond that held them together. She saw him now against a background vastly different from the glitter of that Swivenhall ballroom.

* * *

Next day she avoided the loke and took Joe back for his lunch along more inhabited lanes.

Digby was descending a ladder placed against a chimney breast when they passed the malthouse. As Joe looked up he could see what reminded him of an aerial like he'd seen above their wireless station at the Camp. Only theirs didn't have letters on and, besides, Sally had told him this was where they made malt for the beer and he knew they didn't need signal equipment for doing that.

Fixed to the chimney, horizontally were two parallel metal rods held together in the shape of an H, the ends of which were marked 'N' and 'S', and the centre bar 'E' and 'W'.

Digby decided to explain.

It was a very old windvane, he told Joe, and the reason why it had two arms pointing north and south was 'on account of the prevailing wind coming more often from that direction than from the east or west.' Sally gasped at this whopper of a tale, but Joe was visibly impressed.

Digby removed the ladder from the wall and as he did so he accidentally knocked a piece of ironwork from the masonry, thereby adding considerably to the age of the building. Passers-by could now see it was ERECTED IN 842.

* * *

Sally took care to keep Joe away from the malthouse for the rest of his stay and saw to it that he had plenty of countryside to occupy his attention in preference to the changing face of what had been built upon it. With help from the Byfield family she arranged for him to spend a day in the harvest field but, as it happened, she was taking him from the frying pan and plunging him into the fire.

Hector Byfield was another of Cyrus Galleon's farmhands and Lilian, his daughter, had been a classmate of Sally's at school. It was not difficult, therefore, to get Lilian to persuade her father to look after Joe for the day in return for a flask of ale. Seeing that Cyrus and Benjamin were such good friends, it did not seem necessary to ask the farmer's permission to allow a spectator on the field. Mrs Digby packed Joe a box full of brown bread and butter, a boiled egg, banana and a bottle of beer, typical of the harvester's lunch and known in the neighbourhood as the 'B' ration.

Sally accompanied Joe to the field in which she had been told they would be cutting the corn and promised to return at nightfall.

'Now mind you bring home a rabbit,' she told him 'else we mayn't have any dinner tomorrow.' It was meant as a joke but Joe was aware that meat was still rationed in England and he did not mean to let them down. He went off with Hector to the far end of the field and fell in behind the horses.

He stared at the beasts and then at the barley and watched the blades of the cutter tearing the crop out of the ground and casting it to one side with careless and automatic abandon. He might have been standing in the mid-West of America in the middle of the nineteenth century.

'Do y' mean y' still stack that stuff by hand?' he called out above the noise of the machinery, trying to keep up with the horses.

'Well, it don't stand up on its own!' said Hector, wrapping his arms round another load which had just spewed out of the cutter.

Joe stood back to admire the 'stook' that Hector and two other farmhands were making. As he did so a very frightened rabbit made a dash for the ditch behind them, and asylum in a neighbouring field. By the time Joe had gathered his wits it was through his legs and into the hedge. 'Did y' get him?' asked Hector, knowing well that he didn't.

'Gee, I didn't see him till he almost knocked me down!'

'You want to hit 'em on the back of the neck, boy, that's how to kill 'em. Or else, pick 'em up by the back legs and crack 'em like a whip. They 'on't get away if y' do that to 'em!'

Joe winced, but just then another inmate abandoned its home in the corn. Thinking it was making for the same haven as its predecessor, Joe flung himself in that direction. Even before he had landed, however, the rabbit had altered course and was heading back to the corn. Joe picked himself up and ran after it, only to see it change its mind again and race for the ditch. Passing within a yard of his foot, Joe lunged at it with his stick but stumbled over some stubble and struck his shins instead of the rabbit.

By now the rabbit was well clear of its pursuer, but Joe was incensed at the way it had made him look foolish. With a great rush forward he sped after the animal and leapt over a five-barred gate as the rabbit went underneath. Into the next field they ran together and out at the far end into a third.

'Bang!' went a gun, and Joe nearly jumped out of his skin — the very fate that awaited the rabbit.

'What do you mean by trespassing on my land?'

The voice, like the gun, sounded very close and fierce and Joe looked up to see a red-faced figure in gum boots, duffle jacket and deer stalker hat brandishing what looked like a medieval blunderbuss.

'Trespassing? Yeah, I guess I was. But so was *that*!'

Cyrus looked at the rabbit, which had paid the ultimate penalty, and was so astonished at his marksmanship that he forgot for a moment he had just acquired a prisoner. This being his first encounter with Joe he did not recognize him as the Digbys' guest. He had no doubt, however, about the origin of the accent and that was enough to justify his capture.

238

'You'd better come along o' me, m'lad; I've got a special way o' dealing with poachers so's they don't come back a second time!'

* * *

Os Lawless was cleaning his bicycle when Cyrus called.

'Where be the culprit now, then? Did he get away?'

'No,' said Cyrus, 'he's locked up with the chicks — cackling like hell! And what's worse,' he added, 'cackling with a foreign accent.'

Oswald was quite nice about it when he called on the Digbys later that evening.

'The gen'l'man gave 'is name as Busman or Truckman, or somethin' like that. Said he was stayin' at this address. Of course, I had to ask, because it's me duty to check on everything, but I wouldn't expect you, Ben, to be harbourin' an undesirable alien.'

Sally was more hurt at Joe being called an alien than at the thought of his being held in custody, though had she known the ordeal he was undergoing at the hands of Cyrus and his chickens she might have wished him back in Baltimore. As it was, his return to the cottage that night had to wait until Digby had personally visited the policeman's house and vouched for Joe's identity, and Cyrus had given an undertaking not to proceed with his charge of trespass.

Oswald and Cyrus apologized to Digby for the trouble he had been caused and told Joe he was lucky to have a man like Mr Digby to speak up for him. There was a time, they told him, not so long ago, when men were hanged for stealing livestock from a farmer's land.

Joe wondered, for once, if his admiration for the English and their glorious past had been, perhaps, a little misplaced but, back in the warmth of Digby's cottage with Sally at one knee and the cat at the other, and with Mrs Digby purring attention and Benjamin puffing at his newly acquired pipe, he quickly forgot he had ever doubted their kindness and marvelled again at the magic of Little Missington.

21

On the day after Joe's adventure with the rabbit the story was all over Little Missington that Digby's American visitor had been taken into custody. The number of variations on the rumour of what had been the charge was as large as the number of those who recounted it. One of the most persistent and to some extent plausible explanations was that Bertie had contrived to get him locked up in retaliation for his cutting in on Sally. Remembering Sally's threat to expose the secrets of 'The Forgery' unless he helped to keep Pru from cutting in on Joe, Bertie recognized the irony of the tale and realized it would have made his secret safer if Joe had been kept in custody. But he knew Joe had been released and that renewed vigilance would be needed to keep him and Pru apart.

There was only one place in the village where Bertie felt certain Sally would not take Joe and that was the Coach and Horses. This, then, was the obvious refuge to which he and Pru could retreat.

Pru had never been in a country pub before and everything about it fascinated her, from the sawdust on the floor to the framed fish on the wall, the logwood fire in the grate to the hardwood benches round the bar, the low beams in the ceiling to the trapdoor over the cellar. Viewed from the other side of the threshold it was equally true that Pru fascinated all who beheld her. There were few in the Coach and Horses that evening when she and Bertie entered who had ever seen anything like Pru before.

Tied at the back of her head in the style of a pony-tail, her long blonde hair hung down below her shoulders and across the bright red stitches of her polo neck sweater like a hard trail in the hot sands of a fiery desert. Following the trail with burning eyes, her admirers gasped and perspired, and their gaze fell on prominences beneath her pullover which were talking points in the village for weeks to come. The lower half of her body was closely draped in tight white trousers and underslung with shapely ankles set in a pair of soft blue sandals.

The effect reminded Ted of the tricolour and the gay young French girls he had seen on his way to the front in 1917. He began to whistle 'Mademoiselle from Armentiers'. Others were less tuneful — they just whistled. There was silence, however, when the lady spoke and no mistaking that her accent had crossed more water than the English Channel.

'Sweetie-pie! You didn't tell me it would be like this. Why this is cute. I kind of expected something more like a ... a henhouse, only without any hens!'

For a non-regular customer Bertie found himself being treated like an old reveller and surrounded by more drinks than he cared to consume. Not so Pru, however, for her capacity for 'highballs' was virtually unlimited and her response to flattery infinite. When Bertie suggested they ought to go for a walk before their legs began to fail them Pru looked towards her sandals and judged from the reaction of those around her that *her* legs were in no danger of letting her down.

Sensing it was time to call a round, Pru took from her pocket a small pink purse and offered to buy everybody a drink. Never in all his experience as a publican had Ted Brewer ever seen so many seasoned scavengers rush to put a purse back in anybody's pocket!

The most dreaded moment at any party is when the inveterate bore steps forward to sing a song, or tell a story, or show off a trick that has long gone stale. The moment he saw Jack Thatcher step up to the bar Ted knew something dreadful was about to happen. Thatchers do not use bricks, but Jack was adept at dropping them. Staggering clumsily to collect his glass, he steadied himself on Pru's shoulder.

'You be an American girl, b'aint you?'

'Sure.'

'And you'd know that American boy, what the Digby girl's taken a fancy to …?'

Pru was not sure for a moment who 'the Digby girl' was, but the look on Bertie's face reminded her. 'Joe Buckman? Why sure I know the guy.'

'I thought you did when you talked about a henhouse. I said to Fred, here, that young woman's talkin' about that American boy what got put in with the chickens for rabbitin' in one of old Cyrus's medders.'

It made little sense to Pru at first, but slowly it seeped through that they were making fun of Joe. The President of the United States could not have displayed more patriotism in defence of a countryman.

'Who's chicken around here, buddy? Joe ain't much of a mixer but he's no rabbit neither! You quit the cacklin' mister or I'll show you this chick ain't just built fer cuddlin'!'

She had created a sensation when she entered the pub, and so she did on leaving it. Like the flash of a rabbit's tail when about to move, there was a glimpse of red and white where a moment before there had been trousers and a top; a streak of blue from receding heels, and a trailing plait of golden hair with a pink bow at the end spinning like a toy propeller in her wake.

Bertie slid down off his stool and followed.

'I always said as whisky weren't no good for a woman. If it don't make 'em sick it makes 'em stubborn!' They didn't call Thatcher 'Old Strawhead' for nothing.

* * *

'If it's Joe you want,' said Benjamin when he saw Pru arriving at the cottage, 'he's down at the Comans' with our Sal collecting some eggs.'

Pru looked at Digby with obvious misgiving and asked if he meant that Joe was still in with the chickens. Was it usual, she asked, for a person to be put in a henhouse for punishment and if so for how long were they sentenced to such a fate? And where, she asked, was one put for committing a real crime if that was where you were put for chasing a rabbit?

Benjamin was beginning to get the drift of the enquiry when Bertie caught up with his escaper.

Hearing that Sally and Joe would shortly be returning with eggs from the farm, Bertie decided to intercept them. The chance of persuading Pru to leave the cottage before the others got back was extremely remote and unless he could warn Sally to about-turn the confrontation he had dreaded would be inevitable.

'Look after Miss Peabody for a minute will you, Boss, I've got to see a man about a dog.'

Pru wore her usual expression of bewilderment at the English idiom and said, 'So long as it's not a bitch you're after, go ahead, buster!'

Digby stared at them each in turn and watched Bertie disappear in the direction of the privy.

'Well, don't stand there,' he said to Pru, 'you'd better come in. There's no sense in waitin' where it's uncomfortable when we've got a perfectly good seat for

244

you to sit on in the house. You know what they say about a watched pot, don't you? It never boils!'

The remark was apt for Bertie was hiding himself on a seat in the privy, waiting for a chance to escape once he could be sure that Pru was out of sight. He heard the latch drop on the back door of the cottage and knew that Digby had taken his visitor inside. Stealthily, he slipped out of his cubicle into the yard, trod noiselessly on the pebbles underfoot, and leapt fearlessly over the gate to avoid it squeaking.

Meanwhile, Sally and Joe were returning from the Comans' by way of the back lanes, carrying a dozen new-laid eggs and a pound of butter in a straw-matted bag with string handles. Swinging the bag rhythmically between them, they took care not to jostle the eggs, and silently thought how like their cargo their relationship had become. Poets rarely liken love to an egg, nor companionship to butter, but Sally, who had the practical domestic outlook of a woman, saw the symmetry and smoothness of the shells as sensuous and fragile, and the soft texture of the butter as akin to the pliable natures of two good friends. Joe thought of the eggs as symbols of fertility and the butter as fat to be stored for the future. They were in that romantic phase when everything about them had to be translated in terms of their own relationship.

''Mornin' Miss Sally, 'mornin' Corporal!'

The words broke into their consciousness and they saw the uniformed figure of Os Lawless approaching them on a bicycle. Sally's heart thumped at the prospect of Joe being apprehended again but she soon saw by the grin on his face that Oswald was not about to act in the execution of his duty.

'Keep an eye on him if he sees a rabbit, won't you!'

In Sally's estimation Joe ought to have scowled but instead he called after him, 'Mister, you can tell the bunnies

245

for me they're safe! I wouldn't touch one if you said it was tame.'

Oswald pedalled on, chuckling to himself, while Joe and Sally tried to regain the rhythm of their stride. Their train of thought was broken, however, and it proved difficult to resume on the same track.

Joe cast his mind back to when they were at the farm waiting for Fred Coman in the back parlour. Sally was chatting with Cathy Coman about school friends whose names meant nothing to Joe and he was gazing at the furniture when his eye fell on a strange-looking apparatus under the window which Cathy described as her mother's spinning wheel. For a moment the memory of this scene was superimposed on the more recent memory of Os Lawless, and Joe jumped in surprise.

'Say, can you imagine that! Do you remember that gadget we saw this afternoon called a spinney or somethin'? Well, I've just had a kind o' vision that ought to make you laff. I reckon if you turned that thing the other way up and put a policeman on top he could ride it just like a bicycle.'

Sally was disappointed by Joe's gullibility and wondered if he had been equally taken in by the 'horse-trough' in the Comans' yard which bore remarkable resemblance to a galvanised bath tub. Her desire to pull the wool from over his eyes was tempered by knowing how difficult it would make life with her father if she did.

Sally was spared from agonizing further when she saw Bertie approaching round a bend in the lane just ahead of them.

Keeping their greetings to a minimum, Bertie announced he had brought a message from Mrs Digby. She would like another dozen eggs. This sounded incredible to Sally who could not imagine what her mother would want so many eggs for. Bertie said she had dropped some but Sally was even more surprised by that.

'My mother has never dropped an egg in her life — whatever can have come over her? Is she unwell?'

Bertie suggested it might have been her father who had dropped them and her mother who had picked them up but, apart from the impracticability of picking up a broken egg, Sally thought it extremely untypical of her father to be anywhere near the pantry.

It was evident that argument was proving useless, so Bertie tried winking at Sally and pretending to Joe that he had a piece of grit in his eye. By this time Sally had detected the smell of beer in his breath and accused him of drinking too much. Not wishing to be involved in a brawl, and anxious to discharge the tension which had built up around them, Joe suggested they should return to the cottage, deliver the consignment they were carrying and then go back to the farm on their bicycles. This was not to Bertie's liking.

'The tyres on your bicycle are flat and there's been a visitor to the cottage,' Bertie retorted with some vehemence. At last Sally perceived what Bertie was driving at.

'Is the visitor still there?' she asked.

'Yes,' said Bertie, 'and we were looking forward to an omelette.'

Sally thrust the two handles of the basket into Bertie's hands and bade him return to her mother with what they had got already. She and Joe would go back to the farm, she said, and collect more eggs but she hoped the visitor would not mind eating her omelette without them as they preferred to be alone.

Joe smiled and loyally set off in the opposite direction for yet another visit to the dairy.

Bertie watched them depart with a sense of relief and amusement and, when they were far enough away not to notice, he gave a little jump of exultation, turned back to the cottage, and ... dropped the eggs.

As a result Bertie was not in the best of moods when he returned to the cottage and when Pru complained that the dog, 'about which he had gone to see a man', must have been a St Bernard or an Afghan by the time it had taken him, they began to quarrel. Pru said she wanted to go in search of Joe and Bertie said he wanted to return to the Coach and Horses. Pru said she was not prepared to stand around in a public place while Joe might be suffering somewhere in solitary confinement. Bertie said she had already demonstrated she did not have to stand a round anywhere and Digby wondered how long it would be before they came to blows.

Borrowing one of her own expressions, Bertie said she was a double-dealer: if she still felt that way about Joe, why had she been leading him up the garden path? Pru said Bertie was getting a swollen head because he was a partner in somebody's business, and if he would like to show her the way *down* the garden path she would find her way out. Bertie said if his head was swollen he wouldn't be able to get it through the door to show her anywhere. Pru said he ought to get it seen to, and added, she meant the head not the door.

Benjamin attributed these exchanges to latent affection. He had often confided to Cyrus that the only signs of love he got from his wife, apart from a good meal and a clean shirt, were the contradictions she made to everything he said.

Bertie wondered if he might have misjudged Miss Peabody. He was attracted by her contours but had given little previous thought to her character. Until this insight into her behaviour under stress, he had thought of her as a child thinks of a doll — decorative and cuddly, but definitely not cantankerous!

It is often the case that when two people walk together in the same direction they see only one side of the other's face. Hitherto Bertie and Pru had been going the same way; now, for the first time, they could see another aspect of the other's countenance. Their reactions to what they saw were equal and opposite: Bertie cooled appreciably and recoiled from Pru's intransigence; Pru warmed immediately and admired Bertie's display of independence.

While Digby was looking for a cue to excuse himself from the fray, Pru put her arm round his shoulders and said in a very loud whisper, 'I guess the guy's jealous!'

Bertie used a word that compromised between obscene and indecent, and left the room.

Vera came in to see what was causing the commotion and was in time to hear Pru telling her husband she was really very fond of Bertie. She said she simply loved the way they lived: it was so absolutely 'basic' and Bertie brought out the primitive instincts in her. Benjamin was about to remind her that she had had a similar effect on some of the menfolk in Little Missington when Vera launched into a monologue about the marvellous labour-saving devices she had seen on the camp at Swivenhall.

'Say! Have you been to Swivenhall? Well, that's just dandy!'

Vera explained it was when they went to rescue Sally after the jeep she was travelling in with Joe had broken down.

The reference to Joe was enough to remind Pru that she had been on the verge of leaving. As she turned to go she found Bertie waiting in the doorway.

'You'll only get lost if I don't show you the way. Come on, I'll take you to where I think you'll find him. But, you do realize don't you that he'll probably be with another woman?'

Prudence grabbed his arm and squeezed it. 'Sure, like I'm with another man!' Benjamin looked at Vera and Vera looked at Bertie, but Bertie could only see in his mind's eye the inevitable reunion of Joe and Pru and the awesome consequence of Sally carrying out her threat to betray his secret.

It was clear to Bertie that in her present mood he could no longer prevent Pru from seeing Joe that evening, but as they walked towards the Comans he looked for an opportunity to delay their meeting as long as possible. Seeing a gate open which led to a field of wheat that had recently been cut, he stepped inside and tried to describe to Pru how to deal with rabbits as they ran for cover.

'That's all very well,' said Pru, 'but how do you deal with the farmer when he catches you at it?'

'You run for cover, just like the rabbit,' said Bertie and sped off towards a hay-stack in the far corner of the field.

Pru followed him. 'Say, is this where they dump the corn after cutting it?'

'Sure!' said Bertie, impersonating her accent, 'that's why they call it a 'corner'!'

Bertie's ruse had worked, and Pru was soon chasing him up the steep side of the haystack as he raced her to the summit. Finding it difficult to stand up on the sloping roof of straw Bertie sat down and Pru, instinctively, fell on top of him.

Meanwhile, Sally and Joe were returning from the Comans with their second consignment of eggs and on the way Sally, like Bertie, was on the look out for opportunities to delay their progress. In her case she was hoping that by the time they reached the cottage the 'visitor' would have gone. She had no means of knowing that the 'visitor' was fast approaching from the opposite direction. When she reached the field with the open gate, Sally stopped and remarked to Joe that they would be safe to assume there were no bulls in there. Joe said he was pleased to hear it, but could they be sure there were no rabbits?

'Why don't we go in and find out?' said Sally, grabbing

250

Joe by the hand and leading him across the stubble to the far side of the field. 'Let's sit down for a minute,' she added, when they reached the haystack, 'it will take the weight off our feet.'

This was another expression Joe had never heard before and he chuckled at the thought of their weights being transferred to a part of their anatomy about which the English seemed more shy than the Americans.

In the cool of the evening they soon found themselves lying close together and looking into each other's eyes from an unfamiliar angle. Embracing on a bed of straw is not a perfectionist's idea of paradise but it has the virtue of stimulating eroticism, and a sudden movement can produce a sensation akin to falling or the pain of being pierced through the flesh. They were just beginning to recognize the symptoms when high above their heads Bertie and Pru began to indulge in a bout of horseplay. Dodging her suitor's thrust towards a prominent part of her torso, Pru failed to remember either the elevation or the slope on which she was lodged, and rolled helplessly over the edge. She fell, not on to the bed of straw, but into the arms of the man she had been taken there to avoid.

22

The Digbys had planned a special tea party to celebrate the last day of Joe's leave. Joe called it a furlough but that was unfamiliar to Ben and Vera and they did not like the sound of it. Vera said she would bake a cake and Benjamin thought they ought to produce some paper hats and crackers. Sally, however, urged them not to give the impression they were glad to be seeing the back of their visitor.

Vera suggested that Joe might like to invite a friend from the camp to keep him company but Sally feared he might choose 'the obnoxious Sammy Wainwright'. Benjamin wanted Bertie to be present but Sally vetoed that as well. On this account, and not because of the loss of eggs-in-transit, Vera baked a smaller cake than she might otherwise have done.

Sally returned to the cottage after her adventure in the haystack with mixed feelings towards her companions. Joe's infatuation with the past and the ease with which he had allowed himself to be duped by the crudest faking was a source of concern to Sally and she was cooling a little in her admiration for him. Bertie, on the other hand, was exhibiting erotic behaviour with Pru and this was reviving in Sally a degree of jealousy which she had not experienced since Joe had come between them. So, instead of wanting at all costs to prevent Joe from being attracted by Pru's attention, Sally was now prepared to let it happen.

It came as a surprise, therefore, to her mother and father when Sally announced she had invited Bertie and Prudence to tea on Joe's last day at the cottage and that they had both accepted.

Pru arrived for the party dressed entirely in white: white blouse, white jacket, white trousers and, of course, white shoes. Digby blinked and wondered if she was trying to tell them something, but Vera hastily put out her best linen napkins in case the girl should spill something while at the table.

Despite the fact that food in England was still in short supply, countryfolk were often able to supplement their rations with home-grown produce and by bartering with friendly farmers. Consequently, afternoon tea at the Digbys was no mean bread-butter-and-cucumber affair. It was a colourful and wholesome meal equivalent, in terms of hospitality, to a town dweller's dinner party.

The table was laid with a lace cloth, dainty chinaware and plates of bread and butter, scones and cakes, surrounded by pots of home-made savoury paté, jams and honey, set beside bowls of bottled fruit, cream and jellies. Tea, milk and sugar were served in silver utensils and the aforementioned linen napkins (called serviettes) were placed beside the silver-plated cutlery.

Prudence was astounded at the sight of so much food at a time of day when she expected no more than a snack between lunch and dinner. Joe, however, had come to accept the Digby's habit of making this the last meal of the day and, after a false start at the beginning of his stay when he had over-estimated what would follow in the evening, he had not gone to bed hungry.

That may have been partly because everyone retired and rose earlier in the country than was the custom in urban areas.

Sally and Joe were not there to greet Pru when she arrived for they had been taking a farewell walk along the river bank. By the time they returned to the cottage Pru had been joined by Bertie who appeared unusually uncomfortable with her in the presence of Benjamin and Vera, although they, to their credit, did their best to be hospitable.

'He's a good partner', Digby told Pru, and then, doubting the wisdom of planting a wrong idea in her mind, added, 'and his services are in great demand.'

There was mud on their shoes when Joe and Sally walked into the living room and Joe's discomfort at putting dirt on the carpet was matched by Sally's displeasure at finding Bertie and Pru sitting together on the floor caressing the cat. Vera dispelled the ensuing awkwardness by hastily bringing on the kettle.

Tea officially started when they took their seats at the table but to Joe and Prudence, tea was what went into their cups.

'Guess you guys eat more often than we do in the States,' said Joe, aiming to break the ice and meaning to be polite.

'Maybe more often,' said Bertie, 'but not as much!'

Vera sensed the occasion was about to be marred by transatlantic misunderstandings. 'Well, we may not have the same habits but we do speak the same language.'

Sally was about to question that remark when her father beat her to it. 'Some folk'd say there's only good habits and bad habits and it don't matter much where you come from.'

Sally had doubted if there was really a common language between them but now she realized some words had more than one meaning even in the same language.

Pru was not easily embarrassed but she began to feel there was an edge to the conversation that might lead to unpleasantness if somebody did not change the subject.

254

Searching for something to say that would ease the tension she remembered she had in the pocket of her jacket, a letter addressed to Corporal J. Buckman. This she had taken from his pigeon-hole on her way out of the camp to deliver to him personally as a gesture of goodwill and a signal to Sally of her proximity to Joe's living quarters. His absence when she arrived at the cottage had caused her to forget the mission and it was a sub-conscious sympathy for her fellow countryman in the situation they now faced which reminded her of the charge she carried.

'Say, Joe,' she began, 'I had somethin' special to giv' yer, but as you weren't around when I got here I kinda forgot.'

Bertie jumped to the wrong conclusion and was momentarily jealous.

Joe had no idea what she meant and was mildly embarrassed. 'Yeah?' was all he could say.

Pru fumbled in her pocket and all eyes round the table followed her fingers as she brought out a small envelope conspicuously covered in postage stamps which Sally identified as coming from the United States of America.

'It looked kinda important so I grabbed it from your mail-rack on my way over here.'

Joe thanked her rather unconvincingly and wondered whether to open it or put it in *his* jacket pocket.

'Now weren't that just thoughtful,' offered Mrs Digby.

'Better open it, lad,' said Digby, 'in case you've been recalled.'

Bertie glanced at his partner and shared the sentiment.

Joe accepted the cue and shocked his hostess by using a table-knife to slit open the envelope. Casting a hasty eye over the handwriting he announced it was from his father.

Digby warmed at the way he conveyed respect and endearment for his paternal parent. Bertie felt let down to hear that he had one!

255

'Gee!' said Joe, excitedly. 'The old man's set on coming over.'

Vera knew the expression 'to come over poorly', but was slow to grasp that Joe's father was planning to cross the Atlantic.

Somewhat unkindly, Digby asked if it meant that Mr Buckman Senior was about to rescue his son from the clutches of the Anglo-Saxons. Fortunately Joe had learned to detect the mischief in Digby's voice and a grin on his face confirmed the diagnosis.

'Well, what d'ya know! He says he wants to come and see for himself what's being written about in the Baltimore press.'

The share value of Digby and Woodfellow would have risen sharply on this news had they been traded on a Stock Exchange. What did show a substantial increase after Joe had read from his father's letter was the cordiality of the assembled company. Conversation became lighter and less electric and the atmosphere changed as it does after a storm.

Joe felt he ought to excuse his father's impetuosity, but Digby recognized the opportunity his visit would present for adding credibility to certain historical 'discoveries'. Sally wondered what Joe's father would look like and posed the question by asking Joe if he resembled his father.

'Shucks! I don't think so,' said Joe. 'He's got brains.'

'There y'go again,' said Pru, 'always selling yourself short. I bet your old man didn't get where he is by hiding his light under a bushel.'

'You could be wrong there, Pru,' Joe chuckled, 'he's spent his life digging things up so he might have cheated a little.'

Digby felt a shiver of guilt and tried not to show it, while Bertie looked at Sally to see if she would take the opportunity to betray them. It was her mother who came to their rescue with a typically practical interjection.

'Do y'father hav' a mooter car? Cos if he do, y'd better tell him not to bring it. He'd never get it home again!'

'Mother, how do you think he'd get it here in the first place?'

'Well, I daresay he can drive, can't he?'

Laughter helped to warm the atmosphere even further.

They pressed Joe to tell them more about his father and then turned the conversation to what he ought to be shown when he came to Little Missington, and where he would stay while he was here. The absence of a hotel made it difficult to suggest a suitably independent base and Vera was certain he would expect something better than she could offer. Benjamin thought of asking Cyrus to put him up but Joe spared them further embarrassment by making it clear he would ask for his father to be accommodated at the camp.

'I guess the Old Man will get the VIP treatment, as usual, when they hear he is coming over,' Joe assured them. Vera was not sure whether a VIP was some kind of snake or an acronym for a secret society, but it relieved her to know that she and her husband would not have to give up their bedroom for the occasion.

Digby was full of ideas about the itinerary for Mr Buckman's visit but realized that many of them would involve some degree of subterfuge and camouflage. Joe had explained that his father was a genealogist and a collector of historical relics. Digby was not too sure what a genealogist did but understood Joe to say his father would be interested in anything that was old.

Digby felt sure, therefore, that those who had benefited from selling their ancient artifacts should continue to keep hidden all evidence of the modern comforts and amenities with which they had been replaced.

Bertie's mind was working in another direction. He favoured a more positive approach and conceived the idea of staging a visual ceremony that would convey the impression of continuity with the past.

'When did y'father say he'd be a-comin'?'

'Soon as I can fix him up, I guess,' said Joe.

'Then he could be here for th' *Harvest Festival*?' Bertie suggested.

'My heart, that's a good idea!' Ben added enthusiastically. 'That's the jolliest of all our festivals. It'll knock the one you saw into a cocked hat!'

An apt expression, thought Joe, who vividly remembered his host in the role of the Laughing Cavalier.

Neither Bertie nor Benjamin knew much about the ritual of Harvest Festivals except that they were occasions when the church was filled with fruit and flowers and vegetables, and sheaves of wheat and oats and barley, and the congregation sang hymns like 'Plough the fields and scatter'. Bertie had read somewhere that in years gone by, and perhaps still in parts of Eastern Europe, the population would express its gratitude for a good harvest, or relief at its completion, by a carnival of rustic revelry that ended in much drunkenness and debauchery. It was something on those lines that he had in mind!

By the time all the cakes and desserts had been eaten, Vera was wondering if she had under-provided. Pru reassured her, however, and said she had never enjoyed a meal so much.

Bertie and Benjamin were well satisfied, though fully aware of some hurried preparations they would now be obliged to undertake.

Sally was bemused. On the one hand she warmed again to Joe through the pleasure he displayed towards a reunion with his father, but this also reminded her of the distance between Joe's background and her own. Joe's home was a long way across the sea and hers was right here where she was now. The thought of one or the other having to settle down in a foreign land terrified her. She instinctively resented the prospect of another woman winning Joe's affections, but, if it had to be, she felt she would like it to be Pru because that would make Bertie jealous and she would enjoy that.

23

Back in Baltimore excitement was increasing now that Joe's father, Mr Theodore Buckman, had announced his intention of going to England. As Curator of a Museum of Anthropology, he had persuaded the Board of Managers that he ought to investigate at first hand the revelations being made in a remote corner of old England known as Little Missington.

The people of Baltimore were renowned for their interest in and support for the arts and the unravelling of ancient history was by many considered more an art than a science. Moreover, since most of the local population had their origins in Europe they were predisposed to believe that more ancient history would be uncovered in England than in Maryland, USA.

Joe's companions at his camp in East Anglia had produced photographs and descriptions which indicated a wealth of history to be found in the vicinity of Digby's ruin and Pru's father had succeeded in mounting an exhibition of these photographs in the Peabody Library. Sebastian Peabody never claimed any relationship with his benevolent namesake, but he felt no particular need to disclaim it. Capitalizing on the interest which his photographs created, the local press published an article by the Museum's Curator suggesting some of their boys might at that very moment be living over the tombs of their distant ancestors.

It was not surprising, therefore, that funds for his expedition came flooding in to Theodore Buckman, and an organisation calling itself 'The Friends of Little Missington' was formed to which learned societies and publicity-seeking businessmen eagerly subscribed.

By the time he was ready to book his ticket to cross the Atlantic, Joe's father had enough money at his disposal to take with him a small party of explorers.

In preparation for this invasion, Benjamin and Bertie were busily thinking of ways to present their village as a place of historical interest. Digby's suggestion was to recreate the Little Missington he had known as a child, but the more he looked around him the more difficult he realized that would be. Apart from the fallibility of his own memory, there was the evident unwillingness of his fellow inhabitants to forego the comforts they had recently acquired with income derived from tourists and souvenir hunters.

Bertie proposed a scheme for representing the village as it might have been in the Middle Ages, with stocks and scaffolds, but his partner thought somebody might take advantage of such facilities and condemn a few of their adversaries to a feudal punishment.

The need to work their ideas into a format consistent with Bertie's concept of a Harvest Festival obliged them to seek advice from both Cyrus and the vicar. They decided to tackle the vicar first.

Norman Harper was a melancholy holy man and he did not hold with too much geniality. His advice, therefore, was to be grateful for what the Lord had provided and not to seek ways of ingratiating themselves with an American. He would, he assured them, do his best to have the church decorated with a full range of local produce but he refused to lead a procession through the village or to wear a cassock or carry a staff. He was prepared to consult the Bishop, though not to invite him, and to preach a sermon on the subject of thanksgiving, but definitely not to deliver it in Latin.

The vicar's reaction convinced them they would do better to approach Cyrus in the presence of the Parish Council. Digby, therefore, raised the necessary support to call a special meeting at which he announced the imminent arrival of Joe's father and 'a team of explorers' who, he said, wanted to see for themselves what their folk at the airfield had been writing home about.

'Now is our chance,' said Digby, 'to widen our market. It's a good opportunity we durstn't miss! Those guys will have money to spend and we can show 'em how to spend it.'

Cyrus was impressed at first but then had doubts about the wisdom of entertaining a museum curator who, he expected, would turn out to be a mere collector of unsaleable commodities.

With his mind on Digby's remark about money to spend, Mortimer Lockett spoke as both Treasurer and retailer when he said, 'I aren't a 'goin' t'have nothin' t'do wi' that *lend-lease* nonsense. If they don't pay cash they 'on't get nothin'!'

Ted Brewer said he believed Americans always wanted their beer ice cold and he did not have room in the bar for a refrigerator.

Mr Stubbles thought a curator had something to do with improving people's health and welcomed the idea of consulting him about his lumbago.

George Whackett mistook a genealogist for a gynaecologist and embarked upon a thoroughly misleading dialogue.

O'Hachetty was still pondering the chairman's remarks about a curator and unsaleable commodities. He had been brought up to believe that curing meat was a means of preserving it, so a curator ought to be able to extend the saleableness of whatever it was he sold.

Digby reminded them that the American gentlemen were coming whether they liked it or not and his idea was to take advantage of the visit. There were reminders about the outcome of his last great idea but Digby had broad shoulders and shrugged off the taunt by pointing out how much richer most of them had become since the village began to attract tourists.

Digby's ploy was successful and they started to discuss ways of impressing the visitors from the New World with examples of what they had to offer in the old one.

* * *

While the Parish Council was in session, Bertie was in action rounding up his contemporaries and urging their support for what he said was to be a 'super ceremony'. They listened open-mouthed at his description of a traditional harvest festival and were completely won over by the time he reached the alcoholic content of the occasion. Apart from the processional arrangements there were two items in Bertie's programme which, he explained, would require considerable effort and for which he needed their assistance. The first was to dismantle and convert the red telephone kiosk opposite the church, to serve as a sedan chair in which the visiting dignitary would be carried on his arrival. The conversion, he said would have to be done without the knowledge of the postmaster, who might regard it as theft, or of the vicar, who would see it as vandalism.

The second task would be the erection of a ceremonial arch across the roadway at the entrance to the village through which the Americans would have to pass on their way from Swivenhall.

Sally had assumed that she would be expected to escort

Joe's father around the village and fancied it would add colour and credence to the occasion if she were to wear some Tudor or Elizabethan costume. With this objective she and her mother worked for several nights alongside a pictorial history book and a sewing machine.

To redeem himself after his *faux pas* at the Parish meeting, George Whackett engaged the services of his entire school in composing and rehearsing the Festival Parade. This was to be a series of tableaux depicting Little Missington during the Plague, the Civil War, the approach of the Armada, and the arrival of the Industrial Revolution.

Even the unimaginative Frank Morse was inspired to set up a team of signallers who were to semaphore to each other from vantage points across the village. They spent several evenings practising the code which Frank proudly reminded them bore his name. Most of the team found this fun but one recalcitrant youth had to be dismissed after setting fire to his flag and claiming to be better at sending smoke signals.

A villager who was keen to exploit the visitation to its utmost was Christopher Hopper. He prepared to deck out the village hall for its most splendid Saturday hop and arranged, with some help from Cyrus and Colonel Peters, for live music to be played by the Band of the US Air Force at Swivenhall. This coup had been accomplished on the understanding that he would produce a special brew of barley wine for the occasion.

After his initial misgivings Cyrus joined in the preparations and conceived the idea of throwing The Willows open to the public and arranging conducted tours of the house and gardens. He spent days re-routing the model railway and concealing items of modern comfort which he and his wife had been quietly accumulating. Mrs Galleon was overawed at the prospect of having her furniture fingered or her tapestries torn, but she conceded that the cash from admissions might go some way to compensate for dirty marks and breakages. Her anxiety returned, however, when she thought of the spring-cleaning that would be necessary before the house would be fit to receive visitors and the spadework that would have to be done to repair the state of the garden. To all of this Cyrus turned a deaf ear and returned to his study to design notices for directing visitors around the estate. The one which amused him most was the notice which said WAY OUT: it showed a rope dangling from the branch of a tree, its noose over the head of a scarecrow!

Digby himself was industrious, as ever. He recognized that visitors from America might not understand what was being enacted for their benefit unless it was explained to them. So he borrowed a microphone and loudspeaker from Chris Hopper and planned to broadcast a commentary as the events took place. In order to keep up with them, it would have to be a running commentary so he strapped the loudspeaker to a pole and tied it to the side of a hand-cart. This he proposed to push before him while swinging a handbell and wearing the costume of a town-crier.

When Vera Digby got to hear of this she rebelled and collected a number of like-minded women to form a group of 'martyrs' who would slouch behind the parade in sackcloth and chains . . . wailing!

Preparations for the visit were also in progress at Swivenhall.

Back on camp after his furlough in the village, Joe found himself at the centre of considerable curiosity. His buddies wanted to hear all about the hospitality he had received from the Digbys and, of course, 'how far he had gone' with their daughter. They expected a great deal more than they got, for Joe was reticent to reveal any intimate details of his relationship with Sally yet quick to dismiss any suggestion that he had been bored or impoverished by the rural environment.

On his second day back Joe received a summons from his Commanding Officer. By virtue of his initials and a reputation for fiery behaviour, Simon Abraham Lincoln Peters was known to his men as 'Old Gunpowder' and Corporal Buckman went in dread of a dressing down, convinced that he must have committed another misdemeanour.

'Ah, Corporal,' the CO bellowed, as Joe entered and saluted, 'I've just had a cable from your father. I see he's a curator of a museum and an anthropologist. I didn't know you came from a brainy family, Buckman! Did you know your father was coming to England?'

'Yes sir, I'm afraid I did.'

'What d'yer mean "afraid"? Don't you want to see him?'

'Oh yes, of course, sir . . . only, I thought perhaps I should have warned you.'

'Warned me! Why, is he difficult to deal with?'

The Colonel could see that his corporal was getting into deep water and, uncharacteristically, rescued him. 'I've cabled back to say he'd be very welcome and offered him a room in the Officers' Quarters. Will that embarrass you, Corporal?'

'Why no sir.'

'I hear you've been staying where your father wants to do his research. Sounds like you've set up some first class Anglo-American relations.'

'It sure is an interesting hamlet,' Joe stuttered.

'So I believe. So I believe! In fact, Corporal, I've been there myself. Met a helluva guy called Galleon who farms there. Did y'hear of him while you were there?'

Joe's heart sank. 'Yes sir. I'm afraid I chased a rabbit into one of his fields and he had me arrested.'

'The hell he did!' Old Gunpowder exploded. 'Damn good job you didn't chase one of his cows!'

24

Preparations for the Curator's mission to Little Missington were also proceeding apace in Baltimore.

Theodore Buckman was a resourceful man, as befitted his occupation, and he lost no opportunity to recruit help and encouragement from his many good friends in the neighbourhood. One of these, about whom Angela had spoken in her conversation with Bertie, was Professor Chippendale from the Johns Hopkins University. The Professor was extremely interested in the forthcoming visit and insisted on one of his students joining Theodore's party to trace the history of the snuff box which he declared had belonged to Horatio Nelson.

The Keeper of Druids Hill Park was not an academic but he was a great reader of historical novels and a regular visitor to the Museum of Anthropology. His name was Aidan Groves and hearing of the Curator's plans he asked if he could join the expedition in the hope of finding evidence that the people of Little Missington were of Druid descent.

A photograph which Sebastian Peabody had received from his daughter showing Sam Waterman in his strange looking weedcutter caught the attention of Jeremiah Sticklebach, a Baltimore industrialist. He insisted on sponsoring some research into the design of the craft and accompanying the expedition to indulge his passion for fishing.

The only woman who showed interest in joining the party was the President of the Baltimore League of Needleworkers who believed she might trace some of her family's ancestors in that part of Norfolk, England, where weaving was once a major craft. Mrs Cynthia Thoroughgood was a stout lady with a strong booming voice and an indomitable spirit, which Theodore felt might be useful if they were to encounter any resistance or unfriendliness from the local population.

To keep this lady company, and to protect himself from her if she, rather than the locals, became difficult to deal with, Theodore decided to take his secretary. Doris Fairhart was not pretty but she was competent and that was a combination which Mrs Buckman found attractive and comforting when her husband told her of his intention.

By the time they were ready to leave, the party had grown to six: Theodore and Doris; Aidan Groves; Professor Chippendale's student, Lenny le Measurer; Jeremiah Sticklebach; and Mrs Thoroughgood.

Sally arranged with Joe for him to write and tell her when his father would be arriving so that everyone in Little Missington would be ready for him. The precise date of his arrival was more important than the size of his party.

Digby wanted to be sure that the Americans were given 'a right rural reception' as soon as they entered the village. He and Bertie worked together on the ceremonial arch and George Whackett choreographed a morris dance to be performed on the road a few yards ahead of the arch. Once the vehicle was brought to a standstill, village maidens would appear from the roadside and offer posies of buttercups and daisies while the morris dancers waved their coloured handkerchiefs and clattered their sticks. A run-through of the programme was arranged to be sure that everyone knew what to do, but unfortunately this was not co-ordinated with the cowman and just as the 'stand-in' for the visitor's car arrived at the newly-erected arch, so did a herd of Friesians. The morris dancers were used to stamping in puddles but they drew the line at cow pats.

Transit between America and Europe had yet to become a regular daily occurrence and civilians were still obliged to make the journey by sea. That gave Joe three or four days to prepare for his father's arrival after he left the States. Digby wanted some comparable early warning system to know exactly when to expect him in Little Missington; not just the date, but the time of day, so that his welcoming ceremony could be suitably organized. He asked Cyrus to arrange for Colonel Peters to telephone when the visitors were leaving the camp. Cyrus wanted their departure to be signalled by a low-flying aircraft looping-the-loop over the spire of the church, but Colonel Peters was not prepared to commit the United States resources to this extent. He did, however, agree to the expense of a telephone call.

* * *

The day came, in mid-September, when Sally received a postcard from Joe with the message they had waited for. His father, he said, would be arriving at Swivenhall on the following Friday, and proposed to drive out to see them after lunch on the Saturday. He explained later that he had sent the message on a postcard so that Wilfred Stamp, the postman, would read it and let the whole village know before nightfall.

When Colonel Peters offered Joe's father accommodation at the camp he was not expecting mixed company. A cable from Baltimore announcing their departure led to hurried arrangements being made for an apartment in married quarters to be put at their disposal.

Cyrus got his phone call on the Saturday morning to

say Theodore and his party had arrived at Swivenhall the previous night and would be escorted to the village in the early afternoon. Cyrus signalled the news by sounding the siren with which he had announced the discovery of the ruin. The villagers heard it on this occasion with a mixture of excitement and panic. Some of them were critical of the fuss that was being made to entertain a lot of foreigners but most of them had expectations of making money out of the visit. Nobody was quite ready with their contribution to the festivities but everybody had been given some part to play, even to the role of a spectator.

Lunch in the village was taken with the same haste and apprehension as had preceded the ill-fated road mending exercise from which this present event stemmed. By two o'clock the 'village maidens' were in position in front of the arch and the bearers of the sedan chair were flexing their muscles for the load they were to carry. The Reception Committee of Parish Councillors was hurriedly assembling on the Common under an oak tree where the Salvation Army gathered on Sundays.

Theodore Buckman rode with his son and secretary in the first of three jeeps which set out from Swivenhall after a convivial lunch in the Officer's Mess. Mrs Thoroughgood and Lenny le Measurer followed in the second jeep, and the Colonel, accompanied by Arthur Storker, his adjutant, and Jeremiah Sticklebach, brought up the rear. Each jeep was driven by a United States Air Force driver and the whole procession was headed by a uniformed motor cyclist outrider.

Joe had warned his father to expect a warm reception when he got to Little Missington but Theodore had not imagined anything like the spectacle that confronted him as he reached the village. Draped in large letters from the cross beam of the arch was the greeting:

HIYA UNCLE SAM

Erratic movements at ground level took the visitor's attention quickly from the banner. Unfamiliar with the costume worn by morris dancers, Colonel Peters mistook them for insurgents and ordered his driver to back away and reverse. Fortunately his Adjutant had spotted the village maidens with their baskets of flowers and was able to calm the Commander before his order was carried out.

After a few moments the morris dancers stood aside and formed an avenue of pikes and tambourines through which the jeeps passed slowly, only to be confronted with what still looked rather like a telephone kiosk in the middle of the road. Again the Colonel took fright as he observed that the box appeared to have guns sticking out from two sides of it, with hefty-looking individuals in bandit's uniform clasping the muzzles. This time, before he could give any instructions to his driver, the 'box' was picked up and dropped by the side of the leading jeep and his guest, the Baltimore Curator, was lifted into it.

Seeing Bertie among the onlookers, Joe called out to him and received a reassuring greeting. Bertie was introduced to Joe's father who leaned nervously out of his 'carriage', and the procession moved forward towards the Common where the Reception Committee was waiting.

Cyrus stood boldly in the centre of a raised platform made of builder's planks, surrounded by his colleagues from the Parish Council. Between the platform and the river, a brass band was playing a selection of Sousa marches. This had been as much a surprise to Cyrus as it was to the visitors, for the only musicians in Little Missington were those who played for the Salvation Army. The band behind him had, it was explained, come from the neighbouring town of Myrtlesham at the request of George Whackett who knew the bandmaster.

Introductions at the platform were effected by Colonel

Peters and Cyrus Galleon, who greeted each other like long lost friends, and then struggled to sort out the order in which everyone else should be presented. By mutual consent they ended by announcing their respective parties collectively so they could get on with the programme.

Digby and Sally, who had meantime been found by Joe, then steered the party round a number of stalls that were pitched on the Common with displays of bric-à-brac and harvest produce.

When Digby judged they had seen enough of the static exhibits he signalled the start of the Festival Parade. Horse-drawn floats and costumed footmen, representing various periods in the imagined history of Little Missington, set off from the courtyard of the Coach and Horses and rumbled past the Common on their way to Galleon's Meadow. Assembling such a motley group had been a major task and led to some heated exchanges between the schoolmaster and participants but, apart from an unscheduled trot by one of the farmer's steeds which added incident to a sequence representing the Civil War, the programme went according to plan.

While the parade was in progress the visitors stood by the roadway and mingled with parishioners who had opted to serve as spectators. In their midst was Angela Cotton who had come into the village independently and was looking for Bertie. On hearing the booming voice of a fellow American, Angie moved closer to Mrs Thoroughgood and greeted her with a grin and a 'hi!'. They quickly became friends and it was not long before Angela was telling the story of how she had gone to the workshed of Benjamin Digby and found a snuff box that once belonged to Horatio Nelson. The cottage, she added, was just across the Common, almost in front of them, and Cynthia insisted on being taken there to see what else it might contain.

Seeing them heading towards his cottage, Digby abandoned his party and dashed for home, arriving at the gate in time to greet the two ladies and invite them in for a look around.

Digby's departure was seen by other spectators who also had artefacts to sell and it was not long before they formed a second procession moving counter to the one they were supposed to be watching. Whereas the official parade had been designed to steer the visitors up to the ruin, the unofficial one was luring them in other directions.

Mrs Lockett, for example, was dragging Doris Fairhart towards her husband's stock of jewellery; Mrs Carter had captured Aidan Groves with a view to selling him some pottery; Sam Waterman had hooked Mr Sticklebach on hearing him ask what fish there were in the river; and Barbara Whackett was leading Lenny le Measurer towards the School House where she had promised to show him some articles of local culture.

That left Cyrus with Colonel Peters; Sally with Joe and his father; and Bertie with the Adjutant, heading for Galleon's Meadow supported by a rapidly disintegrating troop of pageanteers who by this time were tired and thirsty.

It is at these moments that adjutants come into their own, and Arthur Storker was accustomed to dealing with such an emergency. He spoke first to Bertie, who took him to Jim Brewer, who led him to his father, who returned to his cellar to withdraw a flagon of ale. This he despatched to the ruin with a tub full of tankards and a portable till on the back of a pony trap driven by his daughter. Kathy might have been less willing to do this had she not been told that Bertie would be waiting to unload it for her.

While those in the meadow were waiting for beer to quench their thirst, those in the village were being served with teas amid articles of varying antiquity, temptingly displayed for sale.

Harvest Festivals normally come at the end of a period of harvesting but on this occasion it was the other way about. There was more to be collected in Little Missington during and after the Festival than had been gathered all summer. The problem confronting the visitors from Baltimore was how to select the wheat from the chaff.

Cynthia Thoroughgood had entered Digby's workshed with the hope of finding something of interest to her fellow needleworkers but once inside she forgot this objective and seized on everything that struck her as curious or unusual. From a large array of glass bottles she selected one that had a particularly long neck and a lip from which to pour, and several very small ones which had evidently held pills or perfumes but which she thought would make pretty ornaments on her bedside table. There were enough pewter tankards in all shapes and sizes to fill the bar of a public house but she chose one with a large and ornate handle which she thought would please her husband. Too big to fit in her handbag, she passed over various items of furniture but made a mental note to tell young le Measurer that some of them might have been Chippendale. In the section which Sally had marked 'Musical' she picked out a colourful and much decorated concertina which Digby insisted on playing to demonstrate its capabilities. Fearing he might repeat the performance with what he described as a kettledrum, she resisted the temptation to add that to her collection but said it reminded her that she had seen elsewhere in the showroom a splendid copper kettle which she could just about manage to carry if he could wrap it up for her.

While Digby set off in search of some brown paper and string, wondering how he could make a parcel of such a shape, Angela led her companion to a collection of snuff boxes. However, since none of them bore any indication of having belonged to Horatio Nelson they settled instead

274

for a strange smelling box labelled 'vinaigrette'. Supposing, without much conviction, that it was possibly meant to contain vinegar, they said they would think of another use for it back in Baltimore.

Loaded to the limit, they left without even a sample of embroidery but vowed to return next day with more cash and containers.

In a bungalow behind the village hall, where the Locketts had converted their front room into a shop, Mortimer was showing Doris his stock of clocks and jewellery. Over the fireplace was a fine example of an old mural clock which Mortimer had bought from the Coach and Horses before the Brewers realized its value as a mark of antiquity. None of the other clocks in the room agreed with it for time and when the hour approached there was a prolonged period of chiming which made it difficult to carry on a conversation. It was the jewellery, however, which fascinated Doris. Accustomed to the bright and cheerful costume jewellery that was popular in Baltimore, she was surprised to find drab looking brooches made of pewter, heavyweight necklaces of local stones and polished pebbles, pendants carrying portraits enclosed in collapsible cases, and bracelets hung with bent and tarnished coins. She wondered if the rings were meant to be worn in the nose rather than on ears or fingers.

Aidan, meanwhile, was making a hit with Mrs Carter and her son Sammy in Cobblers Lane. Each was amused by the other's vernacular and encouraged an exchange of expressions which often left the listener lost for their meaning. The Keeper of Druids Hill Park was particularly interested in some of the superstitions revealed by the Carters, such as not walking under a ladder, throwing salt over their shoulder, not crossing knives at table, and turning money over in their pockets at the sight of a new moon. He felt certain it would not be long before he had evidence of a Druid connection. When he heard Sammy's account of young Coman's experience by Galleon's Meadow and the subsequent discovery of a ruined castle, Aidan was sure his journey had not been in vain.

Among the expressions that Barbara Whackett was fond of quoting to her daughter when she spoke of someone in doubtful circumstances, was that 'birds of a feather flock together'. Hearing that Lenny le Measurer was a university student, doing some kind of research, she instinctively felt she had a duty to introduce him to her husband. The possibility of him being suitable for Kathy occurred to her later.

Neither Kathy nor her father were at home when Lenny was led into the School House where the Whacketts lived, but the schoolmaster's wife found no difficulty in interesting her guest in the collection of paraphernalia which had been neatly arranged in what she called the exhibition room. Lenny was delighted to see such enterprise displayed in what he had imagined would be a backward part of the Old Country, but a glance at the furniture made him realize he was really in a classroom. Chuckling to himself at Mrs Whackett's euphemism, he suddenly noticed a high-backed chair behind the podium where he had expected to see a stool. This he saw was made of mahogany in a style which he recognized as Georgian. It could, indeed, thought Lenny, be a Chippendale . . . and fortunately for him it was not one of Bertie's reproductions.

* * *

Down by the river Sam was recounting to an entranced listener his version of the history of Little Missington as passed down by his father and grandfather before him, culled no doubt by them from earlier generations. It included, inevitably the episode in which Sam himself encountered a fallen tree trunk across the river at a time when mysterious manifestations were appearing in the adjacent meadow. Jeremiah Sticklebach stopped him abruptly and demanded to be taken at once to the scene of the story.

They arrived by boat about an hour later with Jeremiah trailing a spinner from the back seat while old Sam pulled steadily on a pair of oars. There were no motor-driven boats on the river at that time and plenty of fish in it. Despite oaths and cajoling from those above the surface, life beneath it remained unaffected: Mr Sticklebach could see the fish, and once he felt one biting at the line, but he did not catch one. The urge to return and have another go was very great.

Theodore and Joe were sitting on a crumpled parapet listening to Sally describing what she had learned about England in the Middle Ages when they were surprised to see Sam and his passenger coming towards them from the river, having moored their boat to the bank below.

By the time they were due at the Village Hall for the much publicized Harvest Festival Hop most of the villagers and all of their visitors were footsore and weary. In the case of the Hopper family, who had been waiting all day for their big event, it was only true to say they were weary, but in the case of the Swivenhall Band who had been driven to the village in a US Air Force crew bus and made to dismount at the frontier, they were more footsore than weary.

Participants were slow to arrive but when the band began with its customary boogie-woogie the noise emitted from the Village Hall spread through Little Missington and drew the young folk to its source like iron filings to the proverbial magnet.

So much could perhaps have been predicted but what followed in the course of the evening was quite unexpected.

277

Theodore had intended to return to Swivenhall with his son and retinue but was prevailed upon by the younger elements of his party to stay and support their musical compatriots. Colonel Peters was similarly invited to remain, and did not take much persuasion to slip away with Cyrus to The Willows which had been open to the public all afternoon. Arthur Storker took the news philosophically, although it meant breaking a date with a nurse he had intended taking to the camp cinema that evening. Cynthia Thoroughgood was easy prey to Digby's suggestion that she and Angela ought to wait until Vera and Sally returned from the pageant; she then felt it her duty to chaperone Angela who wanted to stay on for the Hop. Aidan had no intention of missing the opportunity to hear more of the mores of those who lived in Little Missington and readily accepted the Carter's proposal that he should accompany Sammy to the Village Hall.

Sam Waterman did not for one moment imagine Jeremiah Sticklebach would want to spend the evening on a dance floor but sensed that he might not refuse a pint or two in the Coach and Horses. It surprised neither of them to find when they got there that Benjamin had steered Theodore in the same direction. The Americans were soon introduced to the regulars like Bob Blackett and Harry Carter and when the word got around they were joined by George Whackett, Frank Morse and Wilfred Stamp. In monetary terms there is no doubt Ted Brewer made a better 'take' that evening than Christopher Hopper, but the Hop was a bigger attraction numerically.

Lenny le Measurer left the Whackett's before Kathy and her father returned to School House but not before Mrs Whackett had shown him a photograph of her daughter and told him she would be at the Hop that evening. Lenny was not such a studious student that he did not appreciate the company of the opposite sex, and the skill of the photographer in highlighting Kathy's feminine qualities made him determined to meet her in the flesh. He was delighted therefore when he discovered that Theodore was not returning to Swivenhall until after the Hop was over.

Doris was also pleased to find that her boss was not in a hurry to get back to Swivenhall because she had learned from the Locketts something of the local gossip about their friend Mr Digby's daughter going out with an American airman called Joe. Joe, she discovered, was none other than Mr Buckman's son to whom she had been introduced that afternoon and felt she would like to know better.

There was only one person missing that afternoon in Little Missington who had made a contribution to our story so far, and that was Pru Peabody. She was at Swivenhall ... on duty ... until nightfall.

25

Joe led his Colonel's Adjutant into the Village Hall as if he were entering a captured city. He was proud of having discovered this gem of an English hamlet and he felt a proprietary claim to everything about it. Sally, in contrast, was subdued for she was thinking of the last occasion on which she had accompanied Joe to such an event. In spite of Joe's enthusiasm she knew that the Harvest Festival Hop would be nothing like the Swivenhall Ball. There would be no chromium plating, and the refreshments would be restricted by rationing which was now more severe than when the war was on. The band would be the same, and the acoustics of close walls and low ceilings might compensate for the lack of electrical amplification, but the lads of the village in their corduroys and grubby jackets would be no match for the American airmen in their smart uniforms and New World outlook.

Joe sensed what was going through her mind. 'Say, honey,' he said, 'this place sure makes a guy feel like he's off duty!' Sally smiled, but his choice of words did nothing to console her.

The adjutant could see he was not wanted and slipped quietly back to his jeep and the nurse he had stood up at Swivenhall.

* * *

It took some time for the band leader to recognize that the youth of Little Missington were not as well acquainted as the airmen at Swivenhall with the rhythms that were then popular on the other side of the Atlantic. Eventually one or two who had returned from the Services gave their rendering of a jitterbug, assisted by young ladies who were already familiar with it from their visits to the neighbouring camp. Most of the villagers, however, stood or sat by the side of the hall tapping their feet and looking shyly at the floor.

By the time Bertie arrived the atmosphere was warming up and Sally and Joe were attempting, from a distance, to copy the experts jiving in the centre of the hall. Before he could make up his mind whether to ignore them or butt in and annoy them, Bertie had been seized by his old admirer, Kathy, and dragged into the fray.

When Doris and Lenny arrived they took straight to the floor; Doris on the look-out for Joe, and Lenny anxious to spot the original of the photograph he had seen at the Whackett's. As soon as he did so, and there was no doubt about his recognition, Lenny asked Doris if she would mind him changing partners 'for a whirl with the girl with a twirl in her hair!' Doris smiled at Lenny's exit line; then cheerfully offered her company to Bertie who was not at all displeased to be dispossessed of Kathy. Sally and Joe continued to circuit and bump while observing with mild amusement the manoeuvres of others.

Cynthia and Angela lost their way from Rose Cottage to the Village Hall because Cynthia insisted on stopping at all the cottages where an 'Antiques' sign was displayed and failed to realize that the way out from some of them was not the same as the way in. Consequently, the hop was well under way when they put in their appearance. Cynthia quickly became aware that she was several years senior to most of those on the dance floor and, seeing Mrs

Hopper struggling to prepare for the interval, she contrived to detach herself from Angela and offered to help in the kitchen. Angela drifted deeper into the hall and joined a group of unattached young ladies standing by the wall.

The frenetic activity of bandsmen on the platform and jivers on the dance floor gave way to a general surge to the back of the hall when the interval was announced. Refreshments were rapidly consumed and many of the less thrusting were left famished and thirsty. Attempts to get reinforcements proved futile and the mood of the unlucky was disagreeable. The Hoppers blamed it all on the Americans who, in turn, attributed it to typical English unpreparedness. Relief came, to all except those who had queued in vain for the cloakroom, when the band resumed playing. Discontent dissolved as the noise level rose.

Lenny returned to the dance floor with Kathy but was beginning to find her reality less endearing than the image. The infatuation he felt for her photograph soon faded. There was just that something about her, he believed, that would be either unobtainable or disappointing. Kathy, on the other hand, was oblivious to such thoughts and kept up a non-stop chatter about nothing in particular.

Bertie was having the opposite experience. He was attached to a pleasant but unglamorous young lady who was bringing out the best in him.

Sally and Joe resumed their partnership with a growing sense of detachment, first to the proceedings and then, oddly, to one another. Then Pru appeared.

When she had first entered the Coach and Horses Pru was a sensation with the elders of the village; now, as she swept into the dance hall, with her long hair flowing and her bright dress glowing, she was a sensation with the young on's. Bertie abandoned Doris with less haste than Lenny had done earlier, but with no more respect for her feelings.

Doris accepted her fate gracefully and waited with the 'wallflowers' for an opportunity to stalk the prey she had set her sights upon. Pru accepted Bertie's assumption that he was her selected partner with a mixture of pride and amusement.

For some time Lenny had been watching a fellow American in Air Force uniform dancing with the same partner and, liking the look of her, he decided to break them up. Next time they passed, he stepped out and asked Joe to excuse him. To her surprise, Sally did not resist, as she had done when she was accosted at Swivenhall, and Joe went quietly to the side of the hall and looked on.

Observing this from the other side of the room was Doris. Immediately she saw Joe on his own she knew her moment had come. Introducing herself as his father's secretary, she invited him to dance with her. Joe said he had no idea his father had such a delightful secretary and Doris said she never realized what a charming son her employer had. Within a short time there developed between them a warmth that owed more to human chemistry than a common country of origin.

Sally was not slow to notice the attention Joe was paying to his new partner and Lenny, in turn became aware that Sally was not listening to his conversation. Sally, therefore, had only herself to blame when she became victim, instead of object, of a sudden 'take-over'. This one, however, had the merit of legality, for Lenny took advantage of the bandleader's call to regard the dance as an 'excuse-me' and led his partner alongside Bertie and Pru for the interception. Pru had already noticed the handsome young student with a Yankee accent and, besides, the idea of Bertie being obliged to dance with his old 'cast-off' appealed to her sense of mischief.

Unaware that a game of 'general post' had been enacted on the dance floor, Kathy was thinking more in terms of 'murder' as she contemplated the humiliation of being 'dumped by a damn Yankee' in favour of 'the Digby girl'. Unable to detect that the gleam in Kathy's eyes was a glare of anger and not the beginning of a mystical trance, the Keeper of Druids Hill Park, who had arrived late on the scene after a brief call at the Coach and Horses, made the unfortunate error of inviting the schoolmaster's daughter to dance with him. It was not long before Mr Aidan Groves realized he was in the presence of a woman possessed and that his hunch about the Druid connection might well be correct. As Kathy clung ever closer to him, he caught sight of Angela leaning idly against a pillar and seized the opportunity to escape.

So, Kathy was dumped again, only this time for another 'damned Yankee'. It had definitely not been her night and she left the hall before any further damage could be done to her pride and reputation. Had she known it, the fact that her absence was hardly noticed would have been the ultimate humiliation.

The last waltz of the evening brought no change of partners to Sally, Doris or Pru for they remained with Bertie, Joe and Lenny respectively but Angela, by this time, had learned of Aidan's quest and taken him on a moonlit trek to the ruin.

* * *

Cynthia accepted an invitation from the Hoppers to spend the night with them at the malthouse. Theodore returned with Digby to Rose Cottage and was persuaded to put his head where his son's had lain a few weeks earlier. Mr Sticklebach asked Sam Waterman if he might sleep in the summerhouse at the bottom of his garden so that he could fish from there at the first sign of dawn. Angela and Aidan failed to return in time to catch their transport back to

Swivenhall and slept rough in a barn on the outskirts of the village.

Joe and Doris went back to Swivenhall as the only occupants in one of the station wagons which brought them to the village in the afternoon, and Lenny and Pru went alone in another. The driver of the third vehicle spent most of the night waiting for his Colonel outside the Coach and Horses not knowing he had agreed to stay at The Willows when he heard that his Adjutant had left for the camp without him. By the time they were back in camp both Doris and Lenny had established close and affectionate relationships with their respective companions.

The Hoppers had to clear the Village Hall before they retired to bed that evening. It was booked for next morning by the Rev Harper to display the gifts of fruit, vegetables, jams, honey, pickles and chutney alongside sheaves of corn and bunches of flowers presented by his faithful parishioners for the Harvest Thanksgiving Service.

* * *

Those who returned to camp slept late in their beds at Swivenhall, but it was not only Mr Sticklebach, Aidan and Angela who rose early in Little Missington. Nor was it only the Harvest Thanksgiving Service that accounted for this. The knowledge that a number of well-to-do Americans were in the village and looking for souvenirs prompted many of the inhabitants to spend the morning preparing to attract and receive their visitors.

Cynthia persuaded the Hoppers to go with her to the Harvest Thanksgiving Service although they were not themselves regular churchgoers. Mr Hopper usually stayed in bed on Sunday mornings after a Saturday night hop, but Gertrude reminded him of the help they had received from Cynthia and said they owed it to her to comply with

285

her wish to go to church. They also hoped to interest her in some articles for sale in their newly constructed 'sun lounge for Sunday visitors'.

Theodore told Digby he wanted to go to church that morning to witness what he said would be 'a rare expression of ecclesiastical eccentricity: the performance of a pagan ritual in modern dress'. Vera looked doubtfully at her Sunday clothes, which were far from modern, but Benjamin assured her she was not meant to take the remark personally.

Jeremiah did not sleep well in the summerhouse despite attempts to do so by counting the number of fishes he expected to catch. When, in the morning, he sat by the water's edge watching his float bobbing idly in the stream he resolved to express his thanks for any fish he might catch by offering them to the vicar. Heaven either failed to hear or did not appreciate the thought because he waited in vain for the float to sink. When Sam came to invite him up to the house for breakfast his thoughts turned to the parable of the fishes and he asked if Sam would be going to church that morning. 'Ah!' said Sam, 'that I will!' . . . Sam knew that after the service all the produce collected by the congregation would be distributed to the elderly and needy of the parish.

Angela awoke to the customary crowing of the cockerels and was comforted to find that Aidan had bedded himself in a bundle of straw on the far side of the barn from where she had been sleeping. Much as she liked the gentleman she had escorted to the ruin, she was not yet ready to grant him any intimate favours. She feared he might be leading her too close to the occult with his obsessive interest in Druids and sought to lead his enthusiasms elsewhere.

'A relic,' she said 'can be a thing of beauty but if you dig too deep you may find nothing but dirt!'

Aidan felt a chill in the air that contrasted with the

warmth of their walk the previous evening. He wondered if, perhaps, he had given offence by some careless act or thoughtless omission. The sound of bells across the meadow lured them to the church where they took refuge and comfort in the pews.

Colonel Peters ate a hearty farmhouse breakfast before telephoning the camp to arrange to be collected. He politely rejected Cyrus's offer to take him there in his pony trap.

* * *

Back at the camp, Joe was having coffee and toast in the apartment allotted to Doris and Cynthia. He had risen too late for breakfast in the mess. In the somewhat unromantic environment of the kitchen they reviewed events of the night before and confirmed their feelings for each other.

After a second brew of coffee, Doris cautiously enquired about Joe's relationship with Sally. He admitted he had been very fond of Sally but said he wondered how much of his interest had been due to the novelty of meeting a pretty English girl in a remote country village far from home. The presence of his father had reminded him of the close attachment he still felt to his family and, not least, to America. Sally, he was sure, felt the same towards her parents and to England. He had, therefore, reconciled himself to the fact that their relationship was a mere passing fancy. Doris took his explanation with a smile and made a mental note to be prepared for a similar epitaph in due course, but hoped, if it came, it would not be until some way into the future.

While Doris and Joe were thus exploring each other in the kitchen, Lenny and Pru were consolidating their friendship in a sitting-room upstairs and mapping out a programme for the next few days. Lenny explained to Pru that his mission was to advise his professor in Baltimore of the connection between Little Missington and Horatio Nelson. Pru was impressed and eager to assist, although she admitted her knowledge of Nelson was limited to his connection with a certain Lady Hamilton.

'Well,' said Lenny, 'maybe we should be looking for her snuff boxes as well!' They laughed into each other's arms . . . and then Lenny nearly spoiled it. Who was the young man, he asked, she had been with when he butted in on the dance floor? Pru stiffened for a moment and then chuckled.

'That was Bertie', she said. 'He's a carpenter. And his other name is Woodfellow. How d'you like that!' Lenny was still not sure of his ground.

'My professor's name is Chippendale,' he said; 'how about that, then!' Pru pursued the theme, for she was enjoying Lenny's discomfort.

'Are you going to take him back some furniture? A chair, maybe? I'm told professors like chairs.'

It was a dreadful pun, but Lenny laughed at it. 'I couldn't afford a Chippendale if I could find one,' he confessed, '. . . if that's what you mean.'

'Ah,' said Pru, who wasn't ready to give up. 'I'll get Bertie to make you a reproduction and you can take that to your professor.' Lenny thought for a moment.

'Hold on! Suppose he thinks it's an original?'

'Well, I guess, if he can't tell the difference it won't matter, will it?'

* * *

Norman Harper knew he would have a larger than usual congregation in the morning but he had not expected it to include so many Americans. His sermon at a Thanksgiving Service was always rather longer than on other Sundays but the content was usually predictable and not particularly memorable. On this occasion, however, he spoke as one inspired and gave his audience much to think about.

There had been, he said, in recent years a glorious victory of good over evil, and they had now returned to times of peace. Why was it then, he asked, that we are not content? They were present that day, he reminded them, to give thanks for the product of their toil, the harvest had been gathered and their food for the winter was assured. Yet they were not content. The highway that had linked them with the outside world had been repaired, with their own hands, yet they were not content. They all had homes to go to, and those who lived in Little Missington had the beauty of a lovely countryside, yet they were not content. I see before me, he told them, more of you than come on other Sundays — yet I am not content.

'What is it we want that we do not have? Is it what other people have? Or could it be that we do not want what we do have and we are made the richer by selling it to other people? Have we forgotten what it was like to be without and are we so greedy that we must have more? No, my friends, I do not believe we are like that at all. We are right to share our possessions, to show our way of life to others who do not live here, to direct their attention to the past and to steer ourselves into the future. Let us be thankful for what we have, for what we used to have and for what we shall inherit.'

The service ended, as it began, with a rousing hymn sung by a boisterous choir, accompanied by a vigorous organist and some unfamiliar dialects in the congregation.

Digby wanted to applaud but Vera grabbed his hand and led him into the aisle. The congregation filed from the church, filled with admiration. Some of them went straight home, some like Sam Waterman to the Village Hall, others went to the Coach and Horses and some just hung around the vestibule chatting with the vicar.

Cynthia beamed and boomed at Angela who overcame her embarrassment and took Aidan by the arm into the graveyard to study markings on the tombstones.

Theodore stayed and congratulated the vicar, while Jeremiah found his way to the Coach and Horses.

The Hoppers returned to the malthouse to prepare the Sunday lunch and Cynthia resumed her tour of the cottages, many of which had been restocked with displays of local craftsmanship including, she was delighted to find, some excellent examples of hand-embroidered aprons, tablecloths and pillow cases. She bought an example of each and they were handed to her in a paper carrier bag, overprinted with the letters COME AGAIN TO LITTLE MISSINGTON.

Angela was finding Aidan's curiosity infectious and she got as much enjoyment out of reading the inscriptions on the tombstones as she had done out of scouring Digby's workshed.

The Digbys left Theodore with the vicar making anthropological enquiries. Vera, like Gertrude Hopper, hurried to get on with the lunch, and Benjamin to get to the Coach and Horses.

* * *

When he returned to the Digbys for lunch Theodore astonished them by playing back his conversation with the vicar on a portable recording machine which he carried in a satchel slung over his shoulder. Vera stared at him with her mouth open as if he were exhibiting some mystical power, but Sally, who had heard of such technology explained to her mother that this was the modern version of a gramophone.

'Better not let the vicar hear about it,' said Digby, 'else

290

he'll probably buy one and give us second-hand sermons for ever after!'

Theodore enjoyed the Digby's hospitality but excused himself after lunch so that he could meet more of the villagers and add to his record of their life-styles. On his way out, however, Benjamin sold him a pewter tankard and a silver sugar bowl.

Throughout the afternoon Little Missington buzzed with excitement. Not with the vicar's sermon, which had been somewhat out of character, but with the presence of the Americans who were making themselves known around the village and spending freely.

Cynthia bought more embroidery and then branched out into brass ornaments and bone china.

Jeremiah stayed at the Coach and Horses and lunched off bread, cheese, pickles and beer. Then he returned to the river and bought a rowing boat from Sam so he could 'go chase that goddam fish that got away the day before'. It was years since Sam had sold a boat but it gave him a good idea and he went in search of Bertie while Jeremiah was afloat.

Aidan and Angela were now in partnership, picking up relics from the past on the principle of what appealed to them, without regard to their origin or any connection with religious rituals. In this way they assembled a collection of untuned musical instruments, outdated implements of farming, and clocks and watches that told the time no more than twice a day. Aidan was sure they would be an attraction to his public back in Baltimore and he planned to exhibit them near the bandstand in a glass-fronted pavilion.

Before leaving that morning Colonel Peters had told Cyrus he would send a station wagon to collect the stragglers who, he learned from his Transport Officer, had not returned to camp the previous evening. Cyrus thought quickly and suggested they might prefer to be collected towards the end of the day so they could share with the villagers the joy of Thanksgiving Sunday. Digby could not have done better!

Joe made no attempt to return to Little Missington in search of his father when he heard of this arrangement but spent the day with Doris showing her around the camp. Lenny and Pru decided it would be fun to go back and pursue their enquiries into a link with Lord Nelson. To do this they resorted to pedal power and cycled together on a borrowed tandem. Needless to say, they never reached Little Missington but remained where they fell off, by the roadside, enjoying the sunshine and the romance of being alone until the cool breeze of evening and a mild attack of hunger led them to remount and retrace their route to Swivenhall.

26

Theodore's companions made several more visits to Little
Missington in the week before they returned to Baltimore
and by the time they bade farewell to their friends in the
village and at the camp they had accumulated a wealth of
local knowledge, an assortment of articles of varying
antiquity and an abundance of anecdotal interest.

Cynthia's trunk was filled with what she later described
to the Customs Officers as 'goods of no commercial value'
and Doris, who had collected more memories than material
things, obligingly provided her with an overflow facility
in the spare space of one of her suitcases. Doris, herself,
spent most of the time after meeting Joe in getting to know
him better and her tangible trophies were limited to a series
of photographs which she donated to Theodore on their
return.

Influenced and encouraged by Angela, Aidan abandoned
hope of confirming a Druid connection but returned to
Baltimore with a determination to establish on Druids Hill
Park a 'Museum of Little Missington'.

The nearest that Lenny ever got to establishing a link
with Admiral Nelson was when he found the Locketts had
a nautical timepiece and ship's barometer which Mortimer
told him had measured the minutes and millibars at the
Battle of Trafalgar. Closer inspection of the casings,
however, revealed that the instruments came from an old

wherry which had sunk in the river below Sam Waterman's boatyard.

Lenny took Pru's advice and introduced himself to Bertie as a student of Professor Chippendale. Bertie thought he might therefore know something about furniture and be a chap worth cultivating. This was borne out later when Lenny asked him if he could produce a Chippendale chair for him to take back to America as a souvenir.

'Daresay I might,' said Bertie, thinking at once of making him a copy, 'but you'll need somethin' special to carry it in. You'll not get that in a suitcase!'

Lenny hesitated and then slyly suggested he would consider taking a miniature copy of one. Bertie suspected Pru of putting the idea in his head but recognized he had a customer and set about proving his skill as a carpenter.

Without realizing it at the time, Lenny's proposal was to lead Bertie to an even more lucrative line of business and one that would allow him to trade more openly than hitherto.

Theodore was fully satisfied with the results of his mission for he had found in Little Missington not only the trace of an uncharted castle but evidence of several migrations among the local inhabitants. This, in turn, had directed his attention to the origin of neighbouring place-names which was to become a source of great interest to his academic friends in Baltimore and elsewhere.

The one member of the party who was not satisfied with his accomplishment was Jeremiah who had consistently failed to catch a fish and was loath to leave so many behind in their native water. All that he had to show for his journey was a flat bottomed boat which he arranged to moor in Sam's dyke until his next visit to England.

Joe was sorry when the time came to say goodbye to his father, but sadder still at the departure of Doris. He urged his father to look after her and puzzled him by saying he must not think of finding another secretary until the American Air Force released him from his enlistment.

Aidan and Angela parted on platonic terms, with Aidan offering Angela an unspecified job when she returned to Baltimore, in the Museum of Little Missington which they had been planning together.

Lenny and Pru were as deeply committed to each other as Joe and Doris and promised to keep in touch by correspondence until they could meet again.

It was, however, a letter from Swivenhall to Little Missington that preceded the flow of letters from Baltimore to Swivenhall. On the morning after the Americans left for home, Wilfred arrived at Rose Cottage with an envelope addressed to Sally. It was too thick to see through but he recognized the writing and, so did Sally.

'Reckon you've got a message there to say they're on their way back to Yankee land!' Sally was not amused and snatched the envelope from him.

When Wilfred had gone, chuckling to himself at the callowness of youth, Sally opened the letter. It contained a warm and sympathetic apology from Joe inviting forgiveness for his behaviour and expressing the hope that she would make it up with Bertie and be happy ever after. A lump came into her throat as she realized the finality of it and tears welled in her eyes as she remembered some of their happier times together. When Benjamin saw the effect on his daughter it brought a lump in his throat, too, but any tears he might have shed would have been for joy, for now he believed the way was open for her to resume her relations with an Englishman.

* * *

With Theodore and his companions gone, and the interests of Joe, Angie and Pru diverted to America, life in Little

295

Missington reverted to its slow, parochial monotony. Benjamin was commissioned to build an extension to the Village Hall in which to store provisions for the Saturday Night Hops and increasingly popular midweek film shows. He also found himself in demand as a funeral director with the sudden death of Reggie Ploughman following a stroke, brought on, some said, by excitement at selling a phoney firescreen to the Americans.

Bertie's diversification into the manufacture of miniatures brought him further riches and he was soon able to offer Sally a salary for her assistance; a step which took his partner pleasantly by surprise.

Cyrus kept up his contact with Simon Peters and they were frequent visitors to each other's territory. Similarly, visitors from the American camp continued to drain the village of its souvenirs and to contribute currency by consuming quantities of cakes and teas on Sundays.

The link between Little Missington and Baltimore, however, seemed to have been broken for Sally heard no more from Joe and nothing more was seen of Angela or Pru. Then, one day, early in December when Wilfred was cursing the weight of a spate of Christmas cards, a letter arrived addressed to the Chairman of the Parish Council bearing a stamp with a portrait of George Washington and the Stars and Stripes.

Cyrus was not a philatelist but he recognized the origin of his letter. It took him a long time, however, to appreciate its contents.

The Museum of Little Missington had been an instant success and the whole of Baltimore was talking about the village and its hospitable inhabitants. So said the writer, who signed himself the Vice-President of a Real Estate Corporation in the State of Maryland. On behalf of the shareholders of that Corporation he was authorized, it said, to offer a large sum of money and all the necessary practical arrangements to purchase and transport the entire village, with or without its population, to a site on the outskirts of Baltimore.

Cyrus read the letter several times, then reached for his decanter. The message was easier to understand after a glass or two of whisky. He decided at once to call an Emergency Meeting of the Parish Council. In the meantime he made a telephone call to Colonel Peters to enquire about the credentials of his correspondent, taking care not to divulge the purpose of the letter. The Colonel promised to investigate and welcomed the opportunity for another visit to The Willows.

If there is any item on an agenda likely to arouse enough curiosity to produce a full attendance at a meeting it is one marked SECRET. SUBJECT TO BE REVEALED. Copies of what came to be known as the Maryland Letter were tabled at the meeting. The response time of the Councillors was no quicker than the Chairman's had been, and they were without the benefit of decanters at their elbows. Digby saw the need in the proposition for a builder but then realized it would be a demolition job on this side of the Atlantic. Syd Stubbles was worried about the significance of the word 'Real' before Estate and wondered if the Americans bought and sold imaginary properties. Cyrus assured them he had obtained confirmation from the Commander of the Swivenhall Air Base that the firm was genuine and reliable. Patrick thought they would be better off in Fairyland than Maryland, but Cyrus said they had to take the matter seriously. It was the Treasurer, Mortimer Lockett, who first asked how much the Americans proposed to pay for the village and thereafter that became the dominant issue. Little attention was paid to the problems of dislocation that would be faced by all the villagers.

George Whackett worked out that if the population of

the village was just over 200 — which he said was about right — and if they were each to be offered a thousand pounds, which Patrick said was not enough, the Americans would have to be willing to pay a quarter-of-a-million pounds to get what they were asking for. Patrick again interjected to say he knew very well what they were asking for and he was quite ready to give it to them! Cyrus called the meeting back to order. Ted Brewer said the Americans didn't pay in pounds, they did business in dollars. The schoolmaster started to do the conversion. Digby directed them to the principle rather than the detail. Did they want money or did they prefer to live as they had been doing, in relative poverty? After all, the letter said 'with or without the inhabitants': they could sell up and go and live elsewhere if they didn't want to go to America. 'And Ben can build us all new houses!' said Patrick, sarcastically.

'There'll be one thing they can't move to America,' said Sam, jubilantly, 'that's the river!'

'Why not?' said Pat, 'they could bottle it first!'

Cyrus could see they were unlikely to reach a decision so he suggested the issue was important enough to hold a referendum. They were too tired to resist and Syd Stubbles was called upon, as Clerk, to prepare a ballot paper. Cyrus impressed upon them how important it was that they should explain to their families and parishioners the consequences of whichever way they voted.

In the days that followed, Little Missington was in turmoil. Would this be the last Christmas they would spend together, or would they remain forever poor? Was that the only alternative, or could they have their cake and eat it? The metaphor seemed apt to those who had been living off the proceeds of cake on Sundays for much of the year. Somebody started a scare by suggesting that if they rejected the offer the Americans might invade and take them over. Nobody really enjoyed their Christmas Dinner, and some of them thought it might be their last.

On the first of January they voted; on the second of January George Whackett, Syd Stubbles and Mortimer Lockett counted, and on the third Cyrus announced the result. It was an overwhelming decision to sell. The lure of capitalism, engendered by the drive to make money out of unwanted articles from their attics, and the realization that profit from their labours providing teas and cakes to visitors was small by comparison, led them to opt for the 'easy buck' and to dream of a wealthy future.

It was the amount of money offered which tipped the scales against those whose native resistance to change, combined with a distrust of foreigners, especially Americans, led them to oppose the scheme. The concept of a million of anything was difficult to grasp and the sound of four million dollars, which was what the Americans were actually offering, was even more magic than the one million pounds which that represented in British currency. Spread evenly over the entire population of Little Missington it meant almost twenty thousand dollars apiece and that was an unimagined fortune in those days. Looked at another way, and they delighted in looking at it in all possible ways, it meant more than fifty thousand dollars per dwelling. Even after the conversion to sterling those sums were persuasive and swamped all other considerations. Only in the morning after the result had been announced did it dawn upon some of them that the manner of distributing the money had not yet been fixed and there was the possibility that those who lived in cottages might expect more than those who dwelled in bungalows. Similarly, if the distribution were to be per capita it might be argued that a new-born baby should count as less than a working man, or a busy housewife more than an idle pensioner. The prospect of a fair distribution looked less and less likely as they viewed the alternatives.

The bar at the Coach and Horses was the customary place in which the strength of feelings was measured and it was here that Cyrus and Benjamin held court both before and after the referendum. Their views were biased towards the valuation of property although they knew that those with large families, like the Comans and Fowlers, for example, would benefit more from a count of heads. In a spirit of compromise Cyrus suggested they commission a professional from Puddlethorpe, or even from the big cities of Norwich or Ipswich. Digby approved the idea in principle but asked Cyrus what particular profession he had in mind.

Estate agents had not yet acquired the experience of handling multiple property transactions and would have found it difficult to put a value on some of the cottages and bungalows in Little Missington since few had changed hands over many generations. The method of pricing by 'willing seller to willing buyer' was, therefore, useless and professional guess work would have been little better than a layman's. Accountants, surveyors, bankers and lawyers were also considered and discounted for the same reason: that their professional experience was unlikely to have much bearing on the worth of property or the people in Little Missington.

Then they remembered that George Whackett had a friend in Myrtlesham who led the military band which had played for them on the day the American visitors first came to the village. As he was well placed in the town among the business community they would ask him for his opinion. That settled, they turned to the next problem which was how to communicate the result of the referendum to the Real Estate Corporation in America. Cyrus thought he ought to go out to Baltimore and negotiate the deal in person. Digby sensed that might not be to everyone's advantage and said they ought to get the distribution problem sorted out first. It was agreed that Cyrus should send a brief reply with words they believed would protect them from all dangers, namely 'subject to contract'. Feeling very satisfied with their deliberations, they bought each other another drink and walked home without noticing there was snow on the ground underfoot.

* * *

It is not unusual for a cold sweat to follow excessive excitement, and that was the condition in which the villagers found themselves, even before the snow began to fall. Families were divided as to whether to stay and seek a new home thereabouts or up and go to America. One or two had heard there were opportunities in Australia but the horizon of most was no further than Puddlethorpe or Myrtlesham. The Digby family was typical in that Vera hankered after the New World with its modern amenities such as she had seen in Swivenhall and Ben was convinced there would be plenty of work for him 'back home' once the Americans had shifted what they wanted. Sally's thoughts lay somewhere between the two, for she also liked the idea of modern living but doubted if she would feel at home in America. Her future might depend on what Bertie had in mind for she no longer considered a future with Joe to be feasible.

Those who had quickly made up their minds were the likes of Patrick O'Hachetty, the Brewers, the Hoppers and the Whacketts whose roots in rural England were not deep and who saw scope for their future where the rewards were greater, on the other side of the Atlantic. Resolved to stay, though where exactly they did not know, were such as Cyrus, Sam Waterman, the Carters, the policeman and old Bob Blackett.

More discomfort came when word got out among the

neighbouring villages. Inevitably facts got garbled and some folk gained the impression that Americans were about to move in instead of the English moving out. Protests were lodged with politicians and the local newspapers carried headlines like 'Americans Go Home' and 'England for the English'.

Eventually the clouds cleared and the climate improved. It was time for a last spring-clean to be started.

27

The bandmaster friend of George Whackett worked in a solicitor's office in the main street of Puddlethorpe and put to his principal the matter which Cyrus had raised. Mr Longwynd, of Longwynd, Seymour and Waite, was a Dickensian character who put caution before action and quality above haste. He knew little about Little Missington except for the scandal of their road work and imagined it was not the sort of place that would be of interest to an American.

'This Mr Galleon, you mention ... is he a ... countryman or a sailor?'

The bandmaster smiled, as duty demanded, and replied that his friend, the schoolmaster, had described him as a very upright gentleman.

'Then he's not taken to hallucinations, or ... fits of fancy?' The bandmaster said it was unlikely.

'Good' said Mr Longwynd, 'Then we must ask him to come and see us.'

Before Cyrus set out to meet Mr Longwynd he received from Baltimore a large package of legal documents which he took with him and placed upon the solicitor's desk.

'You are quite sure, I suppose,' said Mr Longwynd, 'that you wish to go through with this ... er ... transaction?' Cyrus wondered if he had come to the right person. 'You realize, of course, that it will take time to ... to prove your title to the properties you are ... proposing to ... sell?'

'Yes,' said Cyrus, 'and I also realize that Americans are used to cutting corners.'

'Ah, well, we can't have any of that over here, now can we?'

'On my farm,' said Cyrus, 'if the weather turns bad when I'm getting the corn in, I cut corners.'

'When you're ... cutting the corn, you cut corners ... is that what you said?' Mr Longwynd was also hard of hearing.

Cyrus wished he had brought Digby with him.

'Are these the instruments of sale?' asked Mr Longwynd, all of a sudden.

'Yes,' said Cyrus, 'and I would be obliged if you would study them and advise my council how best to proceed. Good afternoon.'

It was a ploy that Cyrus had learned from his father. When the going gets rough, he used to say, take cover. If you can, go ashore; if you can't, go below.

It took a lot to take the wind out of Mr Longwynd, but he was left in no doubt about the calibre of his client.

* * *

Proving title where the resident owner is descended from the original builder is not difficult but finding the owner where the property is rented and the rent paid to a rent collector is not so easy. Among the cases confronting Mr Longwynd was one in which the owner had been killed in the First World War and the cottage left to his sister who was now in a sanatorium. This was the type of complication that kept a lawyer in business.

Some of the dwellings in Little Missington had never been documented and some owners could not be traced. Obliged to value the properties for tax purposes, the professionals relied on the fact that district valuers had no yardstick by which to contradict them. On Mr Seymour's advice, experts were engaged to minimize the tax that would be due on selling The Willows, the malthouse, the church and the Coach and Horses but it taxed their ingenuity to do it.

Such were the complexities faced by the lawyers that Mr Longwynd, Mr Seymour and Mr Waite all became involved in the action and an extra clerk was recruited to do their devilling. Cyrus displayed his usual impatience and asked if they were also short of quills, string and sealing wax.

* * *

In Baltimore the pressure for completion was far greater than in Puddlethorpe for Aidan had now been taken over by Druids Hill Entertainments Inc. whose executives estimated the addition of a complete English village to their possessions would attract half a million more visitors a year. At two dollars admission they calculated they could recover their outlay within five years and thereafter be swimming in profit. They wanted to be first in the field before some other enterprise bought up Stonehenge or Windsor Castle.

On his way back from England, Jeremiah Sticklebach had been persuaded by Aidan to invest in the new company. This he did to such an extent that he soon secured a place on the Board of Directors. In this capacity he was able to arrange a special visit to Little Missington in March to assist the lawyers and make another attempt at catching some fish. Unfortunately, nobody told him this was the close season and he failed again to spike the elusive pike.

* * *

Meanwhile the inhabitants of Little Missington were marking up their belongings and mentally spending money they had not yet received. Representatives from removal firms, investment brokers, travel agencies and sundry charities were constantly calling on them, and relatives they had not heard from for years began to re-appear.

The Rev Harper informed the Church Commissioners of the Baltimore proposal and expected them to object to the sale of their land in the village. Influenced, no doubt, by the size of the rector's stipend, and the shortfall between that and the revenue from weekly collections, the Commissioners agreed to sell both the church and the vicarage and to find Mr Harper another parish. Stung by this sign of ingratitude, Norman resolved to follow the route of the Pilgrim Fathers and to settle in America.

Ted and Daisy Brewer had bought the freehold of the Coach and Horses out of Ted's gratuity and a loan from the bank, so they did not need to seek a decision from a distant landlord. Unless Jimmy were to raise an objection, they were free to move with the property and continue their business in the States. This gave them the idea of inviting the Hoppers to move with them and reopen the malthouse to provide a steady supply of home-brewed beer when they got to the States. After some heart-searching and initial disagreements, the Hopper family eventually saw it as a good opportunity to improve themselves socially and accepted the Brewers' proposal.

Digby was now getting agitated about how the buildings were going to be demolished in such a way as to be re-erectable when they got to America.

'I reckon they'll cheat,' he said, 'and just put up a load of replicas with Yankee thatch and mortar.' Sally was aghast at her father's hypocrisy, knowing of his complicity with Bertie in fabricating antiquity, but he winked at her and added: 'Daresay they could do with some help when it comes to the furnishings, eh?'

Jeremiah arrived in England with more than a fishing rod for company. He came with an army of architects, photographers, surveyors and lawyers who descended on the village to perform their respective tasks for the benefit of their American client. Arrangements were made by telephone and cable for them to be accommodated at hotels and guest houses in the neighbourhood and there they experienced for the first time the English way of living. After the discomfort of draughty bedrooms, the frugality of food rationing, and the notorious weather conditions they were ready for whatever they might find in Little Missington. Their instructions from Baltimore had been to study the character of the village and devise a means of transferring the 'ambiance' of the place to their Baltimore site. The extrovert among them interpreted this to mean 'get to know its characters,' and soon they were overwhelmed with questions of what it was like to live in America.

It was also part of the professionals' brief to sub-contract as much as possible of the manual work, once they had designed an overall plan. With this in mind the architect and surveyor spotted the sign of Builder and Funeral Director over the back gate of Rose Cottage and introduced themselves to Digby. His resources, he explained, were limited but he and his partner, he said, would be pleased to help them. On reflection, it was not clear to the Americans in which capacity he was speaking.

Digby had learned the trade of building from his father and was able to follow the American's questions about structures and materials, but he was still a novice in the technique of demolition. It fascinated him to see the way the Americans were planning to take down a building from the roof groundwards, labelling each slate, tile, brick or stone so that its place was recorded for reconstruction. He smiled as he wondered if they would try to identify each piece of thatch but found that was one of the cases where they did intend to cheat by using local American produce.

When it came to packing and transporting Digby found the Americans were far ahead of the English in their experience of doing things on a large scale. Whereas he had been thinking in terms of boxes and trailers, the Americans were planning to use crates, and to load them onto ships from large articulated lorries.

Excitement turned to frenzy as the inhabitants found out what was being planned and deals were struck as to the order in which homes would be demolished. Wisely, the Americans did not intend to move the entire village in one go, but to phase the operation over several months so that each dwelling could be tackled separately. The possibility of components becoming mixed in the course of transit was thus reduced, although Digby had a mischievous vision of part of the Coach and Horses becoming attached to the vicarage during reassembly.

They were all agreed that the village pub should not be demolished until the last of the residents had moved.

Digby and Bertie were already thinking of what the village would look like when it had been stripped of all its superstructure.

'Guess it'll look a bit like the Somme did after the First War,' said Digby.

'I can't remember that far back,' said Bertie, 'but I reckon it might look like it's been blitzed in the Second.'

'Y'know', said Digby, 'we'll just have to start rebuilding it. There won't be any shortage o' land, now will there?'

'There might be a shortage o' people,' said Bertie wistfully.

'Don't you believe it, boy; they'll come back when their bellies are full o' ice-cream and pop-corn and their pockets empty o' dollars!'

308

There was nothing in the Sale Agreement that said they could not replace a house that was going to America, but there was a clause to prevent them selling it a second time to another American. Digby had plans in his mind to build a Super Rose Cottage on the proceeds of selling the one he was soon to dismantle. There would be room in it, he envisaged, for Bertie as well, if he decided to settle down with Sally. Cyrus also had ideas of getting a new house built, but Gladys wanted a smaller one than The Willows so Cyrus said it would have to be called The Weeping Willow. He asked Digby if he would build it for them and Digby agreed on condition they found someone to recommission the Coach and Horses. Cyrus said he would have a word with Simon Peters who was thinking of settling down in England after his Service days were over.

Frank and Madeline Morse had also decided to stay in England. They had heard that communications in America were more hectic than they were accustomed to and were looking for a sub-post office in Puddlethorpe. Wilfred Stamp said he would like to follow them, so long as he could take his old bike, and find somewhere to live where he could grow vegetables. That seemed to be the ambition of most of those who were not wanting to start a fresh life in the New World and estate agents in Puddlethorpe and Myrtlesham found a sudden surge in demand for low-cost houses with small gardens or allotments.

George Whackett had been loudly cheered by his pupils when he announced that the school would be closing for good at the end of term in July. There were boos, however, when he added that it would reopen in Baltimore in September for those whose parents were emigrating. Juvenile rebellions broke out in many families and nearly resulted in some of them not going.

Undeterred, the Whacketts arranged for the School House to be the first to be demolished and were transported with it half way through their summer holiday. Kathy made a great scene on leaving and threw her arms round Bertie in a last gesture of affection. He was so pleased to see her go that he gave her a lingering kiss and entirely the wrong impression. She pleaded in vain with her father to stay.

Others followed at weekly intervals. Most of the dwellings being much smaller than the School House took only a few days to pull down and despatch. Their occupants were able to travel together on the same shipment and so share the pain of detachment. Tears accompanied them to the docks, but afterwards the novelty of unfamiliar surroundings filled their eyes with wonder and the anticipation of wealth and a new home overtook all other emotions.

By December those who were not going to America had found new accommodation in neighbouring towns or villages. For the Galleons and Digbys, it was of a temporary nature, while they waited for new homes to be built; for the Byfields it was until they obtained permission to settle in New Zealand.

The malthouse was moved before the Coach and Horses to enable the Hoppers to produce some English beer in time for the opening in Baltimore of an English pub. Digby said it was not the first time the Hoppers had put the cart before the horse.

The last sermon delivered by Norman Harper was to a congregation of ten, of whom six were waiting to take the church to pieces as soon as the service was over. It was probably the shortest sermon Norman had ever preached.

Dismantling the ruins began in November, on the anniversary of their 'uprising', but was not completed until New Year's Eve. This was because Digby had insisted that it be done exclusively by local labour 'as a token of respect' … a suggestion that amused the Americans. They did not object, however, and Digby and Bertie did it themselves with minimal help from Cyrus.

Because he was involved in this, and in dismantling other people's dwellings, Digby was not ready to tackle his own until early in the New Year and there was snow on the ground when the first tiles of his cottage were numbered and placed in their crate. Vera and Sally were too upset to watch and retreated to their temporary residence while Benjamin supervised the proceedings.

By now the surrounding countryside had been laid bare and the recent covering of snow made it look like a landscape in Alaska or Russia.

Step by step, or rather stone by stone, the structure of Rose Cottage was taken to pieces until only the foundations were visible. Insisting they should take the lot, including the tightly packed stones on which the cottage had been built, Digby turned his back while the American supervisor, who had arrived on the scene with his superiors to witness the final ceremony, took an exuberant swipe with a pickaxe.

Twenty minutes later the Americans were clustered round a section of the base from which stones had been removed and were staring at the top of what seemed to be an ancient wall. By the end of the day they had unearthed copper coins and broken vases in the remains of a Roman settlement.

Little Missington had had a *Real Ruin* after all.